AFTER SHE VANISHED

S. A. DUNPHY

HACHETTE
BOOKS
IRELAND

First published in Ireland in 2017 by HACHETTE BOOKS IRELAND

1

Cataloguing in Publication Data is available from the British Library

ISBN 978 1 4736 5521 8

Typeset in Bembo Book Std by Bookends Publishing Services, Dublin.
Printed and bound in Great Britain by Clays Ltd, St Ives plc.

Hachette Books Ireland policy is to use papers that are natural, renewable and recyclable products and made from wood grown in sustainable forests. The logging and manufacturing processes are expected to conform to the environmental regulations of the country of origin.

Hachette Books Ireland
8 Castlecourt Centre
Castleknock
Dublin 15
Ireland

A division of Hachette UK Ltd
Carmelite House, 50 Victoria Embankment, EC4Y 0DZ

www.hachettebooksireland.ie

For Deirdre – for ever

PROLOGUE

All Fall Down

1

DAVID DUNNIGAN KNEW HE HAD TAKEN THE corner badly just before the BMW tail-finned – he had been driving the car, a 1982 3 Series, since he was in college, and he knew the workings of the thirty-six-year-old vehicle intimately.

Even though he had been awake for close to fifty hours and was probably only peripherally aware of a lot of things, he felt the tyres on the driver's side lose traction with the road and registered (in a part of his brain that was watching the unfolding disaster with cold objectivity) that he was in trouble.

The rear end of the vehicle suddenly wasn't where it was supposed to be, and then his beloved classic ricocheted off a Fiesta illegally parked on the other side of the road, rebounding into a spin, then bouncing off two cars travelling in opposite directions before it came to a juddering stop in the middle of Pearse Street.

It was all over in less than sixty seconds, and traffic going both ways came to a standstill. The BMW, its bonnet buckled, the passenger-side rear door stove in, steam hissing from the mangled radiator, was effectively blocking all progress, stalled as it was right across both lanes.

A man dressed in the blue uniform of a rail worker gingerly approached Dunnigan's car and tugged at the driver's door. For a second it didn't move, but then, as if shoved hard from the other side, it flew open, and a bloodied, pale David Dunnigan tumbled out.

'Are you all right, lad?' the rail worker asked him. 'You should probably sit down.'

'Get out of my way,' Dunnigan hissed and, shoving aside his Good Samaritan, lurched from the wreckage of one of the few possessions he cared anything about, and staggered in the direction of Trinity College.

2

IT SHOULD HAVE TAKEN HIM FIVE MINUTES TO reach the entrance to the university, but as he started to run, he realised that one of his legs wasn't working properly: every time he put any weight on it, a searing pain travelled upwards right into his groin – the agony was so great that, after a hundred yards, he had to stop and throw up in the doorway of a Spanish restaurant. Looking down, he realised a shard of glass, probably from one of the windows, two of which had imploded in the crash, was embedded in his right thigh, and thick, dark blood was oozing slowly out of the wound.

He contemplated removing it, then reasoned that it might actually be preventing him from bleeding to death so decided to leave it where it was. He stood back up and nearly fainted with pain.

People were milling past, rushing on their way to lunches and business appointments. No one paid him any heed at all, probably thinking him drunk or homeless. He could hear sirens on the wind, and stood up again, favouring his left leg, which was unencumbered by injury. He drew his long grey coat about him to hide the bloodstain that was spreading across his jeans, and hobbled on.

He had an appointment of his own to keep, and he was determined not to miss it.

Ten minutes later, when he reached the Nassau Street entrance to Trinity College, he was drenched in sweat and could feel blood sloshing in his shoes. The doors slid open and he was in the bustling entrance hall of the university. For a second his vision went misty and he fell against a tall youngster, who tutted and shoved on past.

He could not remember finding his way to Bolger's office, but consciousness came back to him, and he was standing outside a door – the sign on it read: *Professor Glin Bolger PhD, Modern History*. Then, as if by magic, he was inside, where a monster was waiting for him.

3

THE PROFESSOR WAS FAT AND BALDING, WHAT little hair he had left Brylcreemed straight back on his round head. He wore a plain white cotton shirt and a sky-blue sports jacket, and when Dunnigan walked in, he was writing in a hard-backed notebook with an expensive-looking fountain pen. The office was decorated with framed Victorian cartoons from magazines like *Punch* and the *Irish Periodical*, and there was a big oak set of bookshelves creaking with untidily organised volumes.

'Ah, Mr Dunnigan – back so soon,' Bolger said, smiling in an indulgent manner. His voice was rich and deep, musical almost.

'I want to speak to you.' Dunnigan swayed, and held onto the arm of a chair to right himself.

'Why don't you sit? It's so much more civilised than having you looming over me looking ill.'

Dunnigan virtually fell into the offered seat.

'So, what can I help you with today?'

'Marian Cooke.'

'This again.'

'And Terri Spears.'

'I've already told you—'

'And Leona Cardwell. And Alanna Morgan and all the others. I want to talk to you about the twenty-five former students who have now given statements that you sexually assaulted them – sometimes in this very office, sometimes in your home, sometimes on research trips to various parts of the country that appear to have been more about rape than they were history. Did you know that, of the twenty-five, fourteen have given evidence that you introduced them to Newton Esmund and Todd Gerard, who seem to have been regular companions of yours on these excursions?'

'Stuff and nonsense.'

'The Sex Crimes Unit has a statement that you were in the company of Newton Esmund in a hotel in County Leitrim in 2010, when you offered Alanna Morgan, whom you brought under the pretence of assisting you in recording interviews with local historians, a sum of five hundred euro if she would bring her niece, who was five, along on the next trip. She says you saw a photograph of the child because she used it as the wallpaper on her phone.'

'More lies. This is really becoming intolerable.'

'I'm almost finished. Terri Spears says she called to your home in Glasnevin at your request in 2007, and arrived just as a woman she did not know was putting a little girl into a car – she says the child was crying. Esmund and Gerard were also there when she arrived, and she says the three of you were either drunk or on drugs of some kind. She alleges you took turns raping her, during which the pair of you bragged about abusing the little girl, whom you referred to as Alice.'

'Mr Dunnigan, are you making your way to a particular point, or must I continue to sit here and listen to these unfounded allegations for the rest of the afternoon?'

'Some of the evidence these women have given dates back to 1994,' Dunnigan said. He was taking shallow breaths now, and fighting to remain conscious. 'We have, among the statements, more than twenty references to you either asking that children be brought to you or of you and your associates being seen with children. Always little girls, and always between the ages of three and ten.'

'I am losing patience, Mr Dunnigan.'

'There are five children within that age range on our books who remain missing,' Dunnigan said. 'And I think you know where they are.'

'Get out of my office.'

Dunnigan fumbled in his jacket pocket, and held out a photograph to the historian. 'Do you know this girl?'

'Get out!'

'Look at the photograph, Professor Bolger.'

'I'm getting Security!'

The academic stood, but before he could move, Dunnigan had flung himself across the desk and had him by the throat. He was screaming, tears mixing with the sweat on his face, hysteria peppering his cries. 'Where is she? Please tell me what you've done with her!'

'Get off me, you lunatic!' Bolger grabbed his attacker by the collar and flung him aside, Dunnigan landing heavily on his injured leg. With a sickening crunch, he felt the glass slice even deeper. He tried to stagger up, but the room had suddenly darkened, and though Bolger was shouting at him, the words were muffled. Then a hole opened and swallowed him, and he was glad to sink into it.

4

HE WAS SUSPENDED WITHOUT PAY WHILE THE powers-that-be fell over themselves apologising to a serial sex offender. They told him he had probably destroyed any chances of bringing a prosecution against Bolger and his fellow deviants, but Dunnigan calmly reminded them that the evidence against the three men was so circumstantial, it would have been years before they could bring charges anyway.

This did not seem to make his superiors any less angry with him, but he had long since stopped caring about that.

He lay in his hospital bed, drank Bovril from a plastic cup and stared at the ceiling into the small hours of the morning because, even with all the pills and potions they pumped into him, sleep proved elusive. Every time he closed his eyes, he saw her face. Every time he drifted into a doze for a moment, she was there, watching from the shadows, reaching out for him.

The doctors told him he was lucky to be alive. He didn't agree.

What he found unbearable was that he had hit another dead end – he had thought Bolger and his foul friends might be able to end his misery, to bring him closure. But he had messed it up. He had failed again.

A week later they sent him home with a bottle of strong painkillers. He stood by the window, alone amid his few items of furniture and the dust, and looked at the pills. He googled their uses and effects: 'Oxycodone,' the internet informed him, 'is a slow-release semi-synthetic opioid, prescribed for severe pain relief. It is also one of the most abused pharmaceutical drugs, as it can cause euphoria, relaxation and reduced anxiety in users.' The script on the bottle advised him to take 15 milligrams every six hours.

He limped into the kitchen and made himself a cup of tea.

Then he sat on his couch and methodically took every pill in the bottle.

He came to consciousness an hour later, vomiting, and realised in a distracted way that someone had their fingers down his throat.

'Come on, you selfish asshole,' the voice of his boss, Detective Inspector Frank Tormey, said, somewhere above him. 'I'll pull your fucking colon out if I have to, but you are not dying on my watch.'

He did not die. He could not even kill himself successfully.

Later, he sat on the bathroom floor while the detective went through all the cupboards and storage units in the flat to make sure he had no further tools to aid him in ending his life.

'You're lucky I decided to call by,' Tormey said, a plastic bag with a couple of half-empty packs of paracetamol and two knives in his hand. 'You are also lucky I had the sense to break in your door when I didn't get an answer.'

'I wanted to die. You stopped me. How is that lucky by any definition?'

Tormey sighed and shook his head. 'Bolger and those sickos – they're not the guys you're looking for. It's all wrong – the profile doesn't fit, and you know it.'

'I don't know anything any more.'

'That's a pity, 'cause I came over to tell you that Bolger has changed his statement. He's not pressing charges, so you can come back to work.'

'I don't understand.'

'He doesn't want to air his dirty laundry in court, so you're in the clear. The traffic accident is still an issue, but with the blood loss you suffered, anyone will believe you were delirious when you left the scene.'

'How lovely for me.'

'That said, you need help, Davey.'

'No.'

'I'm calling your sister.'

'Please don't.'

'With the greatest of respect, Davey, fuck you.'

And he left him sitting with his back against the toilet, his life in tatters about him.

PART ONE
Unwanted Visitors

1

ONE WEEK LATER

'HELLO?'

'Don't pretend you don't know who it is, David Dunnigan. Get out of bed and open the damned door.'

'I'm not at home, Gina.'

'Jesus Christ, I could hear the phone ringing. The walls in this place are made of cardboard. Open up and let me in. I'm gonna kick the door down in a minute. It's made of plywood, probably won't take very much effort.'

Pause. Then: 'I don't want to see anyone today.'

'You said that last week. I'm not leaving, so just pack in the self-pity.'

'There's something wrong with the signal. You're breaking up.'

'Davey, do you think I'm an idiot?'

Another pause.

'No.'

'I'm worried sick about you. Please let me in, just for a minute.'

'Does Clive know you're here?'

'I am a grown woman. I can go where I want without seeking permission from my husband.'

'Does Clive know you've come to visit me, Gina?'

'No, he doesn't, but that's not the point. Now, are you opening the blasted door or am I?'

'Okay. I'm coming.'

'About shaggin' time!'

Dunnigan hangs up.

2

GINA CARLTON, NÉE DUNNIGAN, STOOD IN THE virtually empty space that was her twin brother's flat.

'I know I've said it before,' she put a bag of groceries on the floor, 'but I cannot believe you've been living here for eighteen years.'

'I have everything I need.'

'And that's what scares me.'

David Dunnigan was painfully thin, his dark hair, long and unkempt from neglect rather than design, was shot through with grey. He was dressed in a *Walking Dead* T-shirt that was at least three sizes too large for him and scuffed, baggy jeans – he had not deigned to put shoes on yet, and his toenails needed cutting. The bruises and cuts from the accident were still very much in evidence on his face, but the abrasions had scabbed over and the bruises had begun to turn yellow.

'I'm very comfortable here, Gina. I have no intention of adding unnecessary clutter.'

The room – Dunnigan's main living space – featured a low, threadbare couch, an equally low coffee-table that looked as though it might collapse if more than one cup were placed on it at a time, a folding card table and one chair. A single framed black and white poster of Patrick Troughton as the second incarnation of the science-fiction character Doctor Who hung over a fireplace that looked as if flame had not graced its environs for a very long time.

'Would you at least consider getting a second chair?'

'Why?' Dunnigan asked, without any hint of irony.

Gina – slender like her brother and striking, if not pretty, her dark hair cut short and tight to her head – was dressed in a soft leather jacket, black jeans, a white mannish shirt and black silk scarf. Her Dr Martens boots were polished to a high sheen. 'If you have to ask, there's really no point in telling you,' she said in resignation. 'Let's have brunch.'

'I don't eat brunch.'

'You do now.'

Dunnigan sat at the card table and ate bacon and eggs; Gina sat on the couch, noting that the brother she had made such an effort to visit now had his back to her.

'When was the last time you ate anything other than breakfast cereal?'

'We get lunch at Harcourt Street, you know. They send out for sandwiches. Sometimes they get McDonald's, or have a Chinese takeaway delivered.'

'Well, that's something, I suppose.'

'I'm doing fine, Gina. I promise.'

'Frank Tormey tells me otherwise.' She thought she saw him stiffen, but it was a small movement, and she might have been mistaken. He continued to pick absently at the food. The couple of mouthfuls he'd had seemed to have filled him. A pool of yellow yolk was congealing on the plate. 'Did you hear what I just said, David?'

'Yes.'

'I just made reference to the fact that you almost killed yourself.'

'It was a mistake. I took too much of my pain medication by accident.'

'You are the most precise person I know,' Gina said, a hardness entering her voice. 'You don't make that kind of mistake.'

'I'm not—'

'I'm not one of your students or some poor eejit you've got locked up in an interrogation room. You can't out-manoeuvre me with words or by playing with the facts. I've been trying to break through this horrible wall of pain you've constructed around yourself for more years than I care to remember. I love you, Davey, but even that has its limits. Now, are we going to have a conversation like adults or are you determined to continue this ridiculous game of hide-and-seek you've been playing, with yourself as much as anyone else?'

Dunnigan looked at her and blinked, as if someone had just slapped him. 'I … I don't know how,' he said in a tiny voice.

Gina stood up, went to him, and put her arms around her brother, who sat, rigid and cold, on his lonely wooden chair, as cut off from her as he had been when the front door had been closed between them.

3

SOME TIME LATER THEY SAT SIDE BY SIDE ON THE couch – at least, Gina sat: Dunnigan perched on the edge, still not really looking at her.

'I know how hard things have been for you, Davey,' Gina said, picking her words carefully. 'But it's been really tough for all of us.'

'I'm aware of that.'

'I'm sorry I haven't been around.'

'How could you be around when you were living in London?'

'That's what I mean. I had to get away after … after what happened.'

'That's okay.'

'I thought it might help me and Clive.'

'You've told me all this, Gina.'

'Will you please shut up and let me speak?'

He lapsed into silence.

'I thought that going somewhere new, where we weren't being faced with reminders of Beth every moment of every day, might save my marriage. I'm not sure I realised what a state the rest of the family were in. It wasn't until about a year later, when Clive and I finally did break up, that I realised Mum was on tranquillizers. Dad more or less stopped talking to anyone – just locked himself up in his study with his books and his old films.'

Dunnigan sighed deeply and turned awkwardly to look at her. 'I don't know what you want me to say.'

'I don't want you to say anything. I've come home, Davey. I've rented out the flat in London and got some part-time teaching in Blanchardstown.'

'Why?'

'Maybe because I'm strong enough to be here now.'

'Nothing has changed. Dublin is the same as it was when you left.'

'But I'm different. I wish you were, too. None of this was your fault, Davey. You did not make this … this awful, hellish thing happen. We've all told you that – well, maybe not all of us . . .'

'I haven't spoken to our parents in seventeen years, Gina.'

'Come on, it hasn't been that long!'

'Seventeen years, six months and twenty-two days.'

'Well, at least you haven't been brooding over it!'

Dunnigan narrowed his eyes at her. 'Was that a joke?'

'Yes! Jesus, Davey, we used to laugh all the time! You were funny – people always commented on how witty and sharp you were. Remember?'

'I'm not that person any more.'

'Couldn't you be again? Look, it wasn't easy to rebuild my life! Can't you at least try?'

'I *have* rebuilt my life.'

'You've built something, but I don't think it's a life. Won't you try, even for me?'

Dunnigan said nothing. He was staring at the floor now.

'It was always you and me,' Gina said, putting her hand on his arm. 'I've lost so, so much – don't take my brother away from me too.'

He shook off her hand and walked to the window. 'I know what happened wasn't my fault,' he said, after a long, painful silence. 'Intellectually, I understand that there was not an awful lot I could have done differently – I've been over and over it in my head. But, you see, being able to rationalise it doesn't help. I still *feel* like I was to blame. No matter what I do, I still have that fear deep inside. That it was down to me, in the end.'

Gina got up and stood beside him, looking through the glass (almost medically sterile on this side of the window, grimy with soot on the other) at the milling throng on the street below. A crow had perched on a windowsill opposite them, and it seemed to be staring right at her. 'Davey, I spent years being really, really angry at the world. I raged at everything I could find to rage at. But all that did was exhaust me. Being mad didn't change anything, and it didn't make me feel any better.'

'I'm not angry – at least, I don't think I am.'

'I believe that, underneath a thick layer of ice, you are very, very angry, Davey. You're just scared to let it out. And I think you're terribly, desperately sad. And that breaks my heart.'

Dunnigan continued to stare out of the window. 'I don't think I feel very much of anything, Gina, if I'm honest.'

'Maybe we could try working on that, then.'

'Maybe.'

Gina didn't know if this was progress or not. But it was a start.

Ernest Frobisher

He was bred to believe the world was his, and that nothing could stand in the way of his will.

His father took him to the basement of their house when he was thirteen. It was a room that was used by the man who did their gardens and maintained their property, and it was full of tools – hammers, screwdrivers, saws. In this room there was a man tied to a chair, naked.

'He's yours,' his father had said.

'What should I do with him?'

'That's the point, boy. You can do whatever you want.'

'I want to make him scream.'

'Good boy.'

It took the man weeks to die, and when he did, Ernest was disappointed.

The money, the cars, the houses, the women – all these he enjoyed, but what he loved was the ability to enforce his wishes, his desires on others.

The Yellow Man found him in 1994. Frobisher was in his office in London when the door opened and the Yellow Man came in.

'Who are you?'

'I am the person you've been waiting for,' the Yellow Man said.

'How did you get in?'

'You had only six people on the doors. Now you have me, you won't need so many.'

After that they became great friends. Together, they made everyone bend to Frobisher's will. They did what they wanted, and no one could stop them.

4

DETECTIVE CHIEF SUPERINTENDENT FRANK Tormey glared at Dunnigan, who stared impassively back at him over his cluttered desk. Tormey was an angular man, his dark hair worn in a crew cut, a heavy moustache hanging over his upper lip. Today he was dressed, as per usual, in a nondescript grey suit, his blue tie hanging askew.

'Where's the report I'm supposed to have from you on the Drogheda killing? Like, yesterday?'

'I put it in your mail slot.'

'I didn't see it.'

'I put it in yesterday evening.'

'Why haven't I got it, then? Why isn't it sitting right there among all the other crap on my desk?'

'Because you haven't collected it yet?'

'I collect stuff, or have someone else collect it, at least three times every day.'

'Well, you mustn't have today yet, because I put the report in there last night. Like I've already said. Twice.'

'Are you yanking me about, Davey?'

'No, boss.'

'You'd better not be.'

'I'm not.'

'I won't put up with it, Davey. I've tolerated a very large

amount of rubbish from you over the years, and I'm about fucking sick of it.'

'Did you just call me in here to shout at me?'

Tormey scowled and picked a file up from amid the clutter in front of him. 'The commissioner wants us to give this a look-over. He specifically asked us to get a criminologist's take on it, so that's why it's landing in your lap.'

Dunnigan took the file and flipped it open to the front page.

'Five missing-person reports, one involving a young couple, all filed over the past six months, all in Dublin's inner city,' Tormey said.

Dunnigan ran his eye down the first page in the file, which was a chronology of when the reports had been made – there was no regularity to it that he could see. Two had come in during the same week in March, and there was a two-month gap between the penultimate and final disappearances. 'I take it there's something linking them?'

'They're all homeless.'

Dunnigan looked up at his boss. 'So who says they're missing? They could just be out on the streets somewhere, off the grid.'

'My thoughts exactly. Homelessness is grabbing a lot of newspaper headlines at the moment. I think the commissioner just wants it to look like we're pulling our weight and doing our bit for the cause. Look the file over, see if there's any line of enquiry we can take. If there is, look into it. If there isn't, we can say we gave it a go and file it as closed.'

'How exactly does a simple missing-person case fall under our remit?'

'Two of the missing have been taken in for soliciting – it's tenuous, but I think Head Office just wants to be able to say they've put their best people on it. You should be pleased that, after all the shit you've pulled, you're still considered to be "best people".'

'Yes, boss.' Dunnigan stood to leave.

'One more thing.'

'Yes?'

'I need you to do me a favour.'

Dunnigan remained standing. Tormey, one of the most self-contained men the criminologist had ever met, had never asked for a favour before.

'My wife's cousin is going to be coming here for a day's work experience, which will mostly involve getting a tour, like. I was wondering if you might show him around for a couple of hours, explain about what you do.'

Dunnigan blinked. 'Is he a garda cadet?'

'No. He's … well, he goes to a centre for people with special needs. I've only ever met him once before – I barely know the lad. I promised I'd take him but sure we can't have him wandering around the bullpen looking at evidence, can we? I don't know what I was thinking. He's coming tomorrow. Could you show him the offices, tell him some stories about cases we solved, then buy him some lunch and send him on his way?'

'This really is not my area of expertise, boss …'

'D'ye think it's mine? The lad was put in a home when he was small and my missus feels guilty we never helped out more. She nags me day and night to do my bit for him.'

'But this would be *me* doing your bit for him.'

'Are you gonna help me or not?'

'Do I have a choice?'

'No.'

'Well, then, of course I will.'

'Good. Now, stop fecking about and get on with that case.'

5

DUNNIGAN HAD A DESK IN THE LARGE SQUAD room, which was usually surrounded by a wall of boxes containing evidence and stacks of files. He made some tea in the tiny kitchen at the end of the fifth-floor corridor the Sex Crimes Unit called home, then sat at his desk and began to examine the information Tormey had given him.

One of Dunnigan's gifts as a criminologist was his ability to focus with laser-like intensity on the details of a case, usually finding facts that conflicted with one another, coincidences that were just too convenient, or links and similarities others had missed. His true talent was that he was painstaking and methodical – while others' minds would start to wander after many hours of poring over seemingly insignificant minutiae, Dunnigan's attention would still be razor sharp. He did not seem to experience mental fatigue the way others did.

That day's file was slim enough, though, consisting as it did only of the pro formas that had been filled out for the missing-person reports themselves, and statements taken from those making the reports – it seemed that very little effort had been expended in investigating so far, and therefore the file did not take very long to read from cover to cover. Trevor Murphy, thirty-two years old, originally from Tallaght; Donald Hanks, forty-five, whose family hailed from Skibbereen; Wayne and Fiona Grant, both in their early twenties, he originally from Dundalk, she from Ardee;

Bridget Bates, forty, originally from Wexford; and Paul Myers, twenty-six, last known address Bray. All had been living on the streets of Ireland's capital city for more than a year – in Myers's case, he had been sleeping rough for the last decade, off and on. Dunnigan took a sheet of paper from his printer, folded it into a small square, and began to jot notes on it in a spidery hand.

Murphy had been the first reported missing, by a friend of his, who said he had gone to buy them a meal at a chip shop that tolerated their presence and had not returned. Hanks had been having a relationship with a homeless woman: he was to meet her on a patch of waste ground where they had been sleeping and had not shown up. The Grants had been due to meet a housing charity to discuss temporary accommodation and missed the appointment – when the outreach worker went looking for them, they were nowhere to be found, and a week later were still missing. Bates had been sleeping in the same spot behind Connolly Station for the past three years, and the other homeless people, who had made a kind of shanty village there, had reported her as missing. Myers met a priest weekly for tea and a chat, and it was the priest who had made the report when he failed to appear three weeks in a row.

There were photos of only two of the missing – Myers and Murphy. Dunnigan removed them from the file, tacking them to the back of one of the boxes that formed a kind of cubicle wall around his desk. He sat back and looked at the images. He allowed his body to relax, his mind to begin sifting what he had just read, every detail of the faces in the pictures to imprint themselves onto his consciousness.

He sat like that for close to half an hour as the bustle and chatter of the squad room continued around him. No one paid him any heed.

Abruptly, he stood, pulling his coat from the back of his chair, and stalked out of the door without saying goodbye to anyone. He didn't have much to work with, but he knew where to begin.

6

THE RESPOND HOUSING AGENCY WAS SITUATED IN a small building on Hatch Street, only a short walk from Garda HQ. Dunnigan sat in a small waiting area while a mousy secretary informed the agency's coordinator that he was there.

Greta Doolin was a slim, plainly dressed woman in her early thirties. She welcomed him into her cramped office and offered him coffee.

'Thank you, no. I want to ask you a few questions about the Grants. You reported them missing last March?'

'Yes. Have you found them?'

'No.'

'Oh. I'm sorry to hear that. How can I help you?'

'Well … um … Ms Doolin, how do you know they *are* missing?'

'I do not know where they are. Therefore they are missing.'

'They were homeless, weren't they?'

'Yes.'

'So, as I understand it, they had no fixed address.'

'Not quite correct.'

'No? They did have an address, then?'

'The Grants had been sleeping rough in Dublin for more than two years. They had been heroin addicts, and had both been thrown out, then disowned, by their respective families. They came to Dublin, thinking it would be easier to be homeless in the big city than in the small towns in the north-east where they were from.'

'Is it?'

'In some ways, yes – if you know how to forage, there are a lot more resources in terms of food and, of course, there is a greater population to beg from. However, there is also more competition, so I often think one balances the other out.'

'You said they had a kind of address?'

'Many long-term homeless make a semi-permanent home for themselves – they find a spot and claim it. There are places the homeless congregate – places most of the housed community don't ever go. Many people who work with them refer to this alternative Dublin as the Warrens. You might have heard the phrase?'

'No.'

'Well, the Grants lived in one of those spots – an abandoned car park that was once part of a storage complex near the Guinness Brewery. They slept there most nights, and if you wanted to contact them, that's where you'd go.'

'And when you went looking for them there, they were gone?'

'They were, but their things were not.'

'They had left belongings behind?'

'They left everything behind – things they had collected and looked after since they came to the city.'

'Like what?'

'I can show you, if you wish.'

'That would be helpful.'

She brought him to a storeroom at the back of the building. There, in the corner, was a small pile of items – he saw two worn sleeping bags, tightly rolled and tied with twine, three Lidl shopping bags filled with clothes, another that had paperback books and some ornaments, and a couple of framed photographs of people Dunnigan took to be estranged family members.

'I brought these here when I was sure William and Fiona weren't coming back. They might not look like much, but on the streets everything has a value. Someone would have taken them.'

'I understand.'

'There were some items that were too large for me to rescue – an old, damaged couch they had taken from a skip, and a barrel they had adapted and used as a table.'

'Sounds like they'd made quite a home for themselves.'

'They had done their very best to make themselves comfortable.'

'How can you be sure they haven't just moved on? Maybe they got into trouble with a local criminal or another homeless person and had to run quickly, so they had no time to bring their things.'

'Well, first, they would never have left their sleeping bags – if they brought nothing else, a decent sleeping bag can mean the difference between life and death when you're sleeping rough.'

'And second?'

'We were about to give them their own place. I had a flat they were going to be given the keys to within the space of a week.'

'This was definite?'

'It was. I had done quite a bit of work with the Grants – they were clean and sober, and were, we felt, ready to make the transition back into their own home. In our estates they would have had access to support, so there was help available if they needed it or ran into difficulty. They were so excited. I know they wouldn't have just taken off.'

'Maybe they went home.'

'I called their families. No one has seen hide or hair of them.'

'Could you give me those contact details, please?'

'Of course.'

Dunnigan took a final look at the pathetic pile of personal possessions. 'What do you think happened to them, Ms Doolin?'

'The street is a dangerous place,' the woman said. 'I think they fell foul of someone, probably over the space they were squatting in, and it all turned nasty.'

'You think they're dead,' Dunnigan said.

'I'm afraid I do, yes.'

Dunnigan nodded, and said his goodbyes. He was inclined to agree with her.

7

FATHER BILL CREEDON WAS FIFTY-ONE YEARS OLD, giving him ten years on Dunnigan. He was a couple of inches over six feet in height, with a full head of well-groomed dark hair that was shot through with a little grey about the temples and along the parting. He had broad shoulders and a slim waist, and wore the dark shirt and dog-collar of a Roman Catholic priest, but he combined them with an expensive-looking soft leather jacket and designer jeans – Father Bill was clearly a priest, but not of the usual sort.

Dunnigan noted, as he sat across from him in the dining hall of the Widow's Quay Homeless Project (a plain room with magnolia-painted walls and fourteen tables spread with red-and-white-chequered tablecloths), that the man had some scar tissue and thickening of the flesh about his eyes, and that the his nose had experienced some adversity in the past – it had obviously been broken at least twice. This did not take from the man's appearance, though. If anything, it added to it, giving him character. Father Bill Creedon was a handsome man, and Dunnigan could imagine that his female parishioners (and probably some of the males, too) would be drawn to his good looks and charisma as much as his spiritual guidance.

'Can I offer you something to drink, Mr Dunnigan?'

'Davey, please. And no, thank you, Father. I'm here to ask you about the missing-person report you filed on Paul Myers.'

'What can I tell you about it?'

'You met Paul every Thursday for coffee?'

'Yes. I've known him for many years. He and I would have a coffee and a smoke and catch up on each other's news. He slept here at the shelter from time to time, but he was happy enough on the street – he'd been living that way long enough to be reasonably safe, so I didn't hassle him about it.'

'Where would you meet?'

'Stephen's Green.'

'Always?'

'Yes. There was a bench we'd always sit on for our natter.'

'How did you come to know Myers?'

'He came to me ... oooh ... four years ago, now, and asked for my help. He was a bit of a mess – not looking after himself very well, doing drugs, drinking too much. Together, we sorted him out.'

'How?'

'He was carrying a lot of anger, Davey. He needed someone to talk to.'

'What was he angry about?'

Father Bill smiled and sat back, as if he was considering whether or not to answer the question. Finally he said: 'He had experienced some less than Christian treatment at the hands of one of my associates.'

'Which one?'

Father Bill laughed. 'Does it matter?'

'This is not the first time your name has come up in an investigation, Father.'

'No?'

'Could you please tell me about your relationship with Father Joseph O'Malley?'

'I didn't really have a relationship with him.'

'I'm not surprised. He died. Shortly after Paul Myers went missing, as it happens.'

'Really? I hadn't noticed.'

'One of your staff here, a Ms Diane Robinson, told us that Father O'Malley came here to see you three days before he died.'

'He certainly did. But that does not mean we were friends, or even associates.'

'Father Creedon, you are a priest with a parish here in Dublin.'

'Yes.'

'And Father O'Malley was also a priest with a parish in the city.'

'He was a neighbour of mine, yes.'

'Does that not suggest at least an association?'

'No.'

'I don't follow.'

'Our paths did not often cross, Davey. My territory runs along the waterfront here – my main role is the running of the Homeless Project, but the guidelines laid down by the Church insist I am linked to an actual parish, also. Mine includes the houses, flats and estates between here and Clontarf. Now, while Clontarf is quite well off and resourced, my area is not, and I work very hard, very long hours, to do what I can for my people. I do not have time to … um … to *associate*, as you have put it, with other priests. I'm the only full-time staff at the Project, despite having asked repeatedly for some back-up, and that means my dance-card is rather full.'

Dunnigan nodded, and glanced down at the sheet of paper he had been using to take notes all day – it was, by then, folded into an even smaller square, and was covered, front and back, with his small handwriting. 'But you knew *of* him.'

'Yes. By reputation.'

'Please explain.'

'You know what I mean.'

'Pretend I don't.'

'Joe O'Malley was a predator, Davey. He had a hunger for children, and he thought he could appease that appetite without challenge or consequence.'

'So you believed Father O'Malley was a paedophile.'

'I *knew* he was.'

'How?'

'Several boys who had experienced his attentions came to me for help.'

'Several?'

'Three boys.'

'Do you know their names?'

'Of course I do.'

'Could you tell me them, please?'

'No, I'm afraid I could not.'

'I am a representative of the gardaí, Father. I can compel you to divulge their identities.'

'As I understand it, the seal of the confessional still provides statutory privilege. These boys are my penitents.'

'Was Paul Myers one of the people who asserted Father O'Malley abused him?'

'I am not at liberty to say.'

Dunnigan scribbled something in the margin of his page. 'That's been tested a few times in the Supreme Court, Father. It doesn't always hold.'

'Joe O'Malley was known to the police as a potential risk to the safety of children in his parish. I don't doubt you have several names on file already of children whose parents reported what happened. Why waste your time trying to get me to divulge more names? What difference would it make to your case?'

Dunnigan said nothing for a moment. 'Why did Father O'Malley come to see you?'

'He was angry with some things I said to an interviewer from one of the local radio stations.'

'The interview you gave to Dublin City FM?'

'That's the one.'

'The interview in which you stated there was a priest in a parish near yours who was a risk to children, and that parents should protest outside his church and request the bishop have him moved?'

'And prosecuted. Yes, I believe you have the bones of it.'

'How did the bishop feel about that interview?'

'Oh, he was beside himself. But, then, he and I don't often see eye to eye.'

'You and Father O'Malley had a conversation, then, when he visited here?'

'Words were exchanged, yes.'

'Only words?'

'Well … it got a little heated.'

Father Bill smiled warmly, as if he were enjoying the memory.

'Ms Robinson eventually admitted to us there was a physical altercation,' Dunnigan said. 'She was reluctant to give us too many details.'

'I punched the scumbag right on his filthy nose, Davey. And when he was on the ground, I delivered a sharp kick to his ribs.'

'So the two of you fought.'

'No. I hit him. He was a coward, and was not inclined to try his luck with someone more his own size than the nine- and ten-year-olds he liked to force his attentions on.'

'You grew up in the inner city, Father Creedon?'

'They call me Father Bill.'

Dunnigan ignored him. 'You grew up around here?'

'I did. This is my home.'

'You studied at UCD. That must have been unusual for someone from this area.'

'My parents placed great value on education. They sacrificed a lot so I could do better than them.'

'You father worked on the docks – and he was something of a boxer, I hear?'

'He was an amateur, but he did well enough.'

'You boxed too?'

'For my school, and I did some while at college.'

'Were you any good?'

'I was good, but not great. I went up against Jamesie Cash, a Traveller from Meath, a light heavyweight as well as a bare-knuckle champ. He showed me what great was, and I realised it was time to hang up my gloves. He was an amazing fighter – beautiful to watch, hellish to get in the ring with.'

Dunnigan made another note on his paper. 'Growing up around here, you must have known some of the people who went on to become involved in organised crime.'

'I did and I still do. The gangs serve a dual purpose, Davey. They are, of course, engaged in criminal activity, a lot of which I abhor and work against. But they also provide an important social function: they police areas the gardaí are afraid to go. They offer guidance and a safe haven for children whose parents often don't give two damns about them. They visit the elderly and tend the sick.'

Dunnigan put down his paper and pen sharply. 'They also deal drugs,' he said. 'They murder innocent people. They run prostitution rings and they lead young people into lives that are doomed to end far too early through violence. You present a very one-sided, and might I say naïve, view, Father.'

'Well, you raised the issue.'

'Do you know a man named Tim Pat Rogers?'

'You know I do.'

'Also known as the Janitor?'

'Well, that's what the tabloids have labelled him, yes.'

'You and Mr Rogers were friends growing up.'

'We were.'

'And Mr Rogers is now the leader of a very prominent criminal gang, which operates mainly out of what was Father O'Malley's parish.'

'That is true, yes.'

'You know that Mr Rogers has been investigated due to his alleged involvement in people trafficking.'

'I had not heard that.'

Dunnigan took up his notes again and unfolded a corner to reveal more dense script.'Father O'Malley's housekeeper has stated that, the afternoon before his death, you called to his house.'

'Not true.'

'She says that he refused to see you, but you shouted a number of things down the hall.'

'You're talking about Mrs Scully?'

'Bridget Scully, yes.'

'You know she drinks, don't you?'

'She asserts you shouted that Father O'Malley was to leave Dublin and never return. You also said that if he did not, he would not like what was going to happen.'

'I was here all that afternoon, Davey.'

'Yes. I have been told that.'

'If I was here, how could I have also been bellowing threats at the late Joe O'Malley?'

'And where were you the following night, when he was snatched from the street outside his church by a man in a balaclava, who dragged him into the back of a blue van?'

'I was doing outreach on the Quays that night.'

'All night?'

'Until about midnight, anyway.'

'So you have no idea how Father O'Malley came to be found the following morning, beaten to death, on a patch of waste ground near the bishop's house – the bishop who, despite your requests and imprecations, refused to move him or hand him over to the police?'

'I haven't got a clue.'

'I think you do, Father. Where were you after midnight on the night of April the twentieth 2015?'

'I came back to the centre, here, checked in with whoever was on duty that night, and then went home to bed.'

'I have in my notes that it was Diane Robinson, and it was she who has acted as your alibi. Again.'

'I believe so, yes.'

'Is she working today?'

'I think she's on at three.'

'I'd like to speak to her, please.'

'I'm sure she'd be delighted to chat with you.'

'I'll come back for three thirty. Will you please ask her to expect me?'

'It will be my pleasure.'

8

'MRS BRANDON, YOUR HUSBAND HAS BEEN CLEAN for the past three years, and has been in therapy for two. He poses no threat to your son, and it would, I believe, be a huge help to his reintegration into society to be able to have some access to him, even fully supervised.'

Diane Robinson paused, the phone receiver held between her chin and her shoulder as she scribbled something on a yellow legal pad. Dunnigan stood at the reception desk of the Homeless Project, waiting patiently for her to finish.

'I was in the army myself, Mrs Brandon, for ten years, in fact. Your husband is experiencing post-traumatic stress disorder, which is quite understandable after what he experienced in Somalia.'

It seemed as if Mrs Brandon was not going to give in easily.

'Yes, he is still sleeping rough a lot of the time, but he comes to the Project as often as we can have him, and I can vouch that his progress has been steady …'

Dunnigan studied the young woman. She looked to be in her late thirties, and had strong, intelligent features. Her hair was light brown, tied back in a tight ponytail. She wore a white and black PLO-style scarf, a black leather biker jacket, and had a stud through her nose just above the left nostril.

'Will you at least consider it?' Diane asked, although resignation had entered her voice. 'Okay. Thank you for taking my call, anyway.' She hung up and looked at Dunnigan pointedly. 'You're the detective?'

'I'm a criminologist, actually.'

Diane shrugged and stood up. Dunnigan noted that she was a good two inches taller than him.

'I'm going to have a cup of coffee. Would you like one?'

'No, thank you.'

'You can watch me have one, then.'

They went into the same dining hall in which he had spoken to Father Bill, and Diane busied herself making a cappuccino from a machine that looked as if it might have been built by NASA.

'So, what do you want to know?' she said, when she sat down.

'I'm investigating the disappearance of Paul Myers. I think he was abused by Joseph O'Malley, who was murdered shortly after Myers was reported missing.'

'And?'

'I don't know. My job is to ask around until I find something meaningful.'

'Good luck with that.'

'You provided an alibi for Father Bill Creedon on two separate occasions,' Dunnigan said, giving her the dates.

'And?'

'I want to know why.'

Diane took a long draught of her coffee. 'You don't beat around the bush, do you?'

'Every piece of evidence points to the fact that Father Bill was, at best, instrumental in Father O'Malley's death, and knows more than he's saying about Paul Myers's disappearance.'

'And you think it would be right to put Father Bill in prison?'

'Who said anything about putting him in prison?'

'Isn't that what you're trying to do?'

'He's a curious man. He goes out of his way to help the

homeless community in the city, but he's friends with a mobster who preys on women, children and the poor.'

'I suppose he's complicated. He doesn't see the world in black and white.'

'That's not for me to decide. Why did you lie for him? He might have been involved in the deaths of two men.'

'Would he have gone to the gardaí about Paul being missing if he was trying to cover it up?'

'It adds a layer of credibility to his saying he knows nothing about it.'

'Even if he knows more than he pretends to, I'd ask the question again: do you think putting that man in prison would be the right thing to do?'

'Ms Robinson, my job is to analyse the evidence, expose certain patterns or trends of behaviour, and find the truth of what happened. Father Bill Creedon is a loner with a history of violence. He is in a job that encourages adherence to a moral code that is often at odds with the law, and places its own authority above that of the state. Even among his own people he is a maverick and has become isolated. He expressed openly that he had a grudge against Father O'Malley and not only threatened him but physically assaulted him. It is not my job to decide whether or not Father Creedon's arrest would be a good idea or morally right. My role is to join the dots and hand the information over to my superiors. Part of the information I plan to hand over will indicate that I believe Father O'Malley was complicit in Paul Myers's disappearance, and that Father Bill Creedon either had Joseph O'Malley killed or did it himself, with the assistance of a criminal gang.'

'Do you know anything about the work he does here?'

'I hear he does a lot of good.'

'He does. He is a lifeline to the people of this area. He puts a roof over the heads of countless men who would otherwise sleep in the streets. He raises thousands of euros every month to bring hampers of food to poor families in the flats. He runs a youth club that keeps kids away from crime, and he is single-handedly responsible for more youngsters finishing school and going on to college than any teacher I have ever met.'

'You are very loyal to him.'

'He inspires loyalty.'

In the hallway outside, they could both hear someone singing. It was a clear, tenor voice, and the song was Neil Young's 'After The Goldrush'.

'That's Father Bill. He sings all the time.'

'I heard you say you were in the army.'

'I was. My dad was a soldier – it runs in the family. I did five years of soldiering and another five in the Rangers.' The Rangers: the Irish Special Forces.

'Impressive. Why did you leave?'

'They paid for me to go to college to do psychology. I graduated with a degree and a postgrad in counselling. The deal they offered was an honourable discharge so long as I agreed to counsel soldiers with issues. So I do that and I work here the rest of the time.'

'Father Bill said you were a volunteer.'

'I'm part-time, but I love it here, so I work more hours than he pays me for.'

'You spend a lot of time here, then.'

'I would say that I spend most of my time here.'

'You and Father Bill must be very close.'

'You could say that, yes.'

'He's a good-looking man.'

'What are you getting at?'

'Well, it says in my notes that you're single ...'

'So what? That doesn't mean I'm shagging my boss!'

'No, but it might explain why you're prepared to perjure yourself for him.'

Diane stood, knocking her chair back violently. 'Do your

fucking notes say that I lost my husband in a car accident five years ago? That one of the main reasons I left the army, which I also loved, was that I was a goddamn mess?'

Dunnigan held up a hand to stop her talking, and checked his sheet of neatly written details. 'No – it doesn't, actually,' he said, genuinely surprised.

'Well, fuck you very much.' Diane turned and stalked out of the dining hall.

Dunnigan made a note of this new information and, putting his pen carefully back in his pocket, followed the young woman out.

9

SHE WAS BACK BEHIND THE RECEPTION DESK WHEN he reached the door. She busied herself sorting through a file, and ignored him. 'I'm sorry if my questions seemed insensitive,' he said, to the top of her head, 'but I had to ask them.'

'Goodbye, Mr Dunnigan.'

'Goodbye,' he said, and opened the door to leave.

'Wait a minute,' Diane barked, as he was almost gone.

He stopped dead, and turned to look at her, the door held half open, half closed.

'Did you read the details of what O'Malley did to those boys?'

'What he *allegedly* did to them,' Dunnigan said, correcting her almost instinctively. 'Yes. I am familiar with the case.'

'He was a fucking monster.'

Dunnigan wasn't sure how to respond. He had been working with violent crime for so long, its impact on the survivors had almost stopped occurring to him.

'Father Bill did everything he could to have O'Malley removed from active ministry. He hounded the bishop, he went to the police, he went to the media.'

'And, finally, he went to the Janitor.'

Diane sighed and shook her head. 'Purely hypothetically, would it have been so awful if he did? The damage that animal was doing to those kids – to this community and others around the city – was devastating. O'Malley is gone, and now the people can start healing.'

Dunnigan chewed his lower lip. 'What are you saying, Ms Robinson?'

'You work for the Sex Crimes Unit, yes?'

'It's why I'm here – Paul Myers was arrested for solicitation in the Phoenix Park in 2014, and Father O'Malley has been on our books for some time.'

'How long?'

'I can't tell you that.'

'But a long time, yeah?'

'Yes.'

'Were you close to catching him?'

'I can't tell you that.'

'You weren't, were you? You could have spent the next ten years chasing that twisted fucker, and you would have been no closer. Well – good news, Mr Dunnigan! He's been caught.'

Dunnigan gazed back at her. He had no idea what to say. 'Goodbye, Ms Robinson,' he said finally, to fill the silence.

'Will you do something for me?' she asked him.

'What?'

'Before you file your report, or whatever it is you're supposed to do, go out with Father Bill when he's doing outreach. See him at work and how people respond to him.'

Somewhere in the depths of the building, Dunnigan could now hear Father Bill singing 'Heart of Gold'. 'Do you keep a record of everyone who uses this establishment?' he asked.

'Of course.'

'Is it digital?'

'We get people to sign a guest book, but I log the details on to a spreadsheet every night before closing up.'

'Could you run these names through your books before I go, please?'

He listed the six people – including the two Grants – who were missing.

'They all slept here, except for the Grants, but they used to come here to eat a couple of times a week,' Diane said.

'Could you print up the dates for me?'

Scowling, she did, and Dunnigan took his leave.

Diane Robinson made him uncomfortable. She seemed far too emotional, and her passion for what she did and for the people with whom she worked radiated from her. It was so long since Dunnigan had felt anything like that that it was almost completely alien. He hurried to his car – the ancient BMW had been fixed and looked none the worse for wear – and drove back to the office faster than he needed to.

10

'I'M MILEY TIMONEY.'

The following morning Dunnigan stood at the front gate to Garda Headquarters on Harcourt Street, its three red-brick office blocks rising behind him, looking at the young man he had to entertain for the next two hours. The youngster had his hand outstretched in greeting.

'Um … hello, I'm David Dunnigan,' he said, taking the proffered appendage gingerly. 'I am a civilian consultant with the Sex Crimes Unit of An Garda Síochána.'

'Pleased to meet you.'

'Inspector Tormey says you asked to come here to learn more about what we do.'

'I'd really like to come on work placement.'

'Are you hoping to become a guard?'

'No. I go to a training centre for people with intellectual disabilities. They send us on training programmes, and I did one that had criminology as a module. I really, really liked it.'

'Did you finish the course?'

'I got a distinction.'

'Oh. Um … well done.'

'Thanks.'

'Okay – let's show you around. Is there any aspect of policing that particularly interests you?'

'I like shows about forensics and that kind of thing, Dr Dunnigan.'

'You don't have to call me that.'

'Call you what?'

'Doctor. I don't have a PhD.'

'I read an article that said you were doing one, and that was back in 1999.'

'You read an article about me?'

'I read true-crime magazines. When they told me you'd be showing me around, I remembered I'd read somethin' about you, so I dug out the magazine. It was all about that kid ...'

'I know what it was about, Miley.'

'Oh. Yes. Sorry.'

'I was doing a PhD back then, but I never finished it.'

'Was it because of—'

'Let's just say that life got in the way. Come on. I'll give you the tour and then we'll go and get ice cream or something.'

'I don't want ice cream, thanks.'

Dunnigan did not respond – he was now desperately trying to work out how to fill the block of time he had allocated to that particular activity, which he had hoped would bring him right up to lunch. He turned and began to walk into the large complex that was the operations base for most of the specialist Irish police squads.

'Follow me. On your left are the offices of the Emergency Response Unit.'

'Can we go in and meet them? See what emergencies are happ'nin' today?'

'No. Up ahead is where the Criminal Assets Bureau is based.'

'I don't s'pose we can go in there either. See where they keep all their assets.'

Dunnigan stopped. 'Are you ... um ... are you mentally deficient?' He knew as he asked the question that it flew completely in the face of everything his sister constantly told him about being sensitive and not offending people, but he was starting to wonder exactly how he should pitch the content of his tour, not to mention the entertaining and informative anecdotes he had planned to share – Miley seemed to be a huge fan of cop shows and true-crime magazines, so Dunnigan had just assumed a certain level of understanding. But this kid *looked* so disabled.

'No, Mr Dunnigan, I am *not* mentally deficient. I was assessed as having an IQ of 114, making me the higher end of average.'

'You live in a residential home, though?'

'My father was sixty-five when I was born, and my mother had psychiatric issues. When my dad died, she couldn't cope. I've been in care since I was six.'

'And you're what age now?'

'I was twenty-seven last birthday.'

Dunnigan looked at the young man: Miley was dressed in an ill-fitting anorak, a T-shirt with a picture of Jimi Hendrix showing underneath it, baggy cord trousers and scuffed black brogues. He had a green canvas bag slung across his shoulder. 'Did my question offend you, Mr Timoney?'

A broad grin spread across Miley's face. 'No one's ever called me Mr Timoney before!' he said, unable to suppress a loud laugh.

'Should I not call you that?'

'Call me Miley.'

'All right. You haven't answered my question – did I insult you by asking about your intellectual faculties?'

'Most people don't ask, they just assume I'm stupid,' Miley said. 'You at least considered the poss'bility that I might not be.'

'I still don't know if I hurt your feelings.'

'No. You didn't,' Miley said. 'But thanks for checking. No one else cares if I'm upset or not.'

'It would make the rest of the day uncomfortable if you were,' Dunnigan said. 'Now, these buildings were originally constructed in 1981 …'

And the tour continued.

11

'YOU CAN'T HAVE HIM HERE.' TORMEY LOOKED as if he was fit to kill Dunnigan, who was mildly bemused by his superior's reaction. Through the glass panel of his office door, Tormey could see Miley Timoney wandering about the workroom across the hall, examining some highly confidential photographs of a crime scene that had been tagged to the wall. 'I mean, for fuck's sake, Davey, what were you thinking?'

'You said to give him a tour. That's what I'm doing. We've given people tours of the place before.'

'And they all went through a request process that usually takes about six weeks! I sidestepped the red tape to get him in and out as quickly as possible. And I told you to show him around outside and take him for a fucking milkshake, not bring him in here where we work. I was clear about that.'

'You weren't. How was I to know you hadn't gone through the proper channels? I thought ...'

Tormey shook his head slowly. 'No, you didn't think. Not at all. Take him away, please! If word gets out that I've let one of my crew bring in some yahoo off the street, totally unvetted, we'll all be in the shithouse. I don't know what gets into you sometimes, I really don't!'

'Sorry, boss.'

'Get the fuck out of my sight.'

Dunnigan rose to leave. As he did, Tormey asked him:

'How's that homeless thing going?'

'None of the missing knew one another, or had any connection I can see. They were different ages, from different places, and they went missing in different parts of the city. Some were addicts, some had psychiatric difficulties and some, like the Grants, were clean, sober and close to getting back onto the property ladder.'

'Are you telling me in your long-winded way to close the shagging file?'

'Not yet. They all do have one connection.'

'Which is?'

'They all frequented the Widow's Quay Homeless Project.'

'Bill Creedon's place?'

'Yes.'

Tormey rubbed his moustache. 'I can't see Father Bill knocking off homeless people – unless they were involved in some shit that offended his personal moral code, which, let's face it, means he quite plausibly could have had something to do with it.'

'I never thought the priest killed Myers – I think they were friends …'

'Father Bill is a sociopath. If someone is dead and he's in the vicinity, the likelihood is he was in it up to his neck.'

'Well, I'm going to dig some more.'

'Okay. Keep me posted.'

'Will do.'

'Now would you kindly get him out of here?'

'I'm going.'

'Good.'

12

DUNNIGAN TOOK MILEY FOR LUNCH IN CAPTAIN America's on Grafton Street.

'I heard Uncle Frank shouting at you,' Miley said, as they waited to be served. 'Is that why we had to leave before the tour really started?'

'He was supposed to have you cleared by the Public Relations Department prior to your visit.'

'And he didn't do that?'

'No. He didn't.'

'Did he know he was s'posed to?'

'It would certainly have meant waiting for several weeks, and in the end you might not have been allowed to come at all. He wanted to get it done quickly, and I was supposed to show you around but to keep you away from the main areas where we work. Detective Tormey will be angry with me for a few days, then he'll forget about it, or be angry with me about something else.'

'Is he mad at you a lot?'

'Yes.'

'Don't you mind?'

'No.'

'I hate it when people are mad at me.'

'What can they do? In my experience, two things happen – you either get shouted at, or get given the silent treatment. Neither make much difference in the general scheme of things, and very few people have the energy to keep it up for long.'

'Well, in my 'sperience, other things can happen too, which are a lot worse than that.'

'Such as?'

Miley looked as if he was about to say something, but then the waitress arrived with their food: a burger and fries for Miley, a chicken wrap for Dunnigan (no sauce). Miley tucked in with gusto, covering everything with tomato ketchup, while Dunnigan began methodically to cut his into bite-size pieces, which he then arranged in a tight circle on the plate.

'You were saying?'

'Oh – I forget. We didn't really get to see much in Garda HQ, so can I ask you some questions?'

'All right.'

'You're a criminologist?'

'Yes.'

'What's that like?'

'In what way do you mean?'

'Well, do you like it?'

Dunnigan paused, considering the question as if he had never thought about it before. 'Yes. I think I do.'

'You *think*? Don't you *know*?'

'I used to love it very much.'

'What does a criminologist do?'

'I teach undergraduate students at the university in Maynooth, and, as you already know, I consult three days a week with the Sex Crimes Unit – it was called the National Bureau of Criminal Investigation when I started working there.'

'And what kind of consulting do you do?'

'Mostly I look at the evidence and try to find patterns, coincidences, things that don't make sense. But there are software programs that can do that now, so I'm doing more interviews with witnesses than I used to.'

'Why the Sex Crimes Unit? Seems pretty nasty.'

'I've done a lot of research on violent crime – when I was still a student it was the field I thought I could do the most good in, but it was also where there were a lot of gaps in what we knew, so I felt I might make my mark.'

'And do you have to deal with lots of bad people?'

'Some bad people, yes.'

'D'you ever get scared?'

'Not often. Usually I deal with the case long before arrests are made, and at that stage it's all about constructing the chain of events, processing evidence, checking and cross-checking facts – that kind of thing.'

Miley was listening to all of this wide-eyed, while still shovelling as much ketchup-coated food into his mouth as he could. 'But you've solved a lot of cases, haven't you? I googled you, and your name comes up a lot as being instr'mental in catching loads of baddies.'

'Baddies?'

'Killers! Criminals! Come on, Mr Dunnigan – you're a hero!'

Dunnigan, perhaps for the first time that morning, looked directly at Miley Timoney. 'I don't think anyone has used that term to describe me in a very long time.'

'Are you okay, Mr Dunnigan? Have I said something wrong?'

'No. And, please, call me Davey. Everyone else does.'

'All right, Davey. Are you sure you're okay? You don't look so good.'

'I'm fine,' Dunnigan said, forcing a smile on to his face that did not come anywhere near his eyes. 'Let's talk about something else.'

Ernest Frobisher

Sometimes he would set the Yellow Man tasks, things that were seemingly impossible, just to see how far his powers went, and how strong his loyalty was.

In the first week the Yellow Man was in his service, Frobisher called him to his office. 'I want you to bring me a woman.'

'What are your tastes?'

'I want Margaret Soames.'

The woman he named was married to Giles Soames, a competitor in a bid he was mounting for a hotel chain. The couple lived in a house set in its own grounds in the Dorset countryside, and it was well known the property had a very expensive security system and was well guarded.

'Yes, sir.'

'She will not be returning home, so make sure you leave no trace you were there – but I would like Giles to know it was me who took her, just the same.'

'He will know, but I'll make sure he will have no desire to prove it.'

'I want her unharmed when she gets here,' Frobisher said. 'More or less.'

'Of course.'

Four hours later, Margaret Soames was tied to a bed in Frobisher's basement. He left her there for three days before he started working on her, all the time playing videos he had made of the time some of his previous visitors had spent in the room on a large screen he had affixed to the ceiling directly above her.

When he finally did pay Mrs Soames a visit, she was quite mad.

He had a fine time with her, just the same – a little too fine, in fact, as the end came far too soon. It was short, but very sweet. Near the end, Frobisher felt they had bonded in a strange way.

Only later did he read some of the police reports dealing with Margaret Soames's disappearance – he had one or two high-ranking members of the force on his payroll, so getting the paperwork had been simplicity itself. There had been five security guards on the estate the evening she vanished, as well as closed-circuit cameras all over the property. The woman had been in her room, reading before bed, the last time anyone had heard from her.

She was in her room and then she wasn't.

The camera covering the corridor outside her room had stopped working for three minutes just before midnight. The only DNA found in the room belonged to Mrs Soames, her husband, and one their servants, none of whom reported seeing anything.

The day after his wife had vanished without a trace, Giles Soames withdrew from the hotel business completely, selling all his assets for far less than they were worth – several companies in which Frobisher had an interest were the beneficiaries of these sales.

The Yellow Man had talent. Frobisher would have to make sure that that talent did not go to waste.

13

LATER THAT NIGHT DUNNIGAN SAT ON THE couch in his almost empty flat, the notes he had taken on the disappearances spread out on the flimsy coffee-table before him.

It seemed clear to him that the five cases were not linked. The missing people were too disparate: the parts of the city they frequented were all different; their personalities (so far as he could tell) bore no similarity; their ages ranged from early twenties to mid-forties. The only two details they shared were that they were homeless and had at one time or another visited the Widow's Quay Homeless Project.

'But does that mean anything?' Dunnigan addressed the poster of Doctor Who, which hung over his fireplace. 'Is it not likely that most people who are homeless over the long term will seek aid sooner or later?'

The poster showed Patrick Troughton's second incarnation of the iconic science-fiction character, standing in the control room of the TARDIS, the craft he used to travel through time and space. The Doctor was grinning at the camera, a white-and-blue-striped recorder in one hand, a leather-bound book in the other.

Dunnigan had been a fan of science fiction, horror and fantasy in all its forms for as long as he could remember, a passion he had probably inherited from his father.

David Dunnigan came from a family of academics. His father was a psychoanalyst, his mother an educational psychologist, and his grandfather had been a professor of sociology at University College Cork. Dunnigan had grown up discussing Karl Marx's thoughts on the prison system over dinner. His mother would tell him about Sigmund Freud's views on violence as she sipped from a glass of sherry while he baked cakes for his and his sister Gina's birthday. He was always going to end up involved in the social sciences in some form or other, but it was crime that had grabbed him from an early age. Looking back, it was probably his and his dad's shared love of horror and science fiction that had made him want to know more about the darker parts of the human mind. His father always told him that the films and books they both enjoyed – everything from classics like Bram Stoker's *Dracula* to more recent works like *Alien* or *An American Werewolf in London* – were healthy ways of indulging the darker parts of their personalities: these guilty pleasures helped to purge the violent urges everyone had.

But didn't some people suggest the opposite was true? Dunnigan had asked – this was, after all, the age of the 'video nasty'. *Weren't there those who said violent films, comic books and even video games actually* caused *some individuals to commit violent crimes?*

Dr Stuart Dunnigan, David's father, did what he always did when his gifted son asked a complicated question: he brought the lad into the room that acted as their family library, pointed at a large wall covered from floor to ceiling with books, and told him to research the problem. David did, and ended up agreeing with his father, coming to the conclusion that humans had enjoyed dark and violent fantasies for as long as people had sat around campfires and told ghost stories. He learned a lot about the other side of the argument, too, but after reading countless case studies he decided that most people who committed violent acts after watching horror films were usually psychiatrically disturbed, and just as likely to be inspired to criminality by pieces of music or books unrelated to horror or violence. (*The Catcher in the Rye*, the American novel about adolescence and identity, had been linked to the shootings of both John Lennon and Ronald Reagan.) Sooner or later, they would probably have been triggered by something, even if they had never rented a slasher movie. He wrote an article on the subject, entitled 'Delinquency and the Horror Movie: Taming the Beast Within'. It was his first publication, and he was fifteen years old. He never looked back.

He moved to Cork to get his Bachelor of Arts when he was sixteen, and had a master's degree by his nineteenth birthday.

A job at the university in Maynooth followed almost immediately, and he had been tipped for great things. Within twelve months of Dunnigan's starting lecturing, Tormey had recruited him to the newly formed National Bureau of Crimininal Investigation – Dunnigan had been researching violent crime, and a paper he delivered to the Sociological Association of Ireland on how paedophile rings managed to remain hidden in plain sight was deemed useful by the police. He had spent the last eighteen years sharing his time between the university and Garda HQ. While he had never lived up to his early promise, he could not see himself doing anything else.

'It's surely a matter of statistics,' Dunnigan said aloud in the empty room. 'Statistics matched with probability – how many homeless are there, and how many shelters?' He pulled opened an ancient laptop computer and logged onto Google Chrome.

There were eight homeless shelters dotted across Dublin City – they were of varying capacities. He knew Widow's Quay could accommodate forty on any given night, while the Drumm Street Refuge, according to its website, could take only eight. Adding the numbers of beds on offer across the capital, he calculated that, on any given night, there were approximately 172 temporary beds available in Dublin City.

'That's the supply,' Dunnigan said. 'Now, what's the demand?'

This was less clear: some organisations suggested the figure was somewhere close to three thousand, others closer to two thousand. He decided to come somewhere in the middle, and settled on 2,600.

'But they're not all sleeping rough,' he said, sitting back and looking up at the Doctor. 'That figure includes people in emergency accommodation, B&Bs, hotels and whatnot. So how many would actually require the services of somewhere like Widow's Quay?'

He found an article that had been published just the previous week in an online newspaper, in which an outreach worker for one of the homeless charities stated categorically that at least three hundred people were sleeping rough in the city. This figure was based on a count he and some colleagues had done during a night of outreach work earlier that month. The article acknowledged that such counts could not hope to be completely accurate, however, as they only took in the city streets and some well-known areas where the homeless congregated, so the figure was probably higher by about 25 per cent.

'So, if we include those who are in the shelters, plus those who are not but who would still be competing for beds,' Dunnigan said, making some quick calculations on a sheet of folded paper, 'we come to a total of five hundred and fifty.'

Five hundred and fifty people competing for 172 beds – not to mention food, clothes, whatever other items the shelters and refuges provided. It seemed sensible that anyone who was on the streets for any length of time would certainly utilise a service like Widow's Quay.

Which made that common link far less interesting or compelling.

'But Father Bill is definitely a mitigating factor,' Dunnigan said, standing up and going to the window. Outside it was dark and quiet. 'He's a rogue element, no matter what way we look at it. Inspector Tormey thinks he could well be involved – but wasn't Myers his friend? And doesn't it look like he had Father O'Malley killed as an act of vengeance?'

He turned back to the Doctor. 'It doesn't make sense.'

But then murder, particularly where organised crime and sexual abuse were involved, often didn't.

14

'CRIMINOLOGY HAS BEEN THROUGH MANY STAGES, phases and fads during the course of its development,' Dunnigan said to his class the following morning.

On the board he had projected a photograph of an Italian theorist of the Victorian era named Cesare Lombrosso. His class did not appear to be hugely interested in the topic. 'Signor Lombrosso was an enthusiastic proponent of what he called *criminal atavism*,' Dunnigan continued, 'the idea that certain physical traits, such as, for example, the shape of our skulls, can be used to determine whether or not we have criminal tendencies. Lombrosso carried out a survey of prisons, and came to the conclusion that the type of person most likely to commit a crime had red hair and a wide forehead. It is an early, if wholly inaccurate, form of profiling. Interesting, though.'

He turned to look at the lecture hall. It was half empty, and those who were there seemed half asleep.

'It's easy for us to laugh at Lombrosso's ideas now, but in the late eighteenth and early nineteenth centuries, they were taken very seriously. Police forces were desperate to develop scientific methods, not just for detecting the perpetrators of crime but also for preventing crime taking place. Measuring crania and being suspicious of red-haired people might seem very primitive, but it was the beginning of a more modern, psychological approach to thinking about anti-social behaviour and the people who carry it out.'

A hand shot up from the back of the hall.

'Yes?'

'Do you use profiling in your work with the police, Mr Dunnigan?'

The hand belonged to a pretty blonde girl, whom he could not remember seeing in any of his classes before.

'Yes, to an extent. Most of what I do is about linking disparate pieces of evidence, but profiling is a part of that. I'm not a psychologist, but I have read a good deal of the literature on the subject.'

'And is there, like, a profile database you can refer to?'

'I'm not sure what you mean. Could you expand on your question, please?'

'Say you're working on a case involving an axe murderer, can you go to a website or a book and look up a profile of the type of person who might commit a crime like that, so you can see if there is someone who fits that criteria on your list of suspects?'

'Well, yes and no. There are software programs that have been developed that contain relevant indices and you can feed in the details of a case. They then suggest matches or useful profiles to move forward with.'

'Really?'

'Yes. And several books on your reading list contain discussions of various profiling techniques. Many detectives refer to volumes like that when the need arises.'

The girl was whispering something to a boy sitting beside her.

'Was there something else?' Dunnigan asked her impatiently.

'When your niece was abducted, did you try to develop a profile of who might have taken her?'

There it was – just like that.

Dunnigan froze. He had known that, sooner or later, this

would happen – someone, probably a student looking for ghoulish thrills, would ask him about Beth.

So why was he so unprepared for it now?

He was aware of two things going on inside him at once: his mind trying to process what he had been asked; a terrible, roiling anger that this girl, whom he did not know from Adam, was trying to score points and impress her friends by using his unhappiness. Immediately in the wake of that came the thought that she might be a plant – had one of the many academics who wanted him dismissed from his post put her up to it in the hope he might snap and lose control? He fought the waves of nausea that began to cascade over him. He would not give them the satisfaction of seeing him buckle beneath the strain.

'I believe some work was done on that, but not by me,' Dunnigan said briskly. 'I was considered too close to the case.'

'But you must have a theory about it.'

'No. I have tried not to get involved. I fear I would only confuse things.'

'Come on, Mr Dunnigan. If that was someone in my family, I'd have worked day and night to find out what had happened.'

Dunnigan cleared his throat. There were countless responses to what this girl was saying. He wanted to scream at her, tell her she could not begin to comprehend all the scenarios he had envisaged, the versions of events he had seen in his dreams. He wanted to shake her, ask her how she could be so callous and cruel to bring up something so personal, so painful, in an open lecture like this, whether she was being put up to it or not.

He wanted to say all these things, but he did not. Instead he said: 'Would you all excuse me for a moment?'

Then he walked out of the door of the lecture hall, went to his car and drove away.

As he drove, the events of the day that had destroyed him, overturning everything he believed – about the world and about himself – played on a loop in his head.

Finally, somewhere near Sallins, he had to pull the BMW over. He sat there, tears streaming down his face, unable to move.

It had been eighteen years, but the pain was still as raw, the panic still as visceral, as if it had happened just that morning.

PART TWO

The Vanishing

1

5 DECEMBER 1998

HE REMEMBERED A DINNER, THREE DAYS BEFORE it had happened. He had driven over to Gina and Clive's house directly from Harcourt Street, parking the BMW on the gravel outside the small bungalow where they lived.

Gina and David had been close, back then, and since he had begun working at the NBCI a year ago they had only become closer – it was convenient for Dunnigan to take the trip to see Gina and Clive and their little girl, Beth, for dinner once or twice a week. These visits were the only real social outlet Dunnigan allowed himself, and he treasured them. He suspected that he might never have a family of his own: his career was the main (perhaps the sole) driving force in his life, so he delighted in experiencing the pleasures of home and hearth vicariously through his sister.

And then there was Beth, one of the few people in the world who could melt his heart simply by smiling. She was four years old, had the dark hair and clear blue eyes that he shared with his sister, which they had from their mother, and every time he saw her he was surprised by the intense feelings of love and joy she inspired in him. That day she met him at the door, a grin spread across her chubby cheeks.

'I sawed your car coming in our driveway,' she said, as he scooped her into his arms.

'Did you now?'

'Yeah, and I said to Mammy that I was gonna come and meet you!'

'Well, I'm very glad to be here. What's for dinner?'

'Mammy says it's chicken and pasta. With the creamy sauce.'

'Yummy.'

'I likes passghetti bolognese better. Why can't we have that instead?'

'Beth, I just don't know why we can't eat spag bol every single day.'

'You should tell my mammy that!'

'I think I will!'

Gina was in the kitchen, mixing a salad. 'Clive will be home in about ten minutes, and we can eat then. Carbonara okay?'

'It's fine, although any sane person would favour spaghetti bolognese.'

She threw her older brother a stern look. 'Have you two been plotting together out in the hallway?'

Beth giggled and hugged her uncle, then squirmed out of his arms and shot through the adjoining door to the living room, where the sounds of a kids' show could be heard emitting from the television.

'She's looking forward to your shopping trip on the eighth,' Gina said. 'She won't tell Clive or me what presents she's planning to get us, although I know it's almost killing her to keep the secret.'

The eighth of December is, traditionally, the opening of the Christmas shopping season in Ireland, the day stores and businesses unveil their festive window displays and Santa's grottos. The previous year, Gina and Clive had, after much persuasion from Dunnigan and their daughter, decided to allow their little girl, under the watchful eye of her adoring uncle, to make the pilgrimage into Dublin to buy gifts for her parents and grandparents. The pair had visited Father Christmas and had lunch at a restaurant that Dunnigan had carefully chosen after sampling spaghetti bolognese all over the city centre in a bid to find the perfect dining experience for his fussy niece. They had had such a good time that the decision was taken to make it an annual outing.

'My lips are sealed.'

'She's told you what she's getting?'

'Naturally.'

'And you're not telling either, I suppose?'

'I made a pinkie promise. Those, little sister, are unbreakable.'

'You are older than me by three minutes, buster! Help me lay the table, you soppy git.'

Clive, who was principal of a primary school in Dalkey, arrived just as Dunnigan was making sure all the glasses were correctly aligned, and they sat down to eat.

'So when is the criminology course kicking off?' he asked, as a plate of garlic bread was passed around.

'We've secured approval from the faculty board just this week for the course outline,' Dunnigan said, 'so I think we'll be taking in our first batch of students in September of 'ninety-nine.'

'And how do you feel about juggling the running of a department with your work for the police?' Gina asked, pouring her husband, then her brother, a glass of wine.

'I think it'll be fine. I've asked William Clarke to cover things while I'm away and, let's face it, he's a middle-of-the-road academic and not well liked in the department, so I don't think I need to worry about a hostile takeover from him. The work with the Bureau will still take precedence, but now that I'm off the Cold Case Unit, it's not as labour intensive as it once was. I think I'll manage.'

'And have you found any time for a lady in your life?' Gina asked, in as conversational a tone as she could muster.

'For the moment, it's not a priority,' Dunnigan said.

'Come on, Davey,' Gina chided him. 'No one's asking you to get married. Why not just go on a few dates – there's a lovely special-needs assistant just started at my school!'

Gina taught English part-time at the local secondary.

'No blind dates, Gina,' Dunnigan replied patiently. 'You know I hate being set up. It would only result in embarrassment for everyone concerned.'

'Can't you give it a go? Just the once? I think you'd really like her – she's into all that sci-fi stuff you like.'

'I said no, sis.'

'I think she goes to conventions. She dresses up as someone called – oh, what did she tell me, again? Oh, yes. Professor Bernice Summerfield. Now don't tell me that doesn't get you interested!'

'He said no!' Beth echoed around a mouthful of pasta.

'Thank you, Bethany,' Dunnigan said, patting his niece's hand.

'I'd just like to see you having a life!' Gina said, sighing deeply.

'I have exactly the life I want to have.' Dunnigan grinned.

These words would come back to haunt him in the years that followed.

2

THE CITY CENTRE WAS DENSELY PACKED WITH shoppers, that December 8th. Dunnigan and Beth hit all the toy stores around the main shopping area first, bought a sticky bun and some hot chocolate from a street vendor near the statue of Molly Malone, then spent a happy hour just looking at the myriad artfully decorated windows, taking in all the lights, the sights and the sounds of the glistening winter city. Carols drifted on the air from open shop doorways, and buskers added their voices to the festive chorus. As they stood outside the Stephen's Green shopping centre, listening to a children's choir singing 'Little Donkey' in three-part harmony, Dunnigan felt Beth's tiny hand slip into his and give it a squeeze.

'They sound lovely,' she said, her voice barely above a whisper.

Dunnigan squeezed her hand back in agreement, lost in the music and the delight of it all.

He would replay what happened next countless times in his head, looking for the precise moment his life was decimated, never to be fully right again.

At some point within the next minute or so, as the carolling continued, he felt Beth's hand leave his. He assumed she was just scratching her nose or adjusting her scarf, and it was some moments – certainly not more than twenty seconds – before he cast a look down to check on her and saw she was gone. They had been in a crowd of people who had all gathered to listen to the music, and Dunnigan did not panic immediately. Logic, his old friend, told him that the child had probably wandered over to one of the many shops around them, more than likely attracted by some toy or other – there were several within easy view of where they had been standing, all with windows packed full of tempting dolls, fancy-dress outfits and colourful books of all kinds.

But a quick search did not find her. Still Dunnigan remained calm. He began to walk back down Grafton Street, then changed his mind and paced back to where the choir was still singing.

'Beth! Beth, come back, sweetie! You can't wander off!' he called, causing several people to glance in his direction.

His continued bellows elicited no other reaction, though. He stood right in front of the singers (clearly annoying the choirmaster, who threw him a filthy look) and called for Beth again. Still no response, other than from an old lady who told him to 'move the feck out of the way'.

That was when the panic hit.

3

DUNNIGAN SCANNED THE CROWD FOR HER FACE, looking desperately at the stream of hurrying people moving past in all directions, sure she would be there, looking for him as he was looking for her. But there was no sign of the child. It was as if she had been swallowed by the cobbled street surface.

He wanted to rush into the nearby shopping centre – she could have got confused in the crowd and wandered in there looking for him. He thought about crossing the road and checking the park for her, knowing she associated such spaces with swings, slides and roundabouts. He considered simply screaming for help to anyone who might listen, begging someone to tell him where the little girl had gone.

He reasoned that moving away from where he had last seen her was a mistake – she might well return there, or describe the location to an adult who found her wandering, lost. He paced up and down a little more, then made his way over to the windowsill of a newsagent and perched there, fighting the overwhelming terror he was now feeling.

He lost all sense of time for a while, just remained sitting there, hoping against hope that the diminutive figure of his beloved Beth would emerge from the crowd, perhaps being led by a kindly passer-by who had come upon her. But the vigil was in vain. People walked past on their way to their jobs or their own shopping excursions, all oblivious to the turmoil he was in.

Finally he saw the blue uniform of a police officer through the crowd, and charged over, grabbing the man by the arm. 'Please, I need help. I've lost a little girl.'

'Step back, please, sir,' the garda said, trying to wrest his arm from Dunnigan's fierce grasp.

'But we have to find her!' Dunnigan said, shaking the man as he spoke. 'She's only little and she isn't used to the crowd and I'm meant to be taking care of her!'

'Just calm down. Take a breath.'

'My name is David Dunnigan – I work for the National Bureau of Criminal Investigation. Please call DI Frank Tormey – he'll confirm who I am. Tell him what's happened and that I need the team here right now!'

Every word Dunnigan spoke seemed to take for ever to get out – he was painfully aware of more and more time passing, and even as he tried to make the officer understand what had happened he continued to scan the crowds for any sign of the child. The man listened intently, then spoke into a comlink he had attached to his shoulder, explaining to other officers in the area that a child had been separated from her carer and repeating the description Dunnigan had provided. He also asked that someone contact Tormey.

'We should have her for you very shortly, sir,' the garda said, smiling and patting Dunnigan on the shoulder.

The crowds continued to swirl and the light changed as the day wore on, and for the first time in his adult life, Dunnigan felt tears come to his eyes.

4

THEY NEVER FOUND SO MUCH AS A TRACE OF HER.

By six that evening the city was being combed by police, and the following day volunteers joined the search. News bulletins broadcast pictures of Beth. Gina, Clive, their parents, Beth's pre-school teachers and anyone else who'd had regular contact with her during her four years were interviewed in a bid to assess if any of them had noticed anything unusual – anyone hanging about, acting suspiciously.

No one had.

Dunnigan was given time off work at the university, it being felt (correctly) that he was in no emotional state to deal with the rigours of a teaching schedule, not to mention the new management duties he had taken on. He offered to help the police with their search, but they suggested he take some time to get his head together, and that they would call him in if they needed his expertise.

Two days later a call came, but not to ask for his insights: he was taken in for questioning. He should have expected it, but in his trauma and heartache, it had never even occurred to him that he might be a suspect. Yet, in the deep places inside where he was honest with himself, he *did* feel he was to blame – he should have kept a closer watch on her, he should never have let go of her hand in such a big crowd, he should have kept talking to her as they watched the choir, so that her sudden silence might have warned him sooner of her absence.

The interrogation went on for eighteen hours, by turns gentle, then harsh; friendly then threatening; conciliatory, then accusing. Dunnigan answered the litany of questions openly and honestly – he had, at this stage, been part of this process from the other side of the table, and he knew the methodology: his interrogators were looking for small inconsistencies in his answers; the process of going over the same ground again and again and again was designed to see if he was really being truthful. Liars have to come up with stories to mask the truth, and fictions have holes. He had nothing to hide so he did not attempt to evade or confuse. There was a huge part of him that would have been almost grateful if they had simply locked him up – at one point one of the interviewing gardaí, a detective Dunnigan did not know, who had introduced himself as Corrigan, told him that they had found some of Beth's underwear at his apartment. Dunnigan knew this not to be true, although he did not think there would have been anything so terribly wrong if Beth had slept over. She had asked to often enough, but Dunnigan had always been too busy to arrange it.

'You liked her, didn't you?' Corrigan said, his tone suggesting the liking was something more than platonic.

The detective was a lump of a man, six feet three and all of it hard muscle. He stank of tobacco and cheap cologne, and Dunnigan knew immediately that the man loathed him intensely. 'I liked her a great deal,' Dunnigan said wearily. 'She was my only niece. I loved her.'

'Wanted to have her all to yourself, eh?'

'I was on a shopping trip with her, just her and me,' Dunnigan said. 'I had her to myself.'

'Not very private, though, was it?'

'We were having a really good time,' Dunnigan said. 'We'd been planning it all year.'

Corrigan slammed his fist into the table, knocking a teacup

aside and lunging forward. Dunnigan didn't flinch or budge an inch – he was so numb by then, he didn't care what the huge, angry man did.

'You know, I fucking hate kiddie-fiddlers,' Corrigan snarled, his face centimetres from Dunnigan's. 'I work with all kinds of scum, but cunts who hurt children are just about the worst, as far as I'm concerned. I could beat you to a fucking pulp and none of my bosses would give a damn. I'd never be disciplined, and I can tell you, you pervert, I wouldn't lose a moment of sleep over it either.'

'Go ahead,' Dunnigan said, tears coming to his eyes again, this time in anger and sadness and resignation. 'I didn't take her, but it's my fault she's gone – I didn't look after her properly. I let her down. I don't know where she is, or who has her, or if she's scared or lonely or hurt. So do your worst, because it can't be anywhere close to as bad as what I deserve.'

Corrigan continued to stare Dunnigan down for what felt like a lifetime, then grabbed him by his lapels and flung him across the room, slamming him into the corner with bone-jarring force. Dunnigan felt his head hit the wall so hard he thought his skull would crack for sure, but then he was hitting the ground, and he rolled onto his side and curled into the foetal position. A beating was coming, and the best thing he could do was try to minimise the injuries he was sure to get. The guard delivered three kicks in quick succession, trying to get him in the groin and stomach, but Dunnigan's arms and knees were pulled tight over them. Swearing bitterly, a final blow was delivered to the top of his head, causing him to bite his tongue badly, and momentarily stunning him. He came around as the cop strode out of the room, leaving him sobbing, sick with pain and dizziness.

He remained curled in a ball in the corner until he heard the door unlocking an hour later. A female officer came in, and told him he was free to go.

5

THERE WAS NEVER ANY SERIOUS ATTEMPT TO PIN the blame for the abduction on Dunnigan – in fact, Tormey and the NBCI quickly concluded that it was an opportunistic abduction: someone had spotted Beth, decided she fitted a profile they favoured, and snatched her when they saw the chance. Tormey told Dunnigan that he had probably been stalked as he shopped with the child, and as soon as Beth had let go of his hand in the crowd the predator had grabbed her.

He watched hours of CCTV footage of the area around Stephen's Green, trying to spot anyone suspicious – he watched a grainy image of Beth and him approaching the crowd of people watching the choir. He watched as the crowd absorbed them, like a sponge. He saw himself leave the throng, looking panicked as he realised Beth was gone.

He watched the scene from the other two angles that were available (there had been a camera at the top of a lamppost to the north, one from above the doorway of the Stephen's Green Centre to the east and one on the railings of the park to the south), but none showed Beth being taken.

Tormey begrudgingly gave him some other footage of him and Beth as they moved about the city centre, but this proved no more useful. One man, who seemed in the footage to be wearing what looked to be a cream or possibly yellow suit, showed up at two of the same locations as Dunnigan and Beth, but there was no sign of him at the site of the abduction.

'I'm sorry you had to go through questioning, Davey,' Tormey said. A month had passed since the abduction, and he had called Dunnigan in for a chat. 'We try to look after our own, but you had to be interrogated – you understand.'

Dunnigan nodded.

'I hope they didn't go too hard on you.'

'I don't want to talk about it.'

Tormey sighed and sat back. 'I understand if you would prefer not to work with us any more,' he said. 'This has been very tough for you, and I can only imagine what working on similar cases must be doing to your head.'

Dunnigan's thoughts raced as he tried to comprehend what was being said. 'Are you firing me?'

'I'm giving you the chance to step down.'

'And if I choose not to?'

Tormey rubbed his eyes with the heel of his hand. 'You're not going to make this easy on me, are you?'

'I don't understand,' Dunnigan said.

'You're a mess, Davey,' Tormey said. 'You're just about keeping it together today, but there are mornings you come in here and you're still wearing the clothes you had on you the day before, and it looks like you slept in them, if you slept at all. You don't seem to be eating, you sure as hell don't seem to be washing, you won't talk to anyone, and I think it's a fucking miracle you haven't made a serious mistake on a case yet and either got someone hurt or allowed some pervert to go free. It's only a matter of time, from the way you've been handling yourself.'

'What are you saying?'

'I'm saying that I think you're a liability.'

Dunnigan shifted on his seat, but his eyes never left Tormey. 'All I've got left is my work,' he said, his voice devoid of expression – he had been making a huge effort to keep things bottled up although, from what Tormey was saying, his attempts had not exactly been a success. 'I can't face my parents. My brother-in-law won't – can't – look at me. My sister, Beth's mother, says it's not my fault, but she starts crying every time I talk to her. I don't like being at home because I frighten myself when I'm alone. I … I get very dark thoughts. Please don't take my work away.'

Tormey looked back at the young man he had recruited a little over a year ago. The dapper, slick operator he had met in Maynooth was gone, replaced by a hollow-eyed, unshaven, wrinkled creature, painfully thin and badly in need of a shower. 'Do you know what I think, Davey?'

'No.'

'I think I'm going to give you a chance to get your shit together.'

'Thank you, boss.'

'I'm giving you two weeks' leave. Take it, and do whatever you have to do to get your life back on track. The university tells me your work there has gone to crap, too. Fix what you can, then come and see me. If we're no further on, I *will* let you go. This is not a job where I can be sympathetic, Davey, even if I want to be. You're on a temporary contract, and your negligence might cost someone their life. Sort yourself out, and we'll take it from there.'

Dunnigan nodded, and stood up.

'And, Davey?'

'Yes, boss?' He paused in the doorway.

'I'm awfully sorry about your niece. She seems to have been a sweet little girl. We're doing our damnedest to find her.'

'I appreciate that, boss,' Dunnigan said, 'but we both know the likelihood of Beth turning up is slim to none. Too much time has passed.'

'It happens. Not often, but it happens.'

'Thanks, boss. I'll see you in a fortnight.'

And he left to try to find a way to keep what was going on inside buried so deeply only he could see it.

Ernest Frobisher

When he was a small boy, Frobisher had attended school for only two weeks – his parents had been forced to remove him when he put a third child in the hospital. His mother hired a tutor, but the man only lasted three days, stating in his letter of resignation that Ernest needed specialist treatment. A second and third fared little better, and finally Bertha Frobisher had no choice but to take on the role of educating her son.

It was not a difficult task, as he was very bright. He was reading fluently before his sixth birthday, and he treated arithmetic as if it were a game or puzzle – maths was effortless to him. By the time he was seven, Bertha left him to his own devices, giving him full access to the house's vast collection of books, films and music.

As soon as he was permitted to take control of his own intellectual life he discovered he loved history. His family could be traced back to the times when the Normans had first landed on the shores of Wexford, and he loved to learn about the men who had tamed the wild Celtic landscape and forged a place for themselves out of the barren rock they found themselves marooned upon.

History still held a fascination for him. Now that age had quelled some of his appetites, he lived vicariously through the actions of the Yellow Man, but he still thrilled at the acts of his ancestors. They had left a legacy, had done great things, had taken the rabble and made of them something worthy, something good.

He determined to do the same. One of the few things his mother had taught him was that he was better than other people, that he had the right to do what he thought was right, and that no one should stand in his way.

'No one is like you,' she had said. 'Be all that you can be, and do not allow anything to hold you back. If something or someone gets in your way, remove them.'

He took this lesson very much to heart – it was a truth he held dear.

Bertha came into the drawing room one evening, when he was sixteen, and found him naked with a dead child, she had been very angry with him.

He could never remember afterwards if he had meant to kill his mother, but she would not stop screaming. His father had understood, and her body and what was left of the little boy were taken away and it was never spoken of again – in the Frobisher home, it was as if Bertha had never existed.

He thought of her often, though, and of the things she had said. He had loved her, in the powerful way boys love their mothers. If only she had not become so hysterical. He was just doing as she had taught, after all. He was only doing what he knew to be right.

6

NO RANSOM DEMAND EVER CAME. THERE WERE no sightings of children that might have been Beth, not even any leads that proved to be dead ends – it was as if the earth had opened up and swallowed her.

Dunnigan recognised that he had become useless – self-indulgently wallowing in his loss and the reality that there was nothing he could do to bring her back. He spent the first three days of his enforced leave putting up posters and hounding newspapers to keep the story alive, but Beth was just one more child who had slipped through the cracks. As the months went by, other news items took precedence, and with each one, Beth's face receded further and further in people's memories.

The world was forgetting, and it was almost unbearable.

This was his truth: one cold December morning a child he had loved as if she were his own daughter had been taken from right under his nose, and reality should have stopped there and then in abhorrence of such a cruel twist of fate. But it hadn't: life ground on relentlessly, and people got up and went to work and ate meals and watched TV as if everything was normal.

Where was she? Who had taken her? Had she been afraid? Had she called for him, in those moments of terror? Had they been violent towards her, his niece, who had never known anything but kindness and affection?

Had she been raped?

Had they tortured her?

David Dunnigan lay awake long into the night, these questions and a thousand more revolving in his mind, questions to which he would probably never get answers.

The world had forgotten, but David Dunnigan could not forget.

Though he did try.

Detective Inspector Frank Tormey

Tormey had monthly meetings with the garda commissioner. In the months after Beth's disappearance, Dunnigan featured in all of them.

'We have no obligation to keep him on the payroll,' the commissioner said, glaring at Tormey, punctuating every word with a jab of his finger. 'His behaviour is erratic, his manner is often offensive and, quite frankly, the quality of his work has plummeted.'

'I know that, sir, but I feel a kind of, well, a responsibility towards him. I brought him on to the team to begin with, and I'd like to give him a chance.'

'That was before this awful bloody business with his niece. The whole thing is making the men nervous. Can we be completely sure he wasn't involved in it? I've met him, and he's a very odd fellow.'

'Davey was thoroughly investigated and we're certain he's in the clear. Look at him, anyway – he's devastated.'

'I've heard he was always on the strange side, even before the disappearance. Is he one of those – what d'you call them? One of those Asperger's chaps.'

'I don't believe so, sir. When he was vetted before joining the Bureau we found a report from a child psychologist, done when he was ten years old, that said he had obsessive compulsive traits – OCD. To be frank, sir, I thought that might be a good thing when you consider the kind of work we were asking him to do. I believe the loss of his niece has magnified characteristics that might have been dormant before.'

'Can't you send him for counselling? We have some head shrinkers on retainer, don't we?'

'He's seen two therapists so far, sir.'

'And they couldn't fix him?'

'No, sir. He was not cooperative.'

'Order him to cooperate, then! If you're determined to keep him, then bring him to heel. D'you hear me, Tormey? If I receive one more complaint, he's gone, and you'll have to answer for whatever rubbish he's perpetrated. Are we clear?'

'Completely, sir.'

'Dammit all, Tormey, why are you so stuck on this lad? He's not even a guard!'

'He's one of my men, sir. We look after our own at the Bureau. You taught me that.'

'Oh. Right.'

'And maybe I know something of what he's going through.'

'What d'you mean?'

'You may remember my wife and I lost our first child. Cot death, they called it then. Losing a kiddie – it can mess with your head. I believe he'll come around, sir.'

'Well. Ahem … All right, fair enough. For God's sake, get him sorted out, though.'

'I'll do my best, sir.'

'See that you do.'

PART THREE

Fighting the Good Fight

1

'HELLO?'

'Is that David Dunnigan?'

'Yes.'

'It's me. Miley Timoney.'

'I know. Your number came up on my phone.'

'Oh. Well … how are you doing?'

'I'm fine. What do you want, Miley?'

'I'm very well, thank you for not asking.'

'Was there something you wanted?'

'I was wondering if you wanted to go out for a – a cup of tea or coffee or something with me.'

'No. I do not.'

'How about lunch, then? We could go to Captain America's again.'

'No.'

'I could come over and visit you. We could talk about cases and stuff.'

'You looked at the websites I suggested?'

'I did. I was reading about the Yorkshire Ripper. I wanted to ask you some questions about him.'

'Mmm.'

'So will I call over?'

'No.'

Pause.

'You could call over to me.'

'I have to go to work, Miley.'

'I could meet you after work. Walk you home.'

'I don't know what time I'll be finished.'

Pause.

'Okay.'

Dunnigan hangs up.

2

DUNNIGAN LOOKED UP FROM HIS DESK TO SEE Tormey looming over him.

'I need you to do an interview for me – it's linked to the Grangegorman case.'

'Okay.'

'What are you working on?'

'The missing-person reports. The homeless people.'

'You're still on that?'

'You told me to look into it. That's what I'm doing.'

'It's not a priority. This interview is.'

'I'm on it, boss.'

'Why are you so taken with these missing street people?'

Dunnigan had stood and was pulling on his coat. 'Something about it doesn't add up.'

'What?'

'I don't really know. Father Bill … he makes me uncomfortable.'

'That's 'cause he's a fucking headcase. He *should* make you uncomfortable.'

'I was thinking of maybe … of, um … you know, spending a little more time over there. Doing some volunteering – see what I can find out.'

'You want to do some undercover work?'

'I wouldn't call it that …'

Tormey chewed his lower lip. 'They already know you work for us at the unit.'

'Of course.'

'So you'd hardly be entrapping them, I suppose.'

'No. It would be like doing overt social research.'

Tormey sighed and turned to leave. 'Do it on your own time. Let me know if anything shows up. If anyone asks, I don't know shit about it. Are we clear?'

'Yes, boss.'

'Now go and do the fucking interview I asked you to do five minutes ago.'

3

HE WAS ALWAYS AT THE OFFICE LATER THAN anyone else – as much out of unwillingness to go back to his empty flat as commitment to his work – and at eight o'clock that night he was poring over statements and interviews relating to Father Bill.

He liked the offices when they were quiet, like this: he could hear the rooks that nested in the trees that grew in the yard outside, and he found the sound soothing.

All testimony regarding the priest was glowing – he appeared to be a driven, selfless, fiercely dedicated man, completely focused on the people of his parish, and committed to getting them what they needed, regardless of personal cost. He had graduated top of his class at university – he had initially trained to be a teacher – but he was a deeply religious person, even in his youth, and his faith had pushed him to the seminary. He had excelled there, also, and was tipped for success and fame in the Church. This, however, was not to be.

Father Bill seemed to have his own way of interpreting his spirituality, and he clashed with his superiors almost as soon as he was given a parish: he was blessing gay unions long before the referendum was passed, and he was outspoken about his church's failure to support the women of the Magdalen laundries and the children of industrial schools, standing with them in demonstrations outside the Dáil (the Irish House of Parliament). A stint in South America with the missions had done nothing to quell his inclination to do things his own way, and it was clear to anyone paying close attention that Father Bill was never going to rise above his post as chaplain and coordinator of the Homeless Project.

He was an outsider.

Something about that spoke to Dunnigan. He had not particularly liked the priest – he did not particularly *like* anyone – but he was self-aware enough to acknowledge some kind of fellowship with him.

His natural inclination was simply to write up the report and give it to Tormey, be done with the whole thing, but he felt drawn to Father Bill. And Diane Robinson made him uncomfortable although the discomfort was, in an odd way, not altogether unpleasant.

Perhaps he might learn something about the missing homeless people. Maybe Father Bill was involved, and maybe he wasn't. There was only one way to find out.

He picked up the phone. 'Father Bill? . . . It's David Dunnigan. Would you mind if I came along with you this evening on your outreach work?'

4

THEY MET AT THE PROJECT AN HOUR LATER, AND Father Bill handed Dunnigan a backpack filled with sandwiches wrapped in aluminium foil. The priest donned a slightly larger bag filled with rolled blankets. 'And you can carry one of these,' he said, handing over a huge Thermos of soup. 'There's paper cups in your bag.'

The Project was situated on a side-street off the quays, not far from the 3Arena. Cars moved by on the road, the occasional cruiser passed on the river, and the smell of coffee and fish and chips drifted on the breeze: an ordinary night in Dublin City. The two men made their way along the footpath, then crossed to the riverside. It was a cool night, and the body of water moved sluggishly to their left.

'Do you want to interrogate me as we walk?' Father Bill asked, as they moved along the path.

'No. I want to see you at work.'

'Why?'

'I don't really know,' Dunnigan admitted. 'It just seems the right thing to do.'

'Well, I'm glad of the help,' the priest said, patting Dunnigan's shoulder.

As they walked, Father Bill whistled 'Only Love Can Break Your Heart'. 'Do you like Neil Young, Davey?'

'I don't listen to music.'

'Ever?'

'Not any more.'

The first group they came across was made up of three young men, the oldest of whom looked to be no more than sixteen. They took the food gratefully. Father Bill did not know them, which he later told Dunnigan was unusual. He welcomed the boys to the city, and was at pains to point out that, while he had no beds that night at the Project, if they came early the following day he would do his best to find some space for them.

'Do either of yiz have a phone?' the youngest-looking of the group asked.

The priest shook his head. Dunnigan looked at them blankly.

'Do you have a phone, Davey?'

'I … um … yes, yes, I do,' Dunnigan said, gripping his handset firmly in his pocket.

'I wants to ring me ma to let her know I'm all right,' the kid said.

'Give him your phone,' Father Bill said conversationally.

'I don't want to,' Dunnigan said.

'You are embarrassing me, Davey.' Father Bill took the phone from him and handed it to the boy. 'Make your call. I'll hold your soup for you while you're talking.'

'I use that to read ebooks, to listen to podcasts and I keep my diary on it,' Dunnigan said, his voice as close to anger as it got.

'He'll be back,' the priest said. 'If he was going to run, he'd have gone by now.'

They watched the skinny kid, his shoulders hunched over, talking rapidly into the handset. The conversation lasted for about two minutes, then, looking dejected, his hollow, stubbled cheeks stained with tears, the boy returned. 'Thanks, lad,' he said, giving the phone back to Dunnigan.

'You're welcome.'

'Tough phonecall?' Father Bill asked, giving the boy back his soup.

'She was off her head on smack,' the kid said, wiping his eyes on his sleeve. 'I could tell. Me little sister still lives with her. It freaks me out to think of her there with no one fit to mind her.'

'Where is she based?'

'Finglas.'

Father Bill put an arm around the lad. 'Do you want me to make some calls? I can have someone check in on your sister.'

The boy shook his head. 'That'd just make me ma run – she'd be sure the cops were on to her. It'd make things worse.'

They stayed with the trio of thin, red-eyed kids for half an hour. They all promised to call to the Project for breakfast, but Father Bill told Dunnigan as they left them that he did not have high hopes. 'If they stay locally, it could take me months to build up a relationship with them. If they move on, I would be very worried about what the future holds. They're not tough, Davey, and you have to be to make it on the streets.'

'Don't the streets make you tough?' Dunnigan asked.

'They do – or they break you,' Father Bill said grimly. 'And those lads look half broken already.'

5

THE NIGHT WORE ON. MORE LOST SOULS WERE treated to soup, sandwiches and a listening ear. Some wanted Father Bill to pray with them; others wanted him to hear their confessions. He met everyone with the same calm, gentle warmth he had shown the three kids from Finglas. Dunnigan mostly stayed in the background, coming forward only to allow the priest to rummage in his backpack for the desired sandwich (they had ham, ham and cheese, and egg mayonnaise) or to pour the vegetable soup into cardboard cups.

At a quarter to midnight a cold wind had started to blow up the Liffey, and Father Bill indicated it was time to turn back for home. 'Anyone with half a grain of sense is bedded down for the night now,' he said. 'And those without sense are beyond our help.'

They began to walk briskly back the way they had come. They were passing the Ha'penny Bridge when Father Bill froze.

'What's wrong?' Dunnigan asked, looking in the direction the priest seemed to be gazing.

It was dark, and they were opposite the mouth of an alleyway. Dunnigan could just about make out the shapes of what looked like a group of people in the darkness, but he had no sense at all of what was going on.

'Stay here,' Father Bill said, and, dropping his bag beside

Dunnigan, took off at a run across the street. Dunnigan paused for a moment, then followed.

He caught up with the priest as he reached the entrance to the alley. At this range he could see what looked to be four young men, fashionably dressed, kicking something or someone on the ground. Father Bill did not miss a beat, and before they knew what had hit them, the two closest to him had been dragged out of the way and, using momentum and their own weight, flung into the wall on the other side of the laneway.

On the ground lay a dirty, bloodied man dressed in a torn anorak and jeans that might have been blue once but were now so soiled and filthy they were closer to a dull grey. Father Bill reached down and gently helped him up. 'How are you, Gary?' he said, brushing him down and straightening his coat. 'I see you're having a bad night.'

'God bless you, Father,' the man who was called Gary said, leaning on the priest's shoulder.

'Who the fuck are you?' one of Gary's attackers demanded. The words were spoken in a drunken Dublin 4 drawl.

'I'm a friend of this gentleman,' Father Bill said. 'And as his buddy and confidant, I have to tell you boys that I'm extremely displeased to see him so roughly treated.'

'That scummer tripped me,' another of the group mumbled, his words even more slurred than the previous speaker's. 'I came up the alley to take a whizz and he tried to take the feet out from under me – he wanted to rob me!'

'I was asleep!' Gary said, tears coming into his voice now. 'I was in my sleeping bag, minding my own business, and these boys took to kickin' me – I thought I was dead for sure! I thought it was the Yellow Man!'

'You're a focking liar and a filthy homeless cunt!' The speaker of these words had been standing at the back of the group, and Dunnigan saw that he was taller than Father Bill, and looked as if he played a lot of rugby.

'I want you to go with my friend Davey,' Father Bill said. 'You can sleep on the couch in my office tonight. I'll have a few words with the boys here.'

Gary nodded and shuffled over to Dunnigan.

'Take him back to the Project,' Father Bill said, his eyes fixed on the four youths in front of them. 'I'll be along presently.'

Dunnigan said nothing, just took Gary by the arm and began to lead him away. From the alley, he heard the priest start to sing 'Cortez The Killer', and there was the sound of scuffling and muffled shouts, but then Dunnigan was gone along the street as fast as he could move, fear twisting in his gut and Gary leaning hard on his arm the whole way back.

6

DIANE ROBINSON BROUGHT GARY INTO THE office, placed him on the couch, then got the first-aid box to clean and dress his wounds.

Dunnigan went into the dining hall and put the bags and Thermos flask on the counter top, then sat at one of the tables, rested his hands flat on it and waited.

An hour later, Father Bill Creedon came in, whistling merrily. To all intents and purposes, he looked exactly the same as he had the last time Dunnigan had seen him, except that the knuckles on both his hands were bloodied, cut and swollen. Father Bill nodded at Dunnigan and went to the freezer. He took some ice out of a bag and put it in a bowl into which he also ran some water. Then he sat down opposite Dunnigan, and proceeded to soak his battered hands.

'What did you do?' Dunnigan asked, barely recognising the sound of his own voice.

'I reasoned with them,' Father Bill said.

'Did you kill them?'

The priest looked at him in wonderment, then guffawed loudly. 'For the love of God, no, Davey! I gave them a pretty solid hiding, which they richly deserved, and when they were a little more subdued, I pointed out the error of their ways. They're all business students at Trinity, and I think they learned an important life lesson this evening, one they won't forget in a hurry.'

'Mmm.' Dunnigan shrugged. 'Will they press charges? Aren't you afraid of getting in trouble?'

'Do you think they'll tell? That I took on the four of them – two of whom are rugger players, by the way – and beat hell out of them? They're far too embarrassed. Anyway, Gary is battered and bruised in the office, and will testify that they attacked him and I interceded on his behalf, which is exactly what did happen! I don't see anything illegal in that. Do you?'

'It would probably be thrown out of court on a technicality, if it ever got that far,' Dunnigan said disinterestedly. 'Your friend, Gary – he said he thought they were Yellow Men, or something like that. What do you think he meant?'

Something passed across Father Bill's face. 'I don't know,' he said. 'Probably just the ramblings of a frightened old man.'

Dunnigan was tempted to question the priest some more, but decided not to. He was in no doubt, though, that Father Bill was lying.

7

'DR WILLIAM CLARKE.'

'Hello. It's Davey Dunnigan. You left a message for me to call you.'

'Yes. How are you, David?'

'I'm fine.'

'Good, good. Glad to hear it. I just wanted to talk to you about a project you've set for one of your classes.'

'Which one?'

'Your first-year criminologists.'

'Yes?'

'Do you think it wise to have them doing a research assignment on organised child abduction?'

'I would not have set it as an assignment unless I thought it was wise to do so.'

'Quite. You see, the thing is, David, we've received complaints from some of your group's parents.'

'Complaints? What about?'

'Some of them feel the reading material you've set is a bit, well, a bit heavy – you know two of that first-year group are only seventeen, don't you?'

Pause.

'They are doing a course in criminology, Dr Clarke. It states clearly on the syllabus, which I provided at the start of the semester, that we would be studying violent crime. The word "abduction" is mentioned on the descriptor. How has this come as a surprise?'

'One of the books you recommended on the reading list is a selection of pornographic writings, according to one lady who rang me this morning. She was very distressed.'

'I made no such recommendation.'

'Well, David, I have the book list here in front of me, and the title she is citing is most definitely on it.'

'Which book are you talking about?'

'The one by Sybil Hodge.'

'That is a novella about a young girl who was trafficked into the sex industry, and it is considered to be one of the most enlightened writings on the subject. It is very far from pornography.'

'She was not the only one to complain about it. You suggested the students watch a film called *Chickenhawk*? A film about self-proclaimed paedophiles?'

'That is a documentary about the North American Man-Boy Love Association, who openly campaigned for civil rights for paedophiles in the 1980s. It could not be described as pornography by any definition of the word.'

'David, I am asking you to rewrite the brief for this project, and I am asking you to withdraw the material you have been encouraging your students to read or to view.'

'Which means you are *telling* me.'

'I'm trying to be nice about this, David. Could you send me a list of all the films, books and journals you're using? I think it would be a good idea if we reviewed them. That way, there won't be any surprises.'

Pause.

'Are you still there, David?'

He is not. Dunnigan has hung up.

8

THE NEXT DAY, GINA MET HIM FOR LUNCH. THEY went to Wagamama's, just below the Stephen's Green Centre. Dunnigan loathed the place, but Gina adored it, so he suffered (more or less) in silence. They were given places on benches at one of the long tables, other lunchers chatting and munching noodles and sushi all around them – the place was busy, as always.

His phone rang just as their food came. Glancing at the screen, he saw it was Miley Timoney, and rejected the call.

'Work?' Gina asked him.

'No – well, kind of. It's this guy Tormey asked me to show around HQ.' He told his sister about the young man, and about the repeated calls he had received from him, looking to meet up again.

'It sounds like he had a good time with you.'

'Does it?' Dunnigan was genuinely puzzled.

'Yes, it does! Can't you be pleased with yourself, just for a second? This young man obviously got a lot out of spending time in your company. He's trying to make friends with you. Would it be such a bad thing to maybe go for a cup of tea with him or something?'

'I'm happy he had fun,' Dunnigan said, examining a piece of bok choi and deciding it was not something he cared to consume.

'You said you were going to loan him a book or something?'

Dunnigan dropped the offending vegetable back into the broth whence it had come. 'Oh, yes. I was to give him a copy of Capote's *In Cold Blood*. I thought he might like it. It's a classic of the true-crime genre.'

'Why don't you drop it over to him at the centre where he lives? You'd probably make his day.'

'I was going to give it to Tormey to pass on to him.'

'Can you really see Frank doing that? You said he only ever met him one time, and only brought him to Harcourt Street because his wife nagged him into doing it – and then he got you to do the tour! I don't think he's really committed to the lad.'

'I have stuff to do.'

'Like what? What stuff do you have to do?'

'I've started volunteering at a homeless project on the quays, if you must know.'

Gina snorted. 'Stop making fun of me. Look, Miley obviously thinks you're some kind of super cop, God bless him for his innocence. Could you just spare half an hour and leave the book over to him?'

'I'm going to want it back. In the same condition it was in when I loaned it.'

'Jesus, Davey, I'm sure he'll treat it as if it was a holy relic.'

Dunnigan sighed and gave up on the bowl of noodles with its floating vegetation, putting down his chopsticks at a perfect right angle at the top left corner of his placemat. 'I'll drop in to see him later. He lives in Clonsilla, if I remember correctly.'

'You want to meet him and talk about crimey stuff and *Doctor Who*!' she said gleefully. 'It'll be great for you to have someone to hang out with!'

'I'll call after work. I never said I'd hang out with him again, though.'

'He'll be thrilled. Why don't you both go out for a drink or something?'

'You don't give up, do you, Gina?'

'If I did, we'd have stopped seeing each other fifteen years ago.'

Dunnigan knew she was right, so he shut up.

Gina patted the back of his hand gently. 'I just think it would be nice if you had someone to talk to. I don't want you to be lonely.'

Dunnigan drummed his fingers on the tabletop. 'I don't need you to pick my friends out for me, Gina. I keep telling you – I'm doing all right, thank you very much.'

'I dreamed about her again, last night,' Gina said, and Dunnigan felt himself freeze, as if she had pushed a pause button and the whole world had stopped moving around them. Suddenly it was just him and his sister, alone in the restaurant, everything else fading into mist.

'I dreamed that I looked out of the window and she was there, standing in the garden by the wall, just staring at the house as if it was something strange and new to her. She saw me and she smiled, and it was like it had never happened and we were together again and it was going to be all right.'

'But it won't be,' Dunnigan said slowly, tasting the words as if they were bitter fruits. 'It won't be all right.'

'It has to be what it is,' Gina said, tears gathering in her eyes. 'We have to be who we are now, without her.'

9

HARRINGTON NURSING AND CONVALESCENT Home was set in its own grounds in a residential part of Clonsilla, in north County Dublin. Dunnigan checked the address twice, then put it into Google Maps because he didn't think he could have the right place. It looked like a bungalow, and the garden had been designed very tastefully. Three jackdaws watched him as he walked from the BMW to the glass-panelled front door.

Harrington Nursing and Convalescent Home, according to its web page, was a home for the elderly.

He rang and the bell was answered by a middle-aged woman dressed in a starched white uniform. 'Miley is not available to see visitors,' she said, smiling thinly.

'Oh – is he out?'

'No.'

'Is he ill?'

'Miley has settled down for the night.'

Dunnigan blinked. 'It's six forty-five,' he said. 'I'd like to give him this book, please.'

'I can pass it on to him,' the nurse – he assumed she was a nurse – said, holding out her hand for the copy of Capote. 'Miley Timoney suffers from many of the comorbid symptoms that accompany his condition – he needs his rest.'

'His condition?' Dunnigan said, confused.

'Miley Timoney has Down's Syndrome, Mr Dunnigan. Didn't you notice?'

Dunnigan blinked, running back over his time with the youngster. Now he thought about it, Miley *did* have the physical traits of the chromosomal disorder, not that Dunnigan had ever spent much time around people with disabilities. 'I didn't think it was important,' he said to the nurse truthfully. 'Look, I promised I would give this book to him personally. Even if he has gone to bed, it can't have been long ago so he's probably not asleep. Can I just pop my head in?'

'This is highly irregular.'

'Miley came to do some work experience with me at Garda HQ in Harcourt Street,' Dunnigan said – he was usually loath to use his credentials with the gardaí, but this woman was giving him no choice. 'I would really, really like to see him.'

He saw her bristle, and something akin to a moment of panic pass over her eyes, but then the smile that wasn't quite a smile was back on her face. 'Please follow me,' she said, and he was in.

The nurse left him sitting in a room that reminded him a little of his own flat, except that it had a lot of old furniture and no pictures at all on the walls. Finally he heard muffled conversation, then footsteps coming down the hall, and Miley was in the doorway, grinning from ear to ear. 'Davey!' he said, almost crying with happiness. 'You came to see me!'

'Could you please keep your interactions quiet,' the nurse said tersely. 'Our other residents are asleep.'

Dunnigan said nothing, just gave her a hard stare of the kind Tormey usually gave him, and then she was gone, leaving a sense of disapproval hanging in the air behind her.

'I promised to loan you this.'

Miley took the book, his eyes wide, '*In Cold Blood*,' he said, reading the title page. 'It sounds brilliant!'

'It's one of the first books of its kind,' Dunnigan said. 'They made a couple of movies about it. One of them was quite good.'

'I'll read it tonight and give it back to you.'

'You know what, why don't you keep it?' Dunnigan said, hardly believing the words he heard himself speaking.

'For serious?' Miley said.

'Yes. If you're really interested in criminology, you should own a copy. If you like it, there's a book by a French writer called Foucault I'll get for you next.'

Miley was perched on the edge of one of the ancient, overstuffed armchairs, hunched over the book, turning one page after another, his face very close to the print.

'Why don't we go and get a drink or something?' Dunnigan suggested, wondering as he said it what was coming over him.

'I ... I can't go out at this time of night,' Miley said, so quietly Dunnigan could barely hear the words.

'It's not night,' Dunnigan retorted. 'It's barely past teatime. Come on – there's a pub on the corner just up the road.'

'No. I really can't.'

'Why not?'

'Half six is lock-down. I shouldn't even be talking to you now.'

Dunnigan frowned. 'What do you mean "lock-down"? This isn't a prison, Miley.'

'Every night at half past six, they put the other residents to bed, and I get locked in my room. It's for my own safety.'

'That's nonsense,' Dunnigan said. 'You can't put up with that!'

'What am I s'posed to do?'

'You're an adult, Miley. Just say you want your door left open and you will go to bed when you're good and ready.'

'I tried that, back when I came here first. They sent Bill Tanner after me.'

'Who's Bill Tanner? One of the nurses?'

'No. He's kind of like a caretaker. He's a big guy. He doesn't like me a whole lot.'

'What does he do?'

Miley had gone very red in the face, and he was looking down at his feet, the book closed and clutched to his chest. 'I shouldn't really ought to talk about this, Davey,' he said. 'I think I should go back to my room now.'

'Are you sure?' Dunnigan said. 'I could ask the nurse if we can go out. I'm sure she wouldn't mind.'

'She would. Thanks for visiting, but I have to go now.' And, without looking at him, Miley stood up and walked quickly from the room.

10

DUNNIGAN FOUND THE NURSE IN A GLEAMING, well-stocked kitchen. 'Could I talk with you for a moment, please?'

'Visiting hours are from three to five,' the woman said, her back to him as she organised tins of what looked like rice pudding in an overhead cupboard. 'I would be happy to answer any queries you may have then.'

'What is your name?' Dunnigan asked.

'I am Joan Hayes, and I am the night coordinator of this unit. You have already disrupted things, Mr Dunnigan. It takes us time enough every evening to get Miley settled – he'll be up, pacing and worrying, for hours now.'

'This is an old folks' home,' Dunnigan said. 'Miley isn't even thirty, and he is not intellectually disabled. Why is he here at all?'

'Miley has a chromosomal disorder, Mr Dunnigan. It carries with it a variety of comorbid conditions.'

'Such as?'

'Down's Syndrome is caused by the chance presence of a partial replica of chromosome 21,' Joan Hayes said as, if reciting from a textbook, still organising her tins as she spoke. 'This can cause mental retardation, physical anomalies and congenital health problems. About ninety per cent of people with Down's Syndrome experience mental impairment, most of them functioning at about the level of a ten-year-old. And while Miley has been assessed as being of normal intelligence in some areas, such as literacy and numeracy, he struggles with many simple day-to-day tasks. He needs to be reminded to wash, he cannot tie his shoelaces, he has only a vague concept of the value of money. You must remember, he has been in care almost his entire life.'

'He is more than likely institutionalised. If he had a chance to live independently, get a job …'

'Down's carries distinct physical traits. Can you see anyone hiring someone who looks like Miley does?'

'Why the hell wouldn't they?'

'Miley has almond-shaped eyes and abnormal formation of his fingers. He has the broad facial features so common with the disorder, but he is lucky enough to be one of the thirty-four per cent of people with the condition who do not have a significantly smaller mouth cavity, so his tongue does not protrude that much, and while he has a slight lisp, he doesn't have a major speech impediment. That said, he is immediately recognisable as having what most people believe to be a mental handicap. It is lovely to think our society is open-minded enough that someone like Miley could live a normal life out in the world. Believe me, Mr Dunnigan, he could not. This is where he belongs.'

'In a home for the elderly and infirm?'

'This is a nursing and convalescent home,' Joan Hayes shot back. 'There is a serious shortage of beds in residential units more appropriate to his needs, so he was placed here. He is quite content.'

'Respectfully, Ms Hayes, I don't think he seems content at all.'

She turned sharply. 'You spend the day with him one time – you buy him lunch, fill his head full of wild ideas, then come out here and disturb him even further. You don't know Miley Timoney, Mr Dunnigan, and you certainly are not in a position to know what is best for someone with his particular challenges.'

'I know you lock him in his room at six thirty every night,

and I know he is afraid of someone called Bill Tanner,' Dunnigan said.

'Mr Tanner helps us when patients are difficult.'

'Patients? Is Miley ill?'

'Good evening, Mr Dunnigan. You found your way to the kitchen. I dare say you can find your way to the front door.'

Dunnigan stalked out, wondering what Father Bill might do in these circumstances.

11

HE DROVE STRAIGHT TO GARDA HQ. IT TOOK LESS than five minutes checking and cross-checking various databases to get more information than he needed on Bill Tanner, who was listed as a maintenance officer at Harrington Nursing and Convalescent Home, which was also his address.

The photograph attached to the file for his driver's licence showed a heavyset face, with thick jowls and a slack mouth, hair that might have been dark but was shaved down to little more than stubble. His professional career included a brief stint as a prison officer (he had done relief work at Wheatfield, though his contract had not been renewed) and as a night watchman for a company called Stellar Security, which was no longer in business.

Tanner had been married for three years to a woman named as Maria Tanner – her photo showed a tired, haggard face framed by dishwater-blonde hair. Their divorce papers listed 'incompatibility' and 'irreconcilable differences' as the reasons for parting company, but Dunnigan found three garda reports detailing complaints from neighbours about shouting and sounds of violence. The responding officers stated on each occasion that Mrs Tanner showed signs of physical abuse, but that she refused to press charges and claimed they had been sustained during kick-boxing classes at the local community centre, though no one there remembered her attending.

One officer, James Duggan, wrote that on one occasion he had taken Bill Tanner aside and warned him that if they were brought out again they would be forced to take him in. Tanner had just laughed and told them to leave his home if they were not going to arrest him. There were several other notes on brawls, public disturbances and drunk-and-disorderly charges, none of which had amounted to more than cautions, but it all pointed to the fact that this was a volatile and violent man, but one who must have passed the vetting process required for employment in the caring profession, even as a member of the ancillary staff at a unit.

Dunnigan spent another hour investigating the rates that clients of the Harrington Nursing and Convalescent Home paid for the privilege of living there, and also the welfare entitlements for which someone like Miley would qualify.

A scheme was forming in his mind as he drove home.

12

ON WEDNESDAYS DUNNIGAN TAUGHT CLASSES IN Maynooth. If asked, he would have said that he enjoyed it; he had, after all, originally designed the course, though it was now run by a young academic named Dr William Clarke.

Dunnigan disliked Clarke a great deal, and made no effort to hide his distaste. If only the same could be said for Clarke. To be fair, Dunnigan had difficult relationships with almost everyone he worked with. Frank Tormey articulated his frustration and annoyance with him in the baldest of terms, but at least he was honest. Dunnigan could cope with honesty. Clarke, for his part, obviously thought him a washed-up, unstable wreck, but veiled his low opinion in a barrage of hail-fellow-well-met falsity, laughing just a little too loud and a little too long every time Dunnigan was within earshot, making excuses to 'pop in' to his classes, often asking if he could see his lecture notes or insisting on regrading papers Dunnigan had already corrected. Now Clarke was resetting assignments and vetoing his reading lists.

Dunnigan assumed Clarke's plan was to make his life so uncomfortable that he would, sooner or later, simply resign. What the younger academic didn't know, of course, was that discomfort was something he had long been used to – for Dunnigan, discomfort had become comfortable.

The two jobs he worked created a structure Dunnigan clung

to desperately, and he had no intention of leaving either of them. Going to Maynooth to teach that morning, however, did not suit him. He had a more pressing appointment. He rang and informed Human Resources that he would not be in – he considered telling them he was sick, but decided the hassle of remembering what he was supposed to be suffering from, how long he'd been suffering from it and what its particular symptoms were was just too much hassle. Honesty seemed a better policy.

Then he drove to Clonsilla.

The day-care unit Miley attended each day from 9.30 a.m. until 3 p.m. was called Grasslands, and was in an industrial estate. The reception area was well lit, and pictures painted by the clients were in frames on the walls. It seemed a happy place, but Dunnigan could not help but wonder how Miley felt about being there.

He told the supervisor he wanted to chat to the lad about doing some more work experience at Harcourt Street, and was shown to an office where they could talk.

Miley didn't look very pleased to see him. 'What's wrong, Davey?' he said, clearly unhappy.

'Tell me about Bill Tanner.'

'Bill works in the home. He's the caretaker – the maint'nance man.'

'You said they sent him after you when you complained about being locked in at night.'

'Yes … no … I shouldn't have made a fuss. They care for me very well at the home. I'm lucky to be there, so I am. I could be in a hosp'tal or somewhere bad like that.' Miley spoke in a voice that was little more than a whisper.

'Look at me, Miley,' Dunnigan said gently, going around the desk and squatting down beside the young man.

Miley turned to him, and he was crying.

'Why are you in that place?'

'I don't have anywhere else to go.'

'You are not intellectually disabled. I checked out some things last night – you get payments every week that go straight to the people who run Harrington Homes, and there are several subsidies and monies you're not getting that you should. They're not doing you any favours in the nursing home, Miley. You could afford to get a flat. You could take care of yourself!'

Miley sniffed and Dunnigan saw something that looked very like hope kindling in his eyes.

'I've been in care for as long as I can remember,' Miley said. 'Do you really think I could have my own place?'

'I do.'

'But Bill Tanner, he told me I'd never be able to be on my own. He says it's too hard, cooking and cleaning up and paying for stuff like the 'lectricity and things. I've never done any of that, and I don't really know how.'

'But you could learn. You wouldn't move right away. You'd build up to it. We'd find people to help you.'

'D'you think we could?'

'I know we could. Now tell me about Bill Tanner.'

Miley sighed deeply and sat up a bit straighter in the chair. 'I got sent to the home when I was eighteen. I'd been in 'nother place but they said I couldn't stay there any more 'cause I was a grown-up. When I got there, and I saw it was all old people and sick people, I got scared – I thought maybe I was sick and that was why they sent me there, and I started to cry. They tried to lock me up in my room, but I wouldn't go in, and I fought them and I screamed, and they went and got Mr Tanner.'

'What did he do?'

'I saw him coming, and even though he was big, I was so scared I didn't care – I tried to fight him, too. I pushed and I kicked, and he grabbed me round the neck and he dragged me into the room and closed the door. I made a run to try and get back out, and he punched me hard in my stomach, and then he grabbed me by my hair and he threw me down on the bed. "You are gonna learn real quick who's boss around here, retard," he said to me. "And I'm gonna have fun teachin' you." I didn't cry or give out any more that night.'

'But he didn't stop being mean to you, did he?'

'The next night, they told me to go in my room at half six. I wanted to watch *The Simpsons*, I always watched them in th'other place, but they said that in Harrington, it's early to bed and early to rise. Well, I got mad again. Tanner came and he dragged me into my room, and he hit me in the face and made my nose bleed, but I kept on shouting. He kicked me in – in my private place, and I thought I was going to die it hurt so bad. I kept quiet then.'

'And was he okay after that? So long as you behaved and kept their rules?'

'No. He told me a few days after that that I was his special project. He had to teach me manners. It was for my own good. He would come in my room at night, after they locked me in, and he'd beat me. When I got back from the day-care unit he'd make me do jobs for him – unblocking the drains or cleaning toilets. He only ever calls me "retard".'

'And this is still going on?'

Miley pulled up the bottom of his T-shirt, revealing a patchwork of bruises, some a light yellow, where they had begun to fade, others, more recent, livid red or black.

Dunnigan stood up.

'Where are you going?' Miley asked, looking terrified.

'To fix this,' Dunnigan said, and walked out without saying goodbye.

Miley Timoney

When he looked in the mirror he saw a man who had been born into a body that was marked as different. He could not bring himself to hate what he saw – he thought he had a pleasant, warm face, and he always did his best to be positive and friendly and, most of all, polite. He knew what people thought when they saw him coming, and being polite always helped to put them at ease.

But they still looked down on him, and hardly a day went by when he did not hear the word 'disabled' used in the same sentence as his name.

Miley could read and write fluently. While he was far from a tech geek, he could find his way around most computers and use the internet very well. He was not physically handicapped in that he could walk and run and jump and climb, and he dressed himself and could make his own bed (though they never let him).

Yet, for all of that, he was disabled – at least, that was what they told him. And that was why he still lived in the Home.

He remembered the day he was taken into care. His grandfather had arrived at the house he shared with his mother. He loved his grandfather – he had a nice smile, and he used to give him chocolate biscuits. 'We're going for a drive, Miles,' the old man had said – he always used to call him Miles. He had liked that.

Miley was surprised when his mother came out with a bag, and put it in the boot of his grandfather's car. He saw his favourite teddy bear, Scruffy, was sticking out of the top of it – why was he taking Scruffy on a drive?

He tried to ask her, but she would not meet his gaze. Sometimes she seemed to find looking at him difficult, and he knew not to push her, because when he did she shouted at him, and sometimes smacked him, hard.

He hoped his grandfather was taking him to the zoo. His mother had been promising to take him, but it had never happened. Then they were pulling up at a strange house, and a woman he did not know was telling him that he would be living there from now on, and when he turned to ask his grandfather what was going on, he was already back in the car, turning on the engine – and was his grandfather crying?

Miley Timoney was sixteen before he got to the zoo, and he had to run away from the residential unit to get there. But it was worth the punishment of being locked in his room for the rest of the day. He thought so, anyway.

13

A DIFFERENT NURSE ANSWERED THE DOOR OF the Harrington Nursing and Convalescent Home – Dunnigan remembered that Joan Hayes ran the night shift. This one was younger and her smile seemed genuine as she greeted him.

'Can I speak to Bill Tanner, please?'

'On what business, sir?'

'I'm a friend of Miley Timoney's,' Dunnigan said, stepping inside. 'I want to speak to Mr Tanner about an issue with Miley's room. He was telling me that his … um … his chest of drawers is sticking.'

'He never mentioned it to me,' the nurse said, and left him in the same room he'd been in the night before.

Tanner was bigger than Dunnigan had expected – he was probably six feet four inches in height, with very broad shoulders and a pendulous gut hanging over the belt of his trousers. He was dressed in a fawn jacket, a little like a lab coat, which had a couple of screwdrivers and a pair of pliers showing in the breast pocket.

'What's this about Timoney's storage unit?' he asked, clearly annoyed at having been interrupted from whatever he had been doing. His voice seemed to come from somewhere deep inside him – it was raspy and coarse.

'Miley's room is fine,' Dunnigan said, standing so he felt a little taller. 'I want to know why you lock him up at half past six each evening.'

Tanner laughed, and it was not a pleasant sound. 'You're asking the wrong person,' he said. 'Talk to Joan Hayes or one of the other nurses if you've got an issue with the house policy.'

'Why do you have him cleaning toilets? He is a paying client.'

Tanner took a step closer to Dunnigan. 'He told you that, did he?'

'He says you beat him and call him derogatory names.'

'*Derogatory names?* Who the fuck are you, anyway?'

'I am Miley's friend and I am here to register a complaint with the management of this establishment. I am also going to be asking for the termination of your employment and for charges to be brought against you. We can begin with professional misconduct, but I expect we will be following that up with assault, forced imprisonment, perhaps even enslavement. I haven't checked that one out yet.'

'I don't know what that fucking mongoloid has told you, but I do know you cannot come in here, to my place of work, making those kinds of allegations.'

'I can and I am. You, Mr Tanner, are a bully, a thug and a hateful man, and I am not going to tolerate you mistreating my friend for one second longer.'

Dunnigan went to walk past the giant. Tanner, however, had other ideas.

'Hold on one minute there,' he said, grabbing him by the arm. 'I haven't finished with you.'

'Let me past,' Dunnigan said, trying to prise the ham-like fist from his arm.

'You're not gonna be sayin' one word to anyone,' Tanner said, pulling Dunnigan on to his tiptoes so they were nose to nose. 'Because if you do, I'll hurt you. What I'll do to your little retarded friend … well, I bet you can guess. I have friends who would love to meet him.'

'I'm leaving now,' the criminologist said. 'Whether you like it or not.'

Tanner smiled, and, with no apparent effort, threw Dunnigan across the room, slamming him into the wall opposite with crushing force and knocking all the air out of his lungs. Dunnigan was so shocked he barely registered the pain, and rolled over, regaining his feet unsteadily and gulping desperately to get his lungs working. Just as they did and he sucked in a much-needed breath, Tanner was on him again.

Dunnigan saw hatred and madness in the huge man's eyes, and he realised in an instant that he was not afraid. He did not care what happened to him, how badly this thug beat him. Gathering his strength, he charged into Tanner as hard as he could muster, and was swatted aside as if he were an insect.

To his credit, the criminologist drove his fist into the bigger man's gut, but Dunnigan had never thrown a punch before in his life, and there was little force behind it – all it really achieved was to make his hand and upper arm go numb. Somewhere in his head he registered surprise that hitting someone hurt so much. Tanner certainly did not seem to notice he had been struck, and used both his own fists to wallop Dunnigan across the back of the head with a ferocious blow. It felt like something was exploding in his skull: he saw stars and went down, the room reeling sickeningly, but he was still conscious enough to use the opportunity to sink his teeth into Tanner's calf – at this stage, he felt as if he was watching it all from somewhere above the fracas. The ogre roared and kicked with his other foot, striking Dunnigan in the stomach and winding him a second time, causing him to release his grip. The smaller man tried to roll out of range, but Tanner was faster than he looked, and reaching down, he grabbed Dunnigan by the hair and lifted him into a half-sitting position.

'You made one big mistake—'

Punch – the blow connected with his cheekbone, skinning it and causing lights to flash behind his eyes.

'—coming in here—'

Punch – his ear, this time, something popped inside and he felt wetness stream down his cheek.

'—throwing your fucking weight around!'

Punch – right on his mouth, mashing his lips against his teeth, one of which felt as if it might have been loosened.

His breath coming in gasps, and soaked in sweat now, Tanner dropped Dunnigan back onto the floor of the waiting room. 'I will … I will treat that dumb-arsed retarded fucking loser however I want. Now, when you're feeling up to it, peel yourself off my fucking floor and get yourself the fuck out of my nursing home.' He turned on his heel and stalked out.

When he was alone, Dunnigan reached into his pocket and pulled out his phone. With the one eye that wasn't swollen shut, he peered at the screen, and switched off the app he had been using to record the entire conversation between him and Bill Tanner.

'Good news, Mr Tanner,' he said, through shredded lips. 'You've been caught!'

And then he laughed, long and hard, even though it hurt like hell.

Ernest Frobisher

In 1996 he was in New York on a trip to negotiate the takeover of an oil company – he preferred to finalise deals personally, and while he did not particularly enjoy the process of travelling, he did relish seeing new places and meeting new people.

He liked people. He was always fascinated by their reactions when he said and did certain things, things he knew some would find shocking or offensive and that would amuse or titillate others. Another demographic might be angered or even enraged by his conduct.

It was always a roll of the dice when he dropped these little gems into a conversation, but it was never less than a thrill to wait for the fallout.

After the meeting at which he bought the company for half what it was worth, he invited the main players back to his hotel for some food and a few drinks, all at his expense – he found that a little wining and dining could smooth over damaged pride if it was done with enough grandeur. While, in reality, he did not care what these worker drones thought of him, he did have to continue doing business, and it was worth tolerating their company just a touch longer to iron out the creases his hostile takeover had created.

He had asked the Yellow Man to book the banquet room that took up the entire top floor of the Plaza, and he ordered in beluga caviar from Russia, vintage champagne from France, Iberico ham from Spain, oysters and smoked salmon from Scotland. Some jazz singer or other who was in vogue at the time was paid far more than he warranted to come along and croon for an hour or so, and things seemed to be going wonderfully well.

Too well, in fact. Frobisher felt himself going to a place that he knew was very dangerous indeed – he began to get bored.

He was standing at the back of the room, his hands in his pockets, watching the throng of besuited businessmen shovelling his ridiculously expensive food down their throats, swilling his champagne as if it were cheap lager, and then he realised someone was talking to him. It was Frederick Gillian, the CEO of the company he had just destroyed with a stroke of his pen. Frobisher looked languidly at him, not hearing a word the man uttered, seeing only the beads of sweat on the other man's brow, the way his collar was too tight for his flabby neck, the fact that he had spilled oyster liquor on his lapel.

'I'm going to fuck your wife until her pussy tears,' Frobisher said to him, deadpan.

Gillian stopped dead, a look of horror on his face.

'You heard me. And when I'm done with her, I'm going to have your son skinned while I watch. I'll send you a video of it.'

Gillian had gone deathly pale, then he threw up all over Frobisher's shoes.

He hadn't expected that response.

It was true – travel really did broaden the mind.

PART FOUR

New Beginnings

1

'I CAN'T B'LIEVE THIS IS MY PLACE!' MILEY SAID, AS Dunnigan placed the last of the boxes containing his few meagre belongings on the floor of the one-bedroomed apartment they had found, with the help of Greta Doolin and the Respond Housing Agency. The apartment was in Ringsend, just across the river from the Widow's Quay Homeless Project. Miley would have a bedroom, a small bathroom, a tiny kitchen and an equally small living room – Dunnigan thought it was plenty.

'It's small, but that makes it easier to maintain,' Dunnigan said. 'You've got everything you need to make this work, and I've arranged for a support worker to call in on you a couple of times a week, to help you with the things you didn't get the chance to do in the nursing home – manage your money, organise meals, that kind of thing. If you're in trouble, you can call Greta, and I've written a number for James, your outreach worker, on a card that I've stuck on the wall right beside the phone.'

'Or I could call you!' Miley said. 'I have your personal phone number!'

'Which you use far too much,' Dunnigan muttered.

'Do you think Mr Tanner will be put in prison?' Miley asked, a shadow of fear crossing his face.

'He's already in custody, Miley,' Dunnigan said. 'I might not be a cop, but I work for them, so beating me up was a big mistake.

He'll be going away for a while, at least. So you don't need to worry about him. Anyway, you've got the intercom system I showed you, so no one gets in unless you feel safe enough to let them inside the door.'

'Yeah. I s'pose you're right.'

'This is your place – no one can tell you what to do here,' Dunnigan added. 'Now, I'm going to leave you to settle in.'

'Where are you going?' Miley asked.

'I'm helping at the Homeless Project tonight.'

'Can I come?'

Dunnigan sighed deeply and put his hands into the pockets of his long coat. 'Do you know what we do at the Homeless Project, Miley?'

'You help people who don't have anywhere to live. People who sleep on the streets at night. If it wasn't for you, Davey, I could be like that. I want to help, too.'

The criminologist shrugged. 'Okay. They need all the extra hands they can get. You know where the Project is – why don't you unpack, then come on over?'

Miley's face nearly split in two he was grinning so broadly as he showed his new friend to the door.

2

'YOU LIFT IT FROM YOUR END AND SWING IT around to the right – no, *your* right, not mine. Yeah, that'll do it.'

Diane Robinson came into the dorm of the Homeless Project later that day as Dunnigan and Miley were moving some new beds into a space Father Bill had created by literally knocking out a wall between the original dorm and a storage room they barely used any more.

'Nice to meet you,' she said, as Dunnigan introduced Miley. 'We're just serving dinner if you'd like some. It's Sunday, so there's roast chicken and stuffing.'

'We'll be along in a moment,' Dunnigan said. 'Two more beds to bring in.'

'I'll save you a couple of plates,' Diane said, and left them to it.

After the meal, Dunnigan made some tea for himself, and spent ten minutes working out how to make a cappuccino from the technologically advanced coffee machine, then brought the result to Diane. Father Bill and Miley were at the other end of the long room loading up the backpacks for the nightly outreach run, Father Bill entertaining the few residents who were still lingering over coffees and teas with a rendition of 'Out On The Weekend'.

Diane took the coffee, looking pleased. She sipped and smiled, nodding her approval.

Such simple things made a difference, a fact that was not lost on Dunnigan, though most of the time he ignored such social niceties. Coming to the Project had caused him to recall his first days at Harcourt Street, however, and he had almost instinctively fallen back on old behaviour patterns.

When he had started working at the Sex Crimes Unit, or the National Bureau of Criminal Investigation, as it had been called back then, he had made a point of building as many bridges with his new colleagues as he could. He did not need their approval on an emotional level (Dunnigan had always been self-contained, and the only people he needed any kind of affirmation from were his family), and he did not need their friendship (he had very few friends, preferring his own company), but he knew it would make the job, and progression within it, easier if he had everyone else on board.

So he had treated it like a project, and mapped out a path to systematically becoming part of the community that was the new Unit.

He was good with names (responsibility for large numbers of students had taught him excellent recall) and he greeted everyone he met with a salutation and a smile, regardless of their initial reaction. He never got coffee for himself without asking everyone else who happened to be in the workroom if they wanted any. Every day he arrived at the office with a box of baked goods (he brought doughnuts on his first day and received an unmerciful ribbing for it: *This isn't shaggin'* Hill Street Blues, *you gobshite!* – although the fact that the consignment disappeared rather quickly did not escape him), and within two weeks he noticed that this gesture alone had caused a thawing of the general attitude towards him. His father had always told him that it is difficult to remain hostile to someone who is feeding you something you enjoy, and those words of wisdom had always served him well.

Even though he was snowed under with his own work, he made a point of offering assistance to others if it seemed to be needed. That had resulted in him doing a lot of photocopying and bringing bundles of letters to the administration office to be posted, but he carried out each task, no matter how menial, with good humour and without complaint.

It seemed that applying the same logic to volunteering at the Homeless Project was bearing fruit. Diane certainly seemed to be thawing towards him.

'Where did you meet Miley?' she asked, the mug of frothy coffee held between her two hands as if for warmth.

'At work. He's related to my boss through marriage. My sister kind of insisted I take an interest in him, too.'

'You have a sister?'

'Oh, yes. I have an entire family, actually. Mother and father, the whole set.'

Diane laughed. 'Pardon me – it's just that you often seem so… so *autonomous*, it's hard to think of you as part of a family or as having friends.'

'Miley's not my friend – I'm just helping him.'

'Friends help one another.'

'It's not like that, really. He needed a hand out of some trouble he was in, and I was able to do something about it.'

'Father Bill told me what you did,' Diane said. 'And your black eye hasn't quite faded. That really was something, you know. A lot of people would have walked away from it. You should be proud of yourself.'

'Why?'

'You gave that guy a chance he would never have had otherwise. Like it or not, what you did was an act of pure friendship.'

'I don't understand why people keep saying that.'

'We're supposed to be living in enlightened times, but the reality is, someone like Miley, he doesn't have very many options. That home you found him in, as horrible as it was, that was probably the better end of what a lot of Miley's people experience.'

Dunnigan looked at her in puzzlement. 'What do you mean by Miley's people?'

It was Diane's turn to be puzzled. 'His disability. Down's Syndrome?'

'Oh. That,' Dunnigan said.

'You actually forgot he's disabled, didn't you?'

'He's not disabled. He has a condition, but he's not really handicapped by it.'

'You are a strange one, David Dunnigan.'

'People often say that.'

'You can come across as the hardest, most self-serving person in the world, and then you turn around and behave like you have the softest heart.'

'I'm complicated,' Dunnigan said, and went to join Father Bill and Miley.

'That you are,' Diane said to no one in particular.

3

THAT EVENING, WHILE FATHER BILL AND MILEY chatted with a group of young men who were sleeping in an alleyway just off Amiens Street, Dunnigan offered to cover the patch of waste ground right behind Connolly railway station. It could only be accessed by squeezing through a small gap in a corrugated-iron fence. He did just that, pulling his bag of sandwiches through after him, and entered the Warrens.

Darkness had fallen twenty minutes earlier, and the area was dotted with fires, groups of people huddled together around them talking quietly, some drinking, some smoking, some asleep.

He spent five minutes walking the perimeter, making sure everyone saw he was there and that he was carrying one of the backpacks they would all be able to identify as property of the Widow's Quay Project – he was letting them know he was a friend.

When no one assailed him or reacted with hostility, he approached the largest group, unslinging the bag and taking out some sandwiches. 'Hello, I'm a friend of Father Bill's.'

They nodded, accepting the food wordlessly.

The group was made up of five men and three women, all of indeterminate age (dirt and hard-living rendered many homeless people in a kind of ageless limbo, to Dunnigan at least) and they were all dressed in a motley array of overcoats, anoraks, gloves and hats, although this close to summer it was not really cold.

'I was wondering if you might be able to help me with something,' he said.

All eyes turned to him suspiciously. 'I'm trying to find out about a woman who used to sleep here. Here name was Bridget Bates – she was from Wexford originally. Do any of you know where she went?'

There was some muted muttering from among the group, then: 'She stopt comin' here t' sleep,' one of the women said. 'I tink she might've met a man. She was a pretty wan, was Bridget.'

'Did she tell you she'd met someone?'

'Can't 'member. She might've.'

A tour of the rest of the groups in the camp taught him no more. Later that night he, Miley and Father Bill made their way to the top of Grafton Street, where many doorways contained bodies wrapped in sleeping bags. One porchway held a couple, but they were Lithuanian. Whenever he had a chance, he asked about Paul Myers, or Bridget Bates, or the Grants. No one knew anything.

At midnight they crossed O'Connell Bridge. An old man was slumped over a by now cold cup of tea in a cardboard cup. 'I've got this one,' Dunnigan said.

Father Bill and Miley were already approaching a similar figure on the corner of D'Olier Street, so the criminologist squatted down, took the Thermos out of his bag and freshened the man's drink.

'Do I know you, lad?' the oldster asked him. 'Are you my boy? Are you Norman?'

'No. I'm not related to you,' Dunnigan said. 'Are you hungry?'

'I told Norman not to buy that car,' the old man continued. 'I knew he was bein' robbed, but he wouldn't hear it. I tried to tell him, lad, but he shouted at me.'

'Here, take these.' Dunnigan gave him three sandwiches,

leaving them on the piece of cardboard the old man was sitting on. 'I don't suppose you know the Grants? Wayne and Fiona?'

The man took a deep swallow of tea – Dunnigan was worried he would burn himself, but the old guy seemed impervious. 'The dark people,' he said. 'They went with the dark people.'

Dunnigan shook his head. The man was obviously suffering from Alzheimer's disease. 'What dark people?' he asked, more out of courtesy than anything else.

'They went with them,' the man said, opening a sandwich and cramming most of it into his largely toothless mouth. 'Used to stay near the Guinness Brewery. Had a squat there. Are you my boy? Please tell me about my boy.'

Dunnigan paused. For all his confusion, the old man knew the Grants. 'I don't know your son. Who are these dark people? Where did they take the Grants?'

'To the moon,' the old man said, in a sing-song voice. 'Took them to the moon, they did.'

Shaking his head, Dunnigan stood up. 'Good night, then,' he said, and began to walk away.

'Beware the Yellow Man,' the old man called after him.

4

AT THE END OF THEIR NIGHT'S VOLUNTEERING Dunnigan walked Miley to his apartment block.

'I can't b'lieve so many people live like that,' Miley said, as they reached his door.

'I know. It's a disgrace,' Dunnigan said absently – he was wondering about dark people and yellow men.

'It makes me realise how lucky I am,' Miley said earnestly. 'To have somewhere nice to live, and people who care about me.'

'Yeah, we're blessed,' Dunnigan said. He pushed the confusing things the old man had said out of his mind, and decided he would watch *Quatermass and the Pit* when he got home. It was a British sci-fi horror series from the late 1950s, about a virus gradually turning a scientist into an alien monster – a theme that some modern movies had revisited, but he had a great fondness for the original.

'Speaking of caring about people,' Miley said, a sly smile playing across his lips, 'what's up between you and Diane?'

'What?'

'What's the story between you and Diane? I mean, the sexual chemistry when you two are in the same room is, like, really powerful!'

'I have no idea what you're getting at,' Dunnigan said. 'Now, it's time for me to be getting home, so I'll bid you good night.'

'I'm just saying,' Miley said. 'She really likes you.'

'Good night, Miley.'

'Night, Davey.'

Dunnigan had forgotten he'd even had the conversation with Miley before he was halfway to his car.

5

THE WAREHOUSE HAD NOT BEEN USED FOR FIVE years, according to the Irish Transport and General Workers Union, and the sprawling shell of a building spread for half an acre along the waterfront. Rooks, jackdaws and herring gulls nested in its rafters and on its flat roof, and the yard in which it sat, slowly rusting, was a wilderness of ragwort, thistles and scutch grass.

This remnant of the economic boom had become a favourite haunt of the homeless, part of the network of squats and refuges they created for themselves, and which the vast majority of the population of Ireland's capital city, comfortable in their suburban bliss, knew absolutely nothing about.

'It was built to have three floors, but the upper two are fucking death traps now,' Steve Evans, the supervisor who ran this part of the bustling waterfront, told Dunnigan and Diane Robinson one Saturday morning, the Liffey's dank aroma blown in by a lively wind. He was a short, squat, barrel of a man in his late forties, wearing a high-visibility jacket and a white hard hat. 'I know a lot of homeless people use the place, and I just sort of turned a blind eye to it, but then I started getting reports of some kid sneaking in and out, and that put the wind up me, which is why I called you guys at the Project. I'm a father myself, and I know my own lads would see somewhere like this as a playground. But it's not.

It's really dangerous. I set some cameras up, and we've recorded him coming and going at all hours of the day and night.'

Evans showed them screen shots of a boy, who looked to be eight or nine years old, in the act of climbing through a low window that had lost its glass a long time ago.

'It looks like he's living in there,' the docker said. 'My bosses would blow a gasket if some kid ended up dead because the roof fell in on him.'

'It might be pretty rough on the child too, Steve,' Diane said.

'Yeah, yeah, of course,' Evans said. 'I'm just tryin' to do my job, y'know? I coulda just sent the security guys in with their dogs. I want t' do right here.'

'We'll have a look,' Dunnigan said.

The sounds of machinery pounding, men's voices calling to one another and traffic from the city streets was loud all around them, but the abandoned yard still seemed a desperately lonely place.

Much to Dunnigan's relief, Evans gave them a key, and they didn't need to squeeze through the window the kid was using to gain access. It unlocked a huge padlock and a heavy chain slid onto the wet ground. It took both of them to get the huge rusted door to slide open, and the sound of it grinding across the concrete echoed through the shell of the old building.

Inside the place smelled of damp earth, old iron and human waste. The warehouse had been mostly gutted, so the ground level was open plan, with a few smaller rooms along the walls that had been used for offices. The window the child was accessing opened on to one of these, but it was empty.

'We'll just have to go over it a yard at a time,' Diane said. 'I'll take the north end, you take the south, and we'll meet in the middle.'

Their search yielded not a sign of the young interloper.

'I could have guessed he wouldn't be down here,' Diane said, studying the map Evans had given them. 'The stairwell to the next level is over there.'

'Didn't he say it's not safe?'

'He did, yeah.'

'But we're going up anyway?'

'Jesus, it looks that way, doesn't it?'

The stairs were metal and went in a spiral pattern upwards. The room the child was using was the second they looked in.

'Ah, God – the poor thing,' Diane said.

A bed had been made from a couple of sleeping bags and some cushions that had once belonged to a couch. Posters, one of the Manchester United soccer team and one of Elvis Presley, had been fixed to the walls with what looked to be chewing gum. On the floor by the bed was a battered teddy bear, a few old children's magazines and a well-thumbed copy of Roald Dahl's *The Twits*. The room was surprisingly clean, and Dunnigan noted that the child had taped cardboard over the window, better to insulate it from the cold.

'One bed,' Diane observed. 'He's here alone.'

'Probably a runaway,' Dunnigan said.

'Or abandoned,' Diane mused.

'So what do we do now?'

'We wait,' Diane said.

6

DIANE HID IN THE ROOM NEXT DOOR, AND Dunnigan went back down to the yard, skirting around to the window the child was using as his access point. He obscured himself behind a gorse bush and began his vigil.

Three hours later, they were still waiting.

Four hours later, Dunnigan texted Diane: *This is a waste of time.*

She texted back: *Go back 2 de Project if u like.*

Dunnigan texted back: *Okay.*

And he did.

It was eight thirty before Diane returned to Widow's Quay.

'Well, I've met our mystery boy. His name is Harry Gately, and he's originally from Clare, or that's the story he told me, anyway,' she said to Father Bill – Dunnigan was there, but she completely ignored him.

'And he gave you the slip, I take it?' Father Bill said.

'Without very much difficulty. He looked scared to death when I announced my presence. I told him I was from the Project, and that we only wanted to help him, but as soon as my back was turned, he took off into the bowels of that warehouse and, seeing as we were on the second floor, I was too scared to go after him. The boards looked like they might give way any second.'

'You were right,' Father Bill said. 'I'd prefer to have you back in one piece. We know he's there and he knows we're here, too, so it wasn't a wasted day.'

'He's all alone,' Diane said. 'And he's tiny – he could be as young as six or seven. We can't leave him there, surely!'

'I have no intention of leaving him,' Father Bill said. 'I've informed social services, but they're ludicrously overstretched. I'm worried about him, but we can't channel all our resources into winning him over, either. One of us will head out tomorrow for a while, see if we can't coax him at least to join us for a meal. It probably won't work, so we'll try the following day. But we can't keep doing it for ever.'

'I'd like to have a go,' Miley said.

He had been sitting at one of the long tables at the back of the room, quietly reading the Project's Code of Practice and listening to everything that was going on.

'And so you will,' Father Bill said. 'But it might be best the lad sees a familiar face, for a while at least. Diane should probably keep trying for the moment. Too many of us bombarding the boy will only frighten him off.'

Nigel, a regular user of the Project's services, came in at that point to collect some fresh bedding for the dorm, and Father Bill went to get it for him.

'Thanks for abandoning your post!' Diane turned on Dunnigan, the anger and disappointment plain in her voice.

'You said to go ahead.'

'I was being sarcastic!'

'Oh. I didn't get that.'

Diane sighed and rubbed her eyes, the temper gone as quickly as it had arrived. 'You know what? I actually believe you.'

'Good. I don't think my being there would have benefited the situation, anyway. The end result would have been the same.'

'Yes. I think it probably would.'

Dunnigan nodded, and began collecting up the dirty tea and coffee mugs.

'What nights are you on next week?' Diane asked.

'Tuesday and Thursday.'

'I'm Monday and Thursday. I said I'd cover the weekend too.'

'Okay.'

Diane watched him carefully place each cup in the dishwasher. She noticed that every movement was made with the same economy, the same deft purpose. 'Would you like to go out on Wednesday night?'

Dunnigan did not pause in his task. He took a bag of dishwasher salt and poured some into the correct compartment. 'I think Father Bill has Trevor and Barry with him on Wednesday.'

'No, I mean *out* out. Away from the Project. A recreational activity.'

Then Dunnigan did pause, his finger halfway to the 'on' button of the machine. 'Oh. Um ... where do you want to go?'

Diane laughed. 'I don't know – where do people usually go? We could get a drink somewhere, we could go for a bite to eat, we could see a film—'

'I like films!'

Dunnigan had cut her off before she could get another word out. 'Well, that's good.' Diane was bemused by his reaction. 'Why don't we catch a movie, then?'

The criminologist looked at her with a quizzical expression for a moment, then returned to the dishwasher.

'So will I see what's playing at the IMAX?' Diane prompted. a couple of minutes later, when Dunnigan made no further comment.

'No. I'll find something appropriate.'

'What do you mean by appropriate?'

'Something that isn't really bad,' Dunnigan said, as if it was a very silly question to ask.

'Well, okay, then,' Diane said, still a little puzzled by how this had gone. 'I'd better get back to work.'

'Diane,' Dunnigan called, as she was at the door.

'Yeah?'

'Why do you want to see a film with me?'

Diane stopped, once again brought to a halt by this strange man. 'Because I like you, and I thought it might be nice to get to know you outside the craziness of this place.'

'You *like* me?'

'Is that so hard to believe?'

'Yes.'

Diane shook her head in exasperation. 'Let me know when and where we're meeting.' And she left him looking at the empty doorway.

'I told you,' a voice from behind Dunnigan piped up.

Miley was still sitting at the table, the Code of Practice open in front of him.

'What just happened?' Dunnigan said, sitting down next to him, a look of anxiety on his face.

'I think you just got asked out on a date.'

'Are you sure?'

'Pretty sure.'

'How do you know?'

'Well, she said she liked you and she wanted to get to know you better.' Miley checked the details off on his fingers. 'She also said she wanted to go for a drink, or to get something to eat or to see a film, and those are usually date-night activities.'

'You're probably right,' Dunnigan said. 'I had no idea I was attracting her to such a degree. I wasn't trying to be charming or anything.'

'Well, you've either got it or you haven't,' Miley said. 'And you, my friend, seem to have it.'

7

DIANE WENT OUT THE NEXT TWO AFTERNOONS to try to get through to the boy, Harry, but each day she came back downhearted and upset – she knew the lad was still using the warehouse, but he was cautious now he was aware he was being watched, and she had not seen him again since that first visit.

'Maybe he just doesn't want to deal with us,' Dunnigan said, as she sat with her head in her hands, close to tears, after her second foray proved fruitless.

'He's only a little kid,' she shot back. 'He isn't old enough to decide whether or not he wants our help. He's at risk, and we need to get him somewhere safe. He could be being used for God knows what by God knows who.'

'Well, why don't we try calling social services again?'

'They don't bloody care! He's just another statistic. If we don't get through to him, no one else is even going to try.'

Dunnigan considered this. 'Would you like me to give it a go?'

Diane looked up, suspicion in her eyes. 'Seriously?'

'Yes. Maybe we need to take a different approach. A fresh pair of eyes. It's sort of what I do with the police – look at cases where others have reached a dead end.'

'Thanks.'

'You're welcome.'

'I was being facetious, Davey.'

Dunnigan shrugged. 'Mmm. Do you want me to try or not?'

Diane sighed. 'It can't hurt, I suppose.'

Dunnigan stood up and made for the door.

'You're going now?'

'No time like the present.'

'I have literally just come in after having sat in that awful bloody building for three hours.'

'And I expect he was watching you from some vantage-point or other for a good deal of that, waiting for you to go. He won't be expecting me.'

She threw up her hands. 'Perhaps you're right. Go on, see if you can win him over, because I am at a complete loss.'

Dunnigan nodded once, and left.

8

IT WASN'T QUITE DARK, BUT DUSK WAS SETTLING over the city as he climbed the steps gingerly to the second floor of the warehouse, and fancied he heard the gentle scuttling of feet as he did so – he was moving quietly, but he knew the child would be hyper-aware, and his presence would have been detected as soon as he set foot in the building.

Harry's small room was in darkness, but Dunnigan got the scent of a recently extinguished candle – the waif had not gone far. He unslung his backpack. From inside he took a blanket, which he spread out on the floor, his laptop, and a large plastic bag. He then switched on the torch on his phone, and propped it up in the corner, spilling a bright triangle of light across the floor of the room.

Flipping open the computer, he inserted a flash drive and opened a folder marked 'Retro Games'. Scrolling through its contents, Dunnigan settled on one of the most simple, and addictive, titles he could find.

In a second, the room was filled with the sound of happy electronic music – he made sure the volume was turned up as loud as it would go, hoping the distinctive sound would permeate the crumbling old building. He played the game through a couple of times, allowing his character to get killed quickly, then noisily opened the plastic bag and took out a large packet of crisps, which he tore open equally noisily and began to eat with gusto.

He started up another game, and waited, barely aware of what was happening on the screen.

It took five minutes for a small, grubby face to peer around the door. The child was remarkably quiet – Dunnigan hadn't heard him coming: one moment he wasn't there, the next he was. Dunnigan ignored his presence and kept playing, reaching over with his free hand to take a crisp from the bag and cram it into his mouth.

The boy watched him silently for a minute or so. Then the head disappeared.

Dunnigan didn't move.

A moment later it was back, and this time the boy stepped tentatively into the room.

He had jet black hair, was dressed in a filthy red anorak and tattered jeans, with worn-out trainers on his feet. His cheeks were smeared with dirt, and he had a frightened, but intensely curious look on his face. 'Dis is my place,' he said. His accent was one Dunnigan couldn't place – it had a rural edge to it, but it wasn't strong.

'I know,' Dunnigan said.

The boy stood stock still, watching him. 'What's dat?'

'This?'

'Yeah.'

'It's a video game.'

The boy eyed him, the desire to go over and get a better look almost tangible in him, but he was still very nervous. Dunnigan wondered how many temptations had been offered to him since he started living on the street, and what tortures he'd had to endure when he succumbed to them.

'It's more fun if two people are playing,' Dunnigan said, holding up a joystick he'd brought along. 'I can plug this in and you can use it. I can play with the keys.'

The boy took a step closer. 'What's the game?' he asked.

'Pacman.'

'I don' know how t' play dat.'

'I'll show you. It's easy.'

The boy, Harry, stayed right where he was.

Dunnigan allowed his Pacman to be eaten by a ghost, and looked directly at the boy. 'I'll tell you what,' he said. 'I'm going to put the computer down here. You can see the screen from where you are, right?'

The kid nodded.

'The joystick has a long cable, so you can sit – or stand, if you'd prefer – over there, and still play. I won't move. I'll stay just where I am. That way, no one has to feel uncomfortable.'

He plugged in the joystick, waited for it to sync with his laptop, then placed it on the floor midway between him and Harry. The boy looked at it, then back at him. 'I ain't gonna touch your mickey,' he said, his voice neutral, but the fear evident.

'I'm glad to hear it,' Dunnigan said. 'Let's play.'

Harry, his eyes never leaving Dunnigan, stooped and picked up the controller.

'You're Pacman, the guy who looks like a circle with a mouth,' Dunnigan said, explaining the rules. 'You have to eat the dots and keep away from the ghosts, because they'll kill you. When you eat the fruit, you get extra points, and when you eat the big flashing dots, you can kill the ghosts, but that wears off when *you* stop flashing. Got it?'

'Yeah,' Harry said.

Dunnigan threw him over a bag of crisps and a bar of chocolate. 'And we're off,' he said.

The boy played the first few games standing up, but gradually he relaxed into a kind of squat. In between games four and five he sampled the chocolate and, though it was a large bar, finished it before game five was over. The crisps disappeared during game six, and by then he was half sitting, half kneeling. Dunnigan rolled a can of lemonade towards him.

'You gots any udder games?' he asked, after they had played Pacman for about an hour.

'I have lots. Would you like to choose another one to play?'

A nod.

'Okay. I'll show you some pictures of them, and you let me know which ones you like, and I'll tell you about them.'

'A'righ'.'

After much discussion, they settled on Asteroids.

'D'you have anythin' else t'eat?'

Dunnigan shot a digital piece of space rock, and paused the game. 'I don't have any more sweets, but I do have some sandwiches.'

''Kay.'

'I've got ham and cheese, I've got chicken. and I've got some tuna and sweetcorn.'

'Can I have one of dem?'

'Of course you can. Which would you like?'

'I don' mind.'

'Well, choose one. Here they are.'

Dunnigan spread them out on the floor, within easy reach. The chicken sandwich was grabbed and, seconds later, the ham and cheese.

'You know, they're serving dinner at the Project not far from here. We could go and get some.'

Harry shook his head. 'I has to wait.'

'For what?'

'My mam 'n' dad.'

'Do they live here too?'

The boy nodded.

'But they're not here now?'

'No. Dey's comin' back, dough.'

'Well, what if I promise to bring you right back here as soon as dinner is finished?'

'Can we put de game back on?'

Dunnigan hit the key, sending the virtual asteroids reeling about the screen again.

'Maybe I go t'morrow,' Harry said, and Dunnigan knew he was in.

9

THE NEXT EVENING, HARRY WAS WAITING FOR Dunnigan, and with the promise of a PlayStation in the common room at Widow's Quay, he came with him to the Project.

Diane met them at the door. 'Well, I'm very pleased to see you, Harry,' she said.

The boy looked up at her from beside his new friend, his face expressionless.

'We've got stew for dinner this evening, but how about I get the guys in the kitchen to do you some sausage and chips?'

The boy nodded, barely perceptibly.

'You are an amazing guy, David Dunnigan,' Diane said, and kissed him on the cheek, causing him to freeze for a second, completely unsure how to respond.

'I need to introduce Harry to Father Bill,' he said brusquely, and pushed past her into the building.

Miley arrived when dinner was half-over. Spying Dunnigan, he waved and made his way over, stopping to chat to a few of the Project's regulars as he went.

'Hey, Davey. Is this the fella everyone's been talking about?'

'This is Harry,' Dunnigan said.

'How's it going?' Miley asked, pulling over a chair and sitting down beside the boy.

Harry had a mouth full of chips, and his face, which Dunnigan had managed to wash before food was served, was now covered with brown sauce. ''Lo,' he said.

'I hear there's a Super Mario Kart tourn'ment happening after dinner,' Miley said, with grave seriousness. 'I reckon I'm going to win me that tourn'ment.'

'No way,' Harry said, trying hard not to laugh.

'I have to warn you, I'm pretty good,' Miley said, leaning back and cracking his knuckles loudly. 'I hope you've been practising.'

They gathered in the common room. Some of the younger residents wanted to participate, and most of the others were happy to watch. Father Bill offered a box of chocolate biscuits as a prize, and the games commenced.

'Our young guest seems to have taken quite a shine to Miley,' Father Bill said.

He and Dunnigan were leaning against the wall, watching the merriment unfold. Harry was perched on Miley's knee, clapping and cheering as Charlie, a twenty-something with a shock of red hair, had his turn at the racing game.

'I think what he wants more than anything else is a friend,' Dunnigan said. 'Miley doesn't seem to have an agenda – he's not trying to get him to do anything he doesn't want to do. He's completely non-threatening.'

'And the rest of us pose a threat?' Father Bill laughed.

'He came with me this evening, but I know he doesn't really trust me. He sees me – and you and Diane – as the enemy, albeit relatively benign,' Dunnigan said. 'We're all trying to tame him, to bring him into our world. He doesn't want that – if we're to get him to trust us at all, he has to be allowed to return to the warehouse this evening.'

Father Bill smiled, and patted Dunnigan on the shoulder. 'You learn fast, Davey,' he said, and left the laughing, cheering group to their games.

Diane Robinson

When her husband died, she thought she would die, too. The army is supposed to prepare you to face death, and she had lost friends in action, and it had been awful. Looking back, though, she now realised that none of them had been close to her, and she'd had the mindset some soldiers adopted, the idea that she and, by extension, those she loved were indestructible.

Then one evening her husband, Geoff, an officer in the Irish Navy, had gone to drop a DVD back to the store. She remembered the film had been something stupid and frivolous – one of those Scary Movie spoofs, with the Wayans brothers. It was a trip that took ten minutes, but he was going to get some bread on the way home, which would have added some time to the journey, and he was an outgoing, friendly man, so the risk of meeting a friend or acquaintance and chatting with them for a few minutes was always a possibility, too.

Then she looked up at the clock, and he'd been gone for an hour. She knew instinctively that something must have happened, but she still told herself he had been persuaded to go for a pint and forgotten the time.

When another hour had passed she decided to go out and look for him.

She saw the lights of the ambulance and the fire brigade in the distance, and she knew right away what had happened.

All the psychology and therapeutic training in the world had not helped her to understand why the bottom had fallen out of her world, and she had never quite been able to rebuild it. She found everything a struggle – and it was not until she found the Homeless Project and threw herself into its world that she felt she truly belonged somewhere again.

And then this strange, skinny, untidy-looking criminologist had arrived at the Project, and there was a quality in him she recognised. He could not have been more different from her husband – Geoff had been tall, well-built, with smiling eyes and a booming laugh. Dunnigan almost never smiled, and he looked as if he needed someone to sit him down and fatten him up a bit. He was not handsome, not by any definition, but he had pale, clear skin that was almost porcelain, and the deepest hazel eyes she had ever seen.

And there was a pain in him that somehow met the pain in her.

He interested her.

It was the first time she had felt that since her husband failed to come home.

She had asked him out in spite of herself – in truth, he frustrated her as much as he attracted her. But if she was going to attempt a relationship again, she wanted it to be with someone kind. And, even though he didn't know it, David Dunnigan was *kind.*

10

MILEY BROUGHT HARRY BACK TO HIS LONELY room that night, and offered to pick him up for dinner the following evening.

'Any sign of his parents?' Diane asked.

'Not that I could see,' Miley said. 'He seems to be 'lone, far as I can tell.'

'He's probably working on the assumption that we won't try to put him in care if there's someone looking after him,' Diane said. 'So he's manufactured a mum and dad.'

'Or maybe they're just really, really neglectful,' Miley suggested.

'Or perhaps they're who he's running from,' Father Bill interjected.

'It'd be good to know,' Diane said.

'I'll see what I can find out,' Miley said.

Dunnigan had a fair idea that Harry's parents would not be coming back, but he kept the thought to himself – he was very interested in how Father Bill might deal with this new development.

Dunnigan and the priest were locking up that night when Miley, wrapped up in his duffel coat and the multi-coloured woollen hat he sometimes wore, returned from dropping Harry home. 'Is there a cup of tea going?' he asked.

'I was just about to have one,' Father Bill said, and busied himself about the kitchen, humming the tune of 'Cinnamon Girl'.

'Harry and his family are from Ballyvaughan,' Miley told them, when they are all sitting in Father Bill's office. The priest produced a bottle of Glenfiddich Scotch whisky and poured a liberal dose into his own mug of tea. He offered the bottle to Dunnigan, who declined, and then to Miley, who shrugged and added a much smaller quantity to his.

'Harry doesn't know why they left Clare, or why they came to Dublin, but he swears his mam and dad were with him till a short time ago.'

'So what happened?' Dunnigan asked.

'They'd been making a few euro here and there, begging, but they mostly survived by skip-diving outside supermarkets. Harry says he got the flu, and his mam and dad wanted to get him some medicine, so they went out to beg for cash.'

'Hard to find medicine in rubbish bins,' Father Bill said, sipping his tea.

'Yes,' Miley agreed. 'Harry says they usually worked 'tween O'Connell Bridge and Stephen's Green. They left early last Saturday, and told him to stay in the room where we found him, to keep warm. They had been sleeping in a ruined building near Christ Church, but they heard about the warehouse, and when Harry got sick, they moved in there. Harry says he slept most of that day, and when he woke up it was dark, and they weren't back. So he did like he was told, and waited.'

'And he's still waiting,' Dunnigan said, voicing what they were all thinking.

'Yes,' Miley said.

'They're not coming back,' Father Bill said, and Dunnigan looked up sharply.

'Try telling Harry that,' Miley said.

And they sat there, in the quiet of the night, each thinking of the little boy who needed so much but asked so little.

11

DUNNIGAN MET DIANE AT THE DAME STREET entrance to Trinity College on the night of their date. She hadn't been sure what to wear – it was only a trip to the cinema, but she wasn't certain if they might go for something to eat afterwards. Dunnigan had asked her to meet him at seven thirty, which was quite early and suggested the film might not be the only activity he had planned.

Eventually she had chosen a little black dress, working on the premise that you could never go far wrong with that, and she wore her usual leather jacket over it, not wanting him to feel she had gone to *too* much effort.

He was exactly on time, as she'd known he would be, and she noted that, in terms of his appearance, at least, Dunnigan had gone to no effort whatsoever: he was dressed exactly as usual, in his well-worn long grey jacket, jeans and, tonight, a T-shirt with the words *Blake's 7* written on it, whatever that was. He didn't even seem to have put a comb through his hair, which looked, as it always did, as if he had just got out of bed and had simply run his hands through it in an effort to tame the mess.

For all that, she was glad he had shown up and gave him a smile as he approached.

'Hello,' he said, 'I've booked two tickets to see *Poltergeist* at the Irish Film Centre. They've remastered the original film stock, so I thought you might enjoy it.'

'Oh,' she said, trying to remember if she had seen the film before – she thought she had, at some point, but could hardly remember it. 'Well, that's very thoughtful of you.'

'Come on, we don't want to be late.'

'Right you be,' she said, congratulating herself on not wearing high heels.

The cinema, which was small and intimate, was only half full, so they had their pick of seats.

'The original movie was released in 1982, and was co-written and produced by Stephen Spielberg,' Dunnigan told her. 'It was very successful. They did a remake last year, but that's probably best forgotten.'

'I haven't seen a horror movie in ages,' Diane said.

'Really?' Dunnigan said, giving her an odd look. 'Why not?'

'No particular reason – I just never got around to it.'

'That's not a good enough answer. Ssh. It's starting.'

The film centred on the Freeling family, who had just moved into a housing development that happened to be built on an old graveyard, understandably upsetting the spirits of the deceased interred there. The unhappy ghosts began communicating with the family's youngest, their daughter, Carol Anne, through the television set, and she ended up being dragged into the dimension of the dead via her toy cupboard. Most of the film involved the family's efforts to get her back, with the help of some parapsychologists and a squeaky-voiced spirit medium.

Diane found herself having a lot of fun, although she possibly enjoyed the fact that Dunnigan took it all so seriously even more than she did.

'So, you watch a lot of horror movies then?' she asked, as they strolled slowly back through the city. It was still early and late shoppers continued to go about their business.

'I've been a fan of horror and fantasy movies since I was very young,' Dunnigan said. 'My father and I used to watch them together.'

'You still close with your dad?'

Dunnigan stared fixedly at his feet as they walked. 'No,' he said, after a long pause. 'We don't talk any more.'

'I'm sorry,' Diane said.

'Horror films are, I think, wonderful dialogues on morality,' Dunnigan, said, pointedly changing the subject.

'Really?'

'In horror movies, everything is magnified, so it's very easy to see where the lines are drawn. The villains are monstrous and grotesque, and the heroes are usually very good, and very selfless, and impossibly brave. In most horror films, the evil is vanquished, the maiden is rescued, and everyone lives to fight another day. I think that is an excellent message to get out to the world – because that is the way things *should* be.'

Diane reached out and took his hand – to her delight, he didn't try to pull it back. 'But that's not the way things are,' she said. 'Life is hardly ever as black-and-white as that.'

'I know,' Dunnigan said quietly. 'But that doesn't mean I can't hope.'

'You live in Phibsboro, don't you?'

'Yes, I do.'

'Well, I'm all the way out in Kilmacanogue. Why don't we go back to your place for a cup of coffee, and you can tell me a bit more about horror movies? It's a part of my education that is sorely lacking.'

Dunnigan fell silent for a moment. 'I don't drink coffee,' he said, when at last he did speak. 'I don't even have any in my flat.'

'Well, there's a shop right over there where I can buy some,' Diane said, trying not to be offended.

'You could do that,' Dunnigan said. 'But, you see, I don't own a lot of furniture and . . . well, other than my sister and my boss, I haven't had anyone in my flat – ever.'

Diane spotted a bench and steered them over to it. 'Sit down for a moment, Davey,' she said firmly. 'We need to have a chat, you and I.'

'I don't want to.'

'I don't care.' She angled herself so she was facing him, although he still seemed determined not to look at her. 'Do you understand that I wasn't speaking in code, just now? I am not suggesting we go back to your flat with the intention of having rampant sexual acrobatics. I would like to spend a bit more time with you, and drinking coffee or tea is the socially accepted thing to do during that process. I want to get to know you some more, and maybe try to swing the conversation around in such a way that I might tell you a little bit about me – don't you wonder about me at all, Davey?'

'I wonder about you a lot,' Dunnigan admitted.

'Then why in the name of God don't you ever ask me anything about myself? I was beginning to think you were completely uninterested in what makes me tick!'

'I didn't like to intrude,' Dunnigan said, trying for a moment to hold her gaze, but not succeeding.

'Surely my asking you out sort of meant I want to us to get a bit more personal.'

'In what way?' Dunnigan asked, looking terrified.

'Davey, did you know before tonight that I live in Kilmacanogue?'

'Uh ... no.'

'There you go! Things like that! I'm not proposing we pee with the door open.'

'People do that?'

Diane could not control her laughter now. 'Yes – some people who are in very close relationships do. Davey, have you any idea the trauma I've been going through, and how conflicted I've been about whether or not to try to have a relationship – actually, never mind a relationship – to try to have a *friendship* with you?

You make things so hard, sometimes, it's like you go out of your way to be rude and abrasive. But then there is so much in you that I think is sweet and beautiful and *kind*. There aren't enough kind people in the world, these days.'

'I'm not kind.'

'Yes, you are! How can you think you're not kind?'

'I'm just not.'

'Look, Miley is your best friend – now, I know he's a lovely guy and he gives a hell of a lot back, but the fact you would even consider being close with him ...'

'That's all for my sister. I promised her I'd spend time with him.'

'And you continue to do so to keep her happy?'

Dunnigan shrugged. 'I said I would.'

'I don't believe you, but let's move on. What about Harry? You saw I was upset, and you went out and befriended him! And you were really clever about how you did it – don't tell me that wasn't an act of kindness.'

'You were unhappy, and I didn't want you to be cross or distracted on our date.'

'What?'

'I had booked the tickets by then, and, they *were* refundable, but I wanted to go, and I thought it would help our working relationship if we had something to talk about. I didn't want you to be in a mood – you can be very changeable at times, and I thought it would be better for us both if you were happy and not feeling guilty or inadequate. So I fixed the problem with the little boy. We had a nice time, didn't we?'

Diane looked at him, aghast. 'I don't know what to say.'

'You're welcome,' he said.

'I wasn't thanking you!'

'Oh. Well, you're welcome anyway. Shall I walk you to your bus?'

'I think you'd better.'

They walked on in silence for a while, Diane trying to process the conversation they had just had. 'You know what wrecks my head the most?' she asked him, her voice full of dejection.

'No,' he said.

'I haven't a clue if you're worth the effort or not.'

'I wonder about that too,' Dunnigan said, and she knew he was being completely truthful.

12

DUNNIGAN KEPT MANY THINGS ON THE BIG external hard drive that was attached to his laptop. He had a vast library of science-fiction and fantasy novels, as well as a collection of works on criminology, sociology and abnormal psychology (all in the ebook format) that was almost as large. Some of these he had bought, more he had pirated using torrent streams – his often precarious financial circumstances meant he had developed a loose definition of the word 'theft' when it came to intellectual property.

He had a huge cache of films, again mostly in the science-fiction and horror genre, and a complete collection of the classic *Doctor Who* series, going right back to William Hartnell's era (those the BBC hadn't recorded over or thrown away), as well as the two Dalek movies starring Peter Cushing.

And he had a folder he rarely looked at, containing hundreds of photos, many of which were scans he had made of shots his father had taken when he and Gina were little (the photos were all carefully posed and artfully structured – Dunnigan's father had used his children as models to serve his interest in photography as an artform, not out of sentimentality, something he was always at pains to tell his offspring while he immortalised them on celluloid), and quite a few of images he himself had snapped, almost all of which featured Gina, Clive and Beth – his surrogate family.

He didn't know what had caused him to go to the folder the night after he'd got home from his date with Diane – sleep had eluded him yet again, and he found his finger hovering over the mouse, then clicking and scrolling. The photos were organised with the same painstaking detail as everything else in his files: most were labelled according to the year they had been taken, but some of the later ones were just marked by their subjects: Gina, Beth's First Birthday, Beth Goes to Pre-school, and so on.

There was one photo among them all that was not in a folder, though. It sat apart, all on its own, and was still identified by the registration tag provided by the digital camera on which it had been taken: DSC_0032. He tapped on it, and it was magnified on the screen. Gina had taken it on his camera on the day Beth had vanished, just before he and his niece had got into the BMW to drive to Dublin.

The photo was of the two of them, bundled up in coats, scarves and hats, she standing, he kneeling beside her in the doorway of Gina's house. They were both grinning at the lens, and Beth was waving. They looked relaxed, happy, delighted to be together and heading off on their Christmassy trip.

Dunnigan looked at the photo for a long time. Then he took a flash drive from his pocket, put it into a USB port on the laptop, and saved the image to it.

The next day, he went to a chemist, and had it developed. On his way over to Harcourt Street, he bought a simple picture frame.

13

THE NEXT WEEK THE OLD MAN WAS ON O'CONNELL Bridge when Dunnigan happened to be walking past. He was in almost the same spot, wrapped in his ragged sleeping bag, an old scrap of cardboard insulating him from the cold concrete. It was the lunchtime rush, and streams of people were moving past him where he sat on the bridge, but the cardboard cup only had a smattering of copper coins in it. While Dunnigan was there, no one paid any heed to the old man at all.

'Hello again,' Dunnigan said, squatting down beside him.

The man squinted at him as if it hurt to look at him. 'Are you Mr Greengrass?'

'I don't know who that is,' Dunnigan said. 'Do you remember I was here the other night? We talked about the Grants – Wayne and Fiona? You remembered they used to live over on James Street.'

'The brewery,' the old man said firmly. 'They had a kind of a squat there.'

'Yes. That's right.'

'Are you Bill O'Herlihy? Off the telly?'

'I don't know who that is either,' Dunnigan said. 'You told me something about dark people taking the Grants to the moon. And something about a Yellow Man.'

'That's right. They come and they take them away. To the

house on the moon they go, to be sure. And they don't come back, no, they don't.'

'I don't understand,' Dunnigan said. 'I've tried to work out what you might be talking about, and I can't. Could you explain it for me in another way?'

'No. I could not,' the old man said, sounding like a spoiled child.

Dunnigan sat down beside him. 'I didn't think you could. I just thought I'd ask.'

The old man nodded sagely, and began to sing 'Molly Malone' gently. Dunnigan joined in on the chorus. People walked past and ignored the pair, singing the old Dublin street song to one another.

14

'YOU KNOW, I WAS HOMELESS FOR A TIME,' Dunnigan said to Father Bill, as they walked past the Spire that evening.

'Were you?'

'I slept in my car off and on for a year or so. Sometimes I had flats and bedsits, but often I didn't.'

Father Bill nodded. 'Any of us is just one stroke of bad luck away from losing everything,' he said.

'It didn't feel that way at the time,' Dunnigan said. 'Nothing mattered. If I lived or if I died – none of it made any difference. I couldn't work, I could scarcely think. I suppose I wanted to disappear too.'

'Like your niece,' Father Bill said.

'Yes.'

He didn't know why he was telling Father Bill about this aspect of his life – he had never spoken to anyone about it before. He was in no way certain he trusted the priest, but something in him wanted to expunge some of the pain he had experienced, to share it with another. 'I suppose I ran away.'

He had left the NBCI to go on two weeks' leave, but ended up taking a year. The people at the university seemed relieved when he called them to ask if he could take an extended sabbatical, and Tormey did not appear to be upset. 'I think it's a good thing you've realised you need some headspace,' he said. 'I'll be here when you feel like talking.'

Back then Dunnigan wasn't sure he would ever feel like talking again, but he kept the sentiment to himself.

His savings paid the rent and kept him in the pizzas he ordered every other day (sometimes he went for three days if he just couldn't face food), but when, in his fifth month as a hermit, the landlord called around to see why the rent had not been paid – his contract with the university allowed him just two months' paid leave, and the NBCI had not paid him since he left as Dunnigan invoiced them only for the hours he worked – he knew he was in trouble.

He had always privately thought the apartment in Maynooth was too expensive anyway, so he left in the middle of the night, taking the few items he felt he needed and leaving everything else. 'It seemed the sensible thing to do,' Dunnigan told Father Bill. 'So I just went.'

For four weeks he lived in his car, sleeping on the wide back seat of the BMW, parking it down rural laneways far from the noise and lights of towns, finding spots that were in deep shadow, lying at night listening to the sounds of the trees and the wind and the small things that went about their business once darkness fell.

Hunger finally caused him to seek work, and he got a job in the kitchen of a Chinese restaurant in Offaly, peeling prawns, mashing ginger and boiling rice. The anti-social hours suited him – he lived a kind of twilight existence, eating with the Romanians and Poles with whom he worked the pass. They spoke very little English, and he learned just enough of their native tongues to get by. Silence enveloped him, like a cloud, and he sank into the repetitive nature of the job, the simple tasks he performed acting like a balm. Thought was something he no longer needed or wanted.

One morning he arrived for his shift to be told his hours had been cut – a nephew of the owner had arrived from Birmingham and needed the work – so Dunnigan accepted a fifty-euro severance payment and left.

An ad in the *Evening Herald* had led him to a position doing process serving for a security company based in Dundalk, delivering writs to errant husbands and bad debtors. The pay was terrible but the hours were long and he spent most of his days on the road, chasing his next victims. Finally even Dunnigan could not bear to be the conduit for any more unhappiness, and simply failed to turn in to work.

'It made me feel ill, for some reason, to be doing that work,' he told Father Bill, remembering the feeling in a very objective way, as if it had happened to someone else.

'You knew it was wrong,' the priest said. 'Your spirit rebelled against it.'

'I don't know if it was my spirit,' Dunnigan said, 'but somehow I knew I had to get away from it and the people I was working for.'

No one chased him to see where he was or what had happened, so he drifted on.

He found that he could live on very little if he needed to. He considered asking his father for a loan to tide him over, but while he had not exactly stopped talking to his family, he knew that making contact caused them pain. They had not really bothered to keep in touch with him either, so calling his father wasn't a pill Dunnigan was ready to swallow.

A job unloading cargo from boats in Galway proved too hard for him physically – months of poor diet and erratic sleep patterns were beginning to catch up with him, and he knew he would have to start looking after himself better.

He went to the supermarket and bought a basketful of groceries, then went back to the flat he had rented, and cooked the first meal he had made for himself in half a year. As he sat down to eat, he suddenly realised he was about to tuck into a bowl of spaghetti bolognese. He pushed the food aside, put his head on the table and wept.

'Crept up on you,' Father Bill said, as Dunnigan explained the significance of the meal he had made.

'How could I have done that,' Dunnigan asked, 'make spag bol without even knowing I was doing it?'

'The mind and the heart are strange things,' Father Bill said.

'I thought I saw her, once,' Dunnigan said.

He was walking through a shopping centre in Sligo, close to the end of the time he had been trying to hide from his life. He was looking for a place to get a cup of tea when he spotted a tiny figure, seemingly alone among the throng of people. The way she stood, the cut of her hair, the jacket she was wearing – he was convinced it was Beth and, without even knowing he was doing it, suddenly he was screaming her name and rushing forwards, barging people aside, grabbing the child by the shoulders and spinning her around.

But something was wrong – this girl had someone else's hair, just the wrong shade of chestnut, and her cheeks were too thin and her eyes were brown and she just wasn't Beth. He actually turned her around twice, as if doing so would make her into the little girl he wanted her to be. Then a man was prising her from his arms, and he was shoved to the ground, and a security guard was telling him not to move.

He allowed them to take him to an office at the rear of the mall, and it took all of ten minutes, once the police had arrived, to explain who he was and why he had behaved so oddly. It took them a further three minutes to confirm the truth of his story.

Then there was the pity, with the sidelong looks that told him they thought he was having a breakdown, and he thought that maybe he was. He was starting to wonder if he might be broken so badly he could never be fixed.

'Is there anyone you'd like us to call, Mr Dunnigan?' The female officer spoke gently, putting a hand on his shoulder as she did so.

'No. Thank you. I'll be fine.'

'Do you have somewhere to go?'

'Yes. I live in Galway. I was just here …'

He couldn't tell her why he was in Sligo. The road had just led him there that day.

'Maybe you need a bit of a rest, eh?' she'd said, and he knew she was right.

It was time to stop running.

'You know, everyone has a story,' Father Bill said gently, sitting on a shop windowsill and beckoning for him to do the same. 'People end up on the street for all sorts of reasons. Some have got into trouble financially, some are in the grip of addictions, some are running away from physical or sexual or emotional abuse, some are mentally ill and are released before they're ready to live on their own, some, like you were, are running away from their lives. There's a whole subculture now of families in hotels and B&Bs who have lost their homes because of the shoddy conduct of construction companies and developers, who sell buildings that are not safe to live in – these poor souls buy a house or an apartment in good faith, get their mortgages and other loans organised, then discover they can't live in the home they've just bought, but they can't sell it either, they're in negative equity, and it just goes on and on.'

'Do you know a man called Bernard Roche?'

'Old Bernie! Yes, of course I do. He's been a fixture in the city since I was a lad. He comes to the Project in the cold weather, but when it's warm he prefers to stay outdoors. He hasn't been well over the last few years. I think he's in the early stages of Alzheimer's.'

'Yes. I met him the other night, and again this lunchtime.'

'Ah, yes, when you were doing your investigating.'

'You know about that?'

'I've been informed you're asking around. Little escapes me, Davey.'

Dunnigan looked blankly at Father Bill. The man was a complete mystery to him. He ploughed on: 'Tell me about Bernard.'

'Not much to tell. He got into trouble with the law when he was a young man, did a stint in Mountjoy Prison, got out and couldn't cope, as so many can't, and ended up living rough. He has been ever since.'

'He doesn't seem to be an alcoholic or anything like that.'

'No. Many choose not to rely on booze or drugs. They know it's a trap that can eat them up if they're not careful. They keep away from substances, and from those who use them. It's why Bernie is usually alone.'

'He says he knows the Grants, the couple who are missing.'

'Does he?'

'Yes. He seems very confused about it – he knows where they used to squat, over on James's Street. But then he said something very odd.'

'What was that?'

The two men had started walking again and they turned on to Parnell Street. Already Dunnigan could see three figures huddled here and there along the thoroughfare.

'He said they were taken by the "dark people".'

Father Bill paused, giving Dunnigan a hard look. 'He said what?'

'He said they were taken by the "dark people" to a "house on the moon", or something like that. And he insisted I "beware of the Yellow Man".'

The priest seemed to shudder. 'It's probably nothing, Davey. Look, we have three beds left tonight, and that chap there looks like he might be a minor, so I'd like to bring him in if we can. I'll do the talking. That usually works best.'

And they moved forward.

Dunnigan had seen something in the priest's eyes, though. He had seen a moment of fear. He had no idea what might make Father Bill afraid, but whatever it was, he knew it had to be something very bad indeed.

Ernest Frobisher

He did not believe in friendships. He had never met another person he saw as his equal, but he placed great value on loyalty. To live the kind of life he relished, loyalty was essential. Loyalty and secrecy.

There were only two men now living who knew the full extent of what he was. One was the Yellow Man, and the other a skeletal, myopic albino named Severn, who had been in the employ of his family for years.

Severn was a cleaner, one with an almost preternatural gift for removing evidence of all kinds of activity swiftly and with the minimum of fuss. He was expensive, but it was a price Frobisher was always willing to pay. Severn employed his own staff, two burly Ukrainians, former soldiers for the Red Mafiya, according to the Yellow Man.

They were used to keeping secrets, and both had signed confidentiality agreements. But, then, Severn never told them anything about where they were going or what they were doing other than what was absolutely essential, so there seemed little cause for concern. As long as they were paid, the gorillas would keep quiet about what they had seen in his stronghold in the mountains, and they did not know enough to link to him and his predilections to any of the other scenes they had scrubbed.

Severn was an odd one. The rumours were that he was a gelding – that his twisted, religious zealot of a father had castrated him after catching his son masturbating as an adolescent. The story went that he had nothing left down there – he had to piss sitting down. He got his jollies now by dealing with the aftermath of other people's fun.

Frobisher could live with that – one thing he understood very well was the dark wishes, the shadowy desires that lie in the heart of men. If his own games gave someone else a jolt of excitement, so much the better.

It was the one thing that niggled him about the Yellow Man – he didn't know what made him tick at all. Nothing seemed to get him excited or set his motor running. He carried out his duties without so much as a grin or a smirk.

Frobisher had asked him once: 'Why do you stay with me?'

The Yellow Man had answered without pause: 'I need to serve.'

'You could serve anyone. There are governments that would pay admirably for your skills.'

'I know. I have worked for some, in the past. I choose to work for you. My skills are perfectly suited to your needs. I enjoy the work and the challenges you set me. For now, we are good for one another.'

'For now?'

'Yes.'

'I won't allow you to leave me.'

At that, the Yellow Man had smiled.

There was never a real reason to rant at his agent, but on a couple of occasions he had found fault where there was none, just to see what would happen when he turned his venom on him.

The Yellow Man took the barrage of abuse without flinching. When Frobisher was done, he bowed and left the room. On the second occasion, in his anger, Frobisher had made to strike him. The Yellow Man, without seeming to move, had caught his master's fist in his open hand, stopping the blow centimetres from his jaw.

Frobisher noticed his skin was warm, dry and smooth, almost like leather. He withdrew his hand, and had never raised his voice, or his fist, to the Yellow Man again.

He still did not see them as equals – but he knew to respect him.

And that was a new feeling for Ernest Frobisher.

PART FIVE

Going Hard

1

MILEY AND HARRY BECAME FIRM FRIENDS.

The young man began spending fewer of his evenings at the Project, and Dunnigan suspected he was instead over in the warehouse, keeping the lad company. He voiced his thoughts to Father Bill.

'Yes, I think you're probably right,' the priest agreed.

'Should we talk to him about it?' Dunnigan wanted to know.

'Why?'

'Well, is it safe?'

'You know the building far better than I,' Father Bill said patiently, a set of the Project's accounts spread out on his desk in front of him. 'You and Diane have both said it's not safe at all, but you still ventured inside.'

'I don't mean is it physically safe,' Dunnigan pressed on. 'I mean, is Miley leaving himself open to ... well, to allegations and whatnot? Or what if some bad people arrive and try to interfere with them or something? Miley is very vulnerable.'

Father Bill took off his glasses – he wore bifocals when reading, which he placed precariously on the very end of his nose – and sat back. 'In theory, either of those two things might happen – but I don't think they will. What's really going on here, Davey?'

'I'm just worried about Miley.'

'As you should be, but I think we have to let him have a bit of freedom. He's finding his feet, and helping Harry is a very positive thing for him to do. He needs to see himself as a strong, confident person, which for many years, particularly when he was in that awful nursing home, he probably didn't.'

'But what if he gets into trouble?'

'If he does, I have no doubt he will ask us for help.'

'But what if it's too late?'

Father Bill put his glasses back on, and returned to his ledgers. 'Has it occurred to you at all that Miley needs Harry as much as Harry needs Miley?'

'I don't understand.'

'You set him up in the apartment, and with the Respond people you helped him get furniture, and you loaned him books, and we offered him friendship – but here we have a chap who has spent his whole life in institutions of one kind or another, where there was always someone about, twenty-four hours a day, seven days a week. He was never really alone. Even when he was locked in his room, he could hear the other residents and the staff going about their business. Suddenly Miley is living on his own in an apartment – and that must be very lonely for him. Why do you think he has been spending every spare moment around here?'

'But Harry is only a kid!'

'A lonely, lost kid with no parents. Sound familiar?'

'I still think we should have a talk with him.'

'Oh, I don't think it would do any harm,' Father Bill said. 'I think you miss him a little bit, too, now he's not about so much. Am I right? And that might be good for him to hear.'

Dunnigan snorted and left Father Bill to balance the books.

2

'YES?'

'Miley, it's Davey.'

'I know – your number came up on my phone.'

'I thought we might go for lunch tomorrow.'

'Sorry. I can't.'

'What do you mean you can't?'

'I told Harry we'd have a picnic in the Phoenix Park.'

'Oh.'

'Want to come?'

'Um … well, it's not really convenient for me. I thought you might meet me at Garda HQ. We could go to Captain America's …'

'Well, it's very nice of you to ask. How 'bout the next day?'

'The next day is Sunday.'

'So? Is that a bad day for you?'

'I was going to watch *Doctor Who and The War Games*. It's one of Patrick Troughton's best stories, I've always thought.'

'Okay.'

Pause.

'Would you like to come over to my flat and watch it with me?'

'Yes, please! I'll bring the popcorn!'

'I don't like popcorn. It gets stuck in my teeth.'

'I'll bring the nachos!'

'I don't like nachos – all that chemical flavouring they put on them gets all over my hands.'

'I'll bring the Tayto crisps!'

'Well ... I suppose that would be acceptable. I was planning to begin at two o'clock sharp.'

'Brilliant! Thanks, Davey. Two sharp on Sunday, then.'

'Right. Yes. See you then.'

'Oh – Davey, one thing.'

'What?'

'Where do you live?'

Miley Timoney

Miley was grateful for everything Dunnigan and Father Bill and Diane had done for him. He understood how lucky he was to have been given a chance to lead an independent life. Which meant he didn't have the heart to tell them he was struggling to live it.

The biggest problem was filling his day. Before Dunnigan had come into his world and turned it upside down, Miley had never had to think about what to do with his time – people decided all that for him. Now he was expected to make those decisions for himself, and he was unsure if he was doing it right or not.

In fact, he was unsure about a lot of things. Unsure and afraid.

He was terrified to return to the day-care centre he had been attending when Dunnigan had rescued him. He was convinced the people from the nursing home would be waiting for him there, and, even though he knew Dunnigan or Father Bill would come looking for him if he failed to come home, and he knew Bill Tanner was in prison, his oppressor had always told Miley that he had lots of friends, and what if some of them wanted revenge?

He decided it would be wiser to start afresh – strike out on his own. But that meant he had the vast expanse of the day to get through, which was a challenge.

He was used to getting up early – in the nursing home, things kicked into gear at about five thirty in the morning. He did not feel inclined to rise at such an ungodly hour now he had his own place, but he was wide awake by six, so he killed some time just lying in bed, watching the light spread across his bedroom wall.

A shower and breakfast took another hour, and he had started listening to Marty Whelan's programme on Lyric FM in the mornings – he liked Marty: he played lots of nice music, some of which he knew, and some he had never heard before, and he told silly jokes. Once Miley had texted in to ask for a request, and Marty had read it out and said hello to him, so Miley felt they had a connection now, and he listened loyally every morning and did not leave the apartment until the show was over.

Next on his timetable was shopping – he made a point of allowing something to run out (milk, bread, butter, washing powder) so he would need to go and pick some up. He would walk to Marks & Spencer on Grafton Street and he found that he could spend an hour or sometimes even two wandering around the aisles, looking at all the amazing things they had, things he would never even think of buying – he googled some of them when he got home, and was surprised to learn that pâté was made of mashed-up livers. He couldn't understand why anyone would want that, but he was pleased to know the information, and he now visited the pâtés every time he went shopping,

He would go back to the apartment then, put away whatever he had purchased, and do his housework. He vacuumed the place from top to bottom, scrubbed the surfaces the way he had seen the nurses in the home do, and he would put some clothes into the washing-machine, then out to dry on the clothes horse Diane had given him.

That usually brought him up to one o'clock, and then it was time to go and meet Harry. It was his favourite time of day. He would make them something nice for lunch (not pâté!) and put it into a bag, and then he would walk over to the warehouse. Harry would always be waiting for him, and would run over and give him a hug. Then they would decide where they would go to eat – sometimes they went to Stephen's Green, sometimes to the Phoenix Park, sometimes to a little spot overlooking the river, where they could see the boats as they went past.

Miley spent most of his afternoons with the boy. They always had fun – they would talk about everything and anything. Harry always listened to everything Miley said, and he once told Miley he thought he was really smart. That made Miley feel so proud and happy. No one had ever told him that before.

If Miley was helping out at the Project, Harry would come with him. If he wasn't, he would stay with the lad until it was time for bed. They got take-out food for dinner, and he had bought a portable DVD player so they would go back to Harry's room and watch a film together. Harry loved the Shrek movies, and they watched those a lot. Miley liked them too – he could understand how the ogre felt sometimes: the way people treated him because of how he looked.

Harry usually fell asleep before the movie was over, and Miley would tuck him in and stay for a while, just to make sure he was okay. When he was sure Harry was sleeping comfortably, Miley would drop by the Project before going home. He liked to see Father Bill and the people who slept there (Father Bill called them the residents), and it also meant he didn't have to go back to his empty apartment. He didn't like being there on his own at night. He heard strange noises and he didn't know what they were.

So, he usually stayed at the Project until it they were locking up, and he would be tired enough by then to know he would fall asleep quickly when he went to bed.

He was very grateful to have his own place. He knew he was lucky to have it.

At least, that was what he told himself.

3

MILEY ARRIVED JUST AS DUNNIGAN'S PHONE registered two o'clock precisely. He came in, arms laden with bags of cheese and onion crisps, a huge bottle of Coke and a large box of Oreo cookies. 'These were on sale in the shop – they've just hit the sell-by date, I think, but Father Bill says you should look for the bargains, so I always do.'

'Sit down, please. Would you like a cup of tea?'

'I have a four-litre bottle of Coke here!' Miley said. 'I'm sorted, thanks.'

'Very well. I'll make one for myself, and then we'll get started.'

Miley wandered idly about the living room as Dunnigan busied himself in the flat's tiny kitchen. 'Is this her?' He was looking at the photograph of Dunnigan and Beth, which was now framed and on the mantelpiece.

'Yes.'

'She's lovely.'

'Yes. She was.'

Miley waited for Dunnigan to say something else. He didn't, so Miley said: 'Why do you like *Doctor Who* so much?' He was gazing up at the poster above the fireplace.

'I love everything about it,' Dunnigan said, coming back in. 'The Doctor has had twelve – well, thirteen, if you count

John Hurt – faces, and he can be rude, or gentle, or angry, or funny, but he is always the same person. His essence never alters, no matter what happens. The Doctor's most constant friend, his home, really, is the TARDIS, his vehicle. He always, without question, defends the little people, those who don't have a voice of their own, and even though he's sometimes afraid or sad or, at times, defeated, he never gives up. *Doctor Who* tells us that, yes, there are monsters out there, but you don't have to be frightened of them, because he is out there, too. You might not recognise him when he arrives. Often, you see, he doesn't look very heroic. But when you need him, you'll hear that wheezing, groaning sound, and then you'll know – help is coming. No matter how bad it is, no matter how desperate things might seem, he'll fix it.'

Miley grinned. 'That's a nice thought,' he said.

'It is,' Dunnigan agreed.

'Well, let's watch this series, then!' Miley said, plonking down on the couch, and Dunnigan hit play on his laptop.

'That was cool!' Miley said, four hours and ten minutes later.

'I'm glad you enjoyed it,' Dunnigan said, standing up and gathering the empty crisps packets and his teacup.

'I don't usually like black-and-white films,' Miley continued. 'They always used to want to watch them in the nursing home, and I never had a choice but to put up with it. But I liked that one!'

'How are things going with Harry?' Dunnigan asked, as he went into the kitchen.

'Good,' Miley said. 'Good, I think.'

'You're spending time with him in the warehouse?'

'Sometimes. He won't come to my apartment. But we've gone to McDonald's a few times, and we went to an arcade, and he likes to just walk about the city. He's trying to find his parents. We've spent a lot of time going round the places they used to hang out, but we haven't found them yet.'

'I don't think he's going to find them,' Dunnigan said, coming back in and closing the laptop.

'Harry says his folks were really good to him,' Miley said. 'I mean, he's not got any bruises or anything – he says they din't even smack him. His dad din't believe in it.'

'That doesn't mean they were good parents,' Dunnigan said. 'Neglect comes in many forms.'

Miley paused, thinking about that. 'I know. But, still, he's really, really certain they wouldn't just go off and leave him.'

'Kids like to see their world through rose-tinted spectacles,' Dunnigan said matter-of-factly.

'Will you try to find out what happened to them?' Miley blurted out.

'What?'

'I told Harry I'd ask you to. You find people for a living, Davey! If anyone can track them down, it's you.'

Dunnigan shook his head. 'The cases I get usually come with very large files, which I go through, looking for threads and themes and contradictions in evidence. I have lists of people I can interview and places I can visit to try to recreate what happened. *That* is how I do my job, Miley – by the time a case comes to my desk, a huge quantity of work has already been done.'

'So you're saying you can't?'

'No, I didn't say that.'

'So you will?'

'I didn't say that either!'

'Harry is a little person,' Miley said, looking at Dunnigan with grave seriousness. 'He doesn't have a voice, and no one wants to help him. He needs to know there are people out there who will.'

'I don't know, Miley.'

'Let's help him to hear that wheezing, groaning sound.'

Dunnigan sighed. 'I knew it was a mistake inviting you around!'

'It prob'ly was,' Miley said, grinning in delight.

But Dunnigan was already drawing links in his head between the Grants and Harry's parents and the other four who were still unaccounted for.

4

FATHER BILL LEANED HIS ELBOWS ON THE RUSTED metal railings and looked out at the slow-moving brown water of the Liffey. He and Dunnigan were just across the road from the Project.

'I'm not surprised at Miley wanting to make things right for the wee lad,' he said, taking a box of Silk Cut purple cigarettes from an inner pocket of his leather jacket and tapping one out. 'Don't look so appalled, Davey – I allow myself one a day. I'm in the process of quitting.'

'How long has the process been?'

'About five years. Look, it would be wonderful if we could find Harry's mum and dad – I would be over the moon. But this is not the first time I've come across an unsupervised child sleeping rough, and on the very few occasions where we have managed to find the parents, they were either hopped up to the gills on crack or, in one case, dead from exposure.'

'That doesn't mean we shouldn't look. I'm going to add them to the file I'm already working on.'

'Have you found any reason to believe any of those people you've been investigating are alive?'

'No. But that doesn't mean they're not.'

'Suppose you do find them and they don't want to come back to him?'

'We make them.'

'How? Maybe he's better off without them.'

'No. Children should be with their parents.'

'I wish that were always the case.'

'If they're on drugs, can't we get them help? Addicts can be supported to get clean.'

'They can. But they have to want to. And it can take a long time and a lot of false starts.'

'He's only a little kid. We could help him have years with a loving family.'

'We could – a foster family or an adoptive family. That's what we should be focusing our energies on, Davey. Harry needs to be in care, not sleeping rough, not roaming the streets looking for parents who walked out on him because he was sick and too difficult to care for.'

'I've never heard you speak like this before,' Dunnigan said.

'There's a first time for everything.'

'I don't like it.'

'Well, I apologise for that. But this is a tough world we live and work in. Some of the realities we have to deal with are not pleasant. You'll have to learn that.'

Dunnigan left the priest he'd thought he knew to his tobacco and his thoughts.

5

TORMEY WAS IN HIS OFFICE AT GARDA HQ WHEN Dunnigan got there, and he seemed only moderately irritated when the criminologist knocked on his door – in fact, he seemed to be in an altogether subdued mood. 'Break it to me gently, Davey,' he said, as Dunnigan sat down opposite him. 'What have you done? How much paperwork and how many apologies is it going to take for me to clean it up?'

'That only happened once,' Dunnigan said, 'and I think it's very unfair of you to keep bringing it up. I'm here to update you on the missing homeless people.'

Tormey tried to stifle a smile. 'You've got something? Have you cracked it?'

'Well … no. I want to add another couple to the list.'

'So, not only have you not found any of the people we're looking for, you actually lost two more?'

'You know I've been volunteering at the Widow's Quay Homeless Project?'

'Bill Creedon's place, yes. What about it?'

Dunnigan briefly told him about Harry, and the boy's request that he try to trace his parents.

'I don't know what you want me to say,' Tormey said, rubbing his eyes wearily.

'I've never started from ground zero in an investigation before,'

Dunnigan said. 'I was wondering if you could suggest where I should begin looking.'

'No one knows the Warrens like Father Bill.'

'He won't help. He said they're probably either high on crack or dead, and Harry is better off without them. He doesn't care.'

Tormey shifted on his seat. He had one of those chiropractic things strapped to the back of it – wooden balls woven into the shape of the chair. 'I've known Father Bill for an awful lot of years, and I have to tell you, the man has many attributes I don't like, but not caring isn't one of them.'

'He knows something about what's been happening. I think you're right – I believe he's involved, somehow.'

'And what has his reaction been to this kid?'

'He said I should be focusing on getting Harry into care.'

'There's a lot of sense in that.'

'I know, but I think we owe it to Harry at least to try to find his people. What if they're hurt or fell foul of some gang or other, or even got picked up by the police for something, and are in prison?'

Tormey reached over and swung the monitor of his computer around so it was facing Dunnigan. 'Jesus, Davey, you can check that right now.'

'I already did. It just annoys me – Father Bill is the one everyone looks up to, and he doesn't seem to give a damn one way or the other about this boy's predicament.'

'That's not true,' Tormey said.

'It is,' Dunnigan retorted.

'I came across Bill Creedon when I was still a rookie,' Tormey said. 'He was fresh out of the seminary, and was a curate over in Dolphin's Barn. I'll tell you, he shook things up back then. This was the eighties, and the Church still ruled with a rod of iron. Father Bill, for reasons he always kept to himself, did not follow any of the rules. Now, what I am about to tell you is partly urban myth, some it comes from surveillance records, and there's a bit of guesswork filling in the blanks, but I can promise you, this is what I believe happened.'

'I'm listening.'

'There was a young woman in Father Bill's parish – she was a lone parent, or an unmarried mother, as they were called then – and she wanted to have her baby baptised in church, with her family and friends around her. The parish priest, Father Bill's boss, refused on the grounds that she was not married, and the child was the product of sin or whatever the terminology was, I don't remember.'

'I think that was common enough back then,' Dunnigan said.

'Oh, it was,' Tormey said. 'This girl, she was pregnant by Mitch Bowers, who was a fairly significant gangster, and he was not happy about the PP's decision. He started to make his feelings known. He and his associates would hang around outside the services, threatening the people who were attending mass, letting them know that, if his child could not be given the sacrament of baptism in that church, then no sacraments of any kind were to be taken there – the church was blacklisted.'

'And the parishioners went along with it?'

'They did. As scared as they were of eternal damnation, they were more afraid of Mitch and his cronies. Getting communion in the next parish over was a bit of a pain in the arse, but it was better than earning the ire of the Bowers crew. Within a week, the pews were empty.'

'Did the priest know why people were staying away?'

'He would've had to be blind, deaf and stupid not to. But he was old school, and he figured he would just have a bit of an old pray and the man upstairs would fix things. His young curate, however, was a bit more hands on in his approach, even then.'

'What did Father Bill do?'

'He went door to door, and asked everyone to come back to the church the following Sunday. He told them that, if Bowers's men were still outside, they could just keep on walking and take mass in Crumlin, as they had the previous Sunday. He gave them his word, though, that there would be no gangsters barring their way – that he would've fixed the problem by then. And they all agreed to come over and see for themselves.'

'*Did* he fix it?'

'Father Bill knew that Mitch Bowers's wife—'

'He had a wife?'

'Oh, yes – did I forget to mention that?'

'You did!'

'Well, see, his wife used to have a bunch of her lady friends over for cheese and wine at the Bowers homestead every Wednesday lunchtime. So, the following week, just as they're sitting down to enjoy their Liebfraumilch and fucking gorgonzola, they hear a racket outside. Father Bill has set up a little altar in the front garden – they lived in one of those posh estates out in Clonsilla – and he's dressed in full clerical regalia, and isn't he only saying mass at the top of his voice. He'd brought along an amplifier and microphone powered by an old car battery, just to be sure everyone in the area could join in on the responses. When Mrs Bowers goes out to ask him what he's up to, he tells her that her husband has made it impossible for him to perform his holy duties in his own church so he has decided to bring God to the suburbs. And then he goes right on with the ceremony.'

'How did Bowers react?'

'Predictably. He worked from an office at the back of the house, and his missus marches in on top of him, and demands he have Father Bill removed, as he's upsetting her lunchtime gathering. Bowers sends one of his thugs to reason with Father Bill, only, as you have probably already guessed, the good father was not of a mind to see reason. When the thug decided to apply a little brute force, Father Bill applied right back, and left him lying where he fell. And then he went on with mass.'

'That sounds like Father Bill.'

'Ten minutes later, two more hard men come out, and Father

Bill doesn't even wait for these guys to speak – he comes around the altar, mid-prayer, and kicks one in the family jewels and nuts the other one in the forehead. End of round two. Mrs Bowers is beside herself at this stage – her lunch is ruined and she has been humiliated in front of her lady friends. The ugliest, craziest side of what her husband does has been brought right to her front door. I mean, this fucking mad priest is giving a sermon on her lawn about loving thy neighbour, and there are three footsoldiers bleeding all over the driveway.'

'What happened?'

'Bowers had to go and speak to Father Bill himself. From what I can gather, Father Bill told him that, while the black mark remained on his church, he would come out to Clonsilla every day to say mass for the Bowers family and anyone else who happened to be there. If the ban was lifted, of course he could happily ply his religious trade where it was meant to be plied.'

'And?'

'And the ban was lifted. A hit was put out on Father Bill, but it was a pretty half-hearted one as, back in the eighties, there wasn't a gunnie in town who would take out a priest. No one needed that on their record when they stood in front of the Pearly Gates. There's nobody more worried about that kind of shite than criminals.'

Dunnigan nodded. 'What has any of this got to do with Harry?'

'The weekend after people came back to mass in Dolphin's Barn, Bowers's baby mama got a call from Father Bill, asking her to come to the church with the kid and some friends. When she got there, he had the whole place decked out with flowers, he had asked some of the more progressive parishioners to come along to pad out the crowd, and he baptised the baby. He caught hell for it from his parish priest – he ended up being sent to fucking South America or somewhere as a punishment, if I recall it right – but he didn't care. He performed that baptism because he knew it was the right thing to do. He could have done it right away, and prevented that boycott happening, not to mention saved himself the hassle of all the business out at Bowers's house, but, see, he didn't do it because he was scared of Bowers, or to keep the old villain happy – and he absolutely didn't want him to think he did. He did it for the girl and her child.'

'Why are you telling me this?'

'Don't ever tell yourself Father Bill doesn't care. Don't get me wrong. I think he's a very dangerous man, and I believe he's been involved in more than one murder in my city over the past twenty-five years, but in his own strange way, he cares. If he tells you this kid is better off without his parents, then he probably is. That doesn't mean he wasn't involved in their disappearance, but if he was, it was probably to help the kid in some twisted way.'

'I'm still going to look for them, boss.'

'I know that, Davey,' Tormey said. 'I just thought I'd try to talk you out of it.'

'Why?'

'Damned if I know, Davey. Damned if I know.'

6

'ARE YOU GOING TO ASK ME OUT AGAIN, DAVID Dunnigan?' Diane was gazing at him fixedly as he unloaded linen from the washing-machine at the Project.

'No,' Dunnigan said. 'You were hurt and offended by some of the things I said on our last date, so I thought it best we … um … we discontinue any plans for a romantic association.'

'Davey, if I were to stop seeing every guy who pissed me off, I would never have got beyond a first date, never mind actually getting married.'

Dunnigan shook out and began to fold a pillowcase. 'You obviously have very poor taste in men,' he said.

'Oh, my God, you have no idea.'

Dunnigan didn't know what to say to that, so he said nothing and continued to fold the linen.

'So?'

'So what?'

'So are you going to ask me out again?'

Dunnigan took a deep breath. 'Am I correct in thinking this means you want me to?'

'That would be a good guess,' Diane said, giving him a thumbs-up.

'If I do, will you promise not to be angry if I get things wrong, or say things you don't like?'

'Will you promise to try to learn from your mistakes and be a bit more thoughtful?'

'I'll try to do that, yes.'

'Well, then, I'm going to assume that means you've asked me to go out with you again. And I have accepted your invitation. I've checked the roster – we're both free tomorrow night.'

'How do you know I don't have an engagement somewhere else?'

'Because I know you, Davey. Bring me somewhere nice, and make a bit more of an effort this time, okay?'

'I'm not sure how to do that.'

'Figure it out.' And she walked off, leaving the subtle scent of perfume and shampoo in the air, and a slight fluttering in his stomach, which he could not explain, and which he did not quite want to stop.

7

DIANE LOOKED STUNNING: SHE HAD HAD something done with her hair, a process Dunnigan couldn't name, which made her look different: he could see more of her neck, and her cheekbones looked different too. He thought perhaps she had tried some new trick with makeup.

She was not wearing her leather jacket, which seemed odd, but then he saw what she *was* wearing, and realised he might have misjudged Diane's expectations quite badly. She had some sort of expensive-looking piece of clothing, which was sort of a scarf and sort of a shawl draped around her shoulders, and the shawl-scarf thing matched a dress that was quite short, and which showed the rise and fall of her body very clearly beneath it. Her shoes had heels that were extremely high, and he noticed she had to change the way she usually walked to move about in them.

As stunning as she looked, Dunnigan was pretty sure she was cross with him again.

'We're going to see another film?'

'You said you liked the last one. I did as you said, and learned from my mistakes. You enjoyed the film, so I got us tickets for another. You didn't like it when I told the truth so I'll try not to do that.'

'You're trying not to tell the truth?'

'Yes.'

'So when I asked you if I looked nice, you lied?'

'You look quite different from how you usually do. I think it's ... very lovely.'

'Thank you. I think. How far is this place? Because my feet are killing me.'

'I didn't know you'd be wearing shoes like that.'

'I thought I'd push the boat out a bit.'

'We should take a taxi.'

'At last he gets it!'

A theatre in Ballsbridge was showing James Whale's classic *Bride of Frankenstein*. Dunnigan had seen the movie about thirty times – it was one of his favourites. Diane did not seem as enthused.

'It's in black-and-white? Jesus, Davey, does it have subtitles?'

'No. The dialogue is in English.'

'Do they sell popcorn here?'

'There is a concession stand in the lobby, as far as I know.'

'Good.'

There was only one other couple in attendance. They watched the movie, Dunnigan's eyes wide, his attention completely focused on the tragedy unfurling before them. Diane watched him more than she watched the film – in fact, she hardly watched the film at all.

When it was over, they stood outside.

'Davey, please take me for a drink or for something to eat. I'm dressed up like a Sunday roast and I want to go somewhere I can show off how feckin' gorgeous I look rather than sit in an empty cinema watching a film made during the Stone Age.'

'I don't really know this part of town,' Dunnigan said, looking about him uncomfortably. 'How would we know which was a good place or which was a bad place?'

'I don't really care. It's not about the food. Oh, for God's sake, Davey – can we have a date where we actually talk to each other?'

'Aren't we talking now?'

'I mean an actual, proper conversation!'

'When you and I have conversations, you usually end up angry with me. In fact, I think you're angry now.'

Diane laughed bitterly, pulled her scarf-shawl about her shoulders, spun on her too-tall heels, and walked away from him up the street. He did not know if he felt relieved or upset. In fact, he had not known how he felt all evening. He realised that he was enjoying watching her walking away – he liked seeing how she moved.

He stood there for five minutes, until she was out of sight, then discovered he was frozen to the spot. In him there was a kind of blind panic – he understood, somewhere in his deeper consciousness, that he did not just want Diane in his life: he needed her.

And parallel with that was the knowledge that he had almost no idea how to make that happen.

As an academic, Dunnigan's go-to response to a problem to which he had no answer was to do research – he would go to the library, surf the internet, ask someone who had skills in the particular field. Yet he felt a sense of urgency about this. It would not – *could not* – wait.

He decided he needed to talk to someone, and quickly.

His choices were limited.

8

'TO WHAT DO I OWE THIS PLEASURE?' MILEY ASKED, holding open the door to his apartment and allowing Dunnigan in.

'I need help, and when I thought about who to ask, you were the only name I could come up with.'

'Sit down. Do you want some tea, or some Coke, or a juice box or something?'

'No. Thank you.'

Miley pulled a chair over so he was facing his friend. 'What can I do for you, Davey?'

'I went out with Diane again this evening.'

'Where'd you go?'

'To the Palace Theatre in Ballsbridge.'

'Did you see a play?'

'They were showing *The Bride of Frankenstein*.'

'Did Diane know that was your plan in advance?'

'No. She wanted me to organise what we were doing, so I did.'

'She probably wouldn't have minded if you'd *asked* her what she wanted to do and then set it up.'

'Indeed. I probably should have. She looked like she was dressed to go somewhere ... well, somewhere different from the cinema.'

'Oh. Like how?'

'She had on makeup. And a dress. A small one.'

'A *small* dress?'

'Yes. It fitted her very ... very well.'

Miley pondered this. 'Do you think she wanted you to do kissing and stuff with her?'

Dunnigan looked aghast. 'I don't know. It's possible, I suppose. I don't know what to do, Miley.'

'You must have had girlfriends before,' Miley said.

'I did, but that was … that was before.'

Miley nodded. 'Can't you remember how you did things then?'

Dunnigan shifted uncomfortably on the couch. 'Not very well. Before things went bad, everything I did was about work – I saw some girls, but I wasn't ever really terribly interested in them. Going out with them just seemed the right thing to do.'

'Maybe you're gay,' Miley offered.

Dunnigan blinked at him. 'Are you suggesting I'm homosexual?'

'Are you?'

'No. No, I don't think I am.'

'How d'you know?' Miley asked.

Dunnigan thought about that. 'I've never been attracted to men,' he said finally.

'You don't seem to be very 'tracted to women either,' Miley said plainly.

'I think I am attracted to Diane,' Dunnigan said. 'She makes me feel odd. I can't remember ever feeling this way before.'

'So you *want* to do kissing and stuff with her, then!' Miley said. 'Well, that's the problem solved, isn't it?'

'No, it isn't!' Dunnigan said, exasperated. 'Every time I'm with her, I find myself saying things that upset her. I can't seem to organise my thoughts, and even when I try really hard to get it right, I still make a mess of things.'

'I once knew this girl, Josie,' Miley said. 'She was the cutest kid in the day-care centre, and everyone wanted to sit next to her at lunch. Cliff, he was the alpha male of the place – he had cer'bral palsy, and he used to put on this Christy Brown act, pretend he was all intellectual and cultured. I saw right through it, but Josie lapped it up. I knew I had to bring out the big guns if I was to have a chance with her, so I saved up my money and I bought her a bunch of flowers – they were only from the petrol station across the road from the centre 'cause I wasn't 'lowed to go into town or anything, but I used my allowance and I bought them for her. The next day, when she came in, I stood in the door so she couldn't fit her wheelchair through, and I handed her the flowers, and I said: "Josie McGrath, I'm crazy about you. Can I sit beside you at lunch today?"'

'Did it work?' Dunnigan asked.

'Hell, no! She laughed at me, then drove right over my toes. Sat next to Cliff just like she always did, him and his left bloody foot.'

'How does this help me?'

'I made a bags of it that first time, but I didn't let it stop me. I got her choc'lates the next week, and perfume the week after that. And each time, she smiled and zoomed on past. But I made an impression. When she finally got bored of Cliff, guess who was called upon to take his place?'

'So you won her over in the end?'

'I did.'

'Why aren't you with her now, then?'

'It turned out she was pretty as a picture but really, really boring. After two days, I made my excuses and moved back to my usual spot in the lunch room – I preferred to read my *X-Men* comics over the break than listen to her go on about the latest episode of *Home and Away*.'

'I don't think Diane is boring.'

'Make your best play, then! Don't let her slip through your fingers.'

'Flowers? Chocolates?'

'Davey, I've spent the last five years locked up in an old folks' home,' Miley said. 'My technique is probably a bit rusty.'

But Dunnigan wasn't listening any more. Miley had given him an idea.

9

THE FOLLOWING DAY DUNNIGAN CAME OUT OF Eason's bookstore. He hadn't bought anything, as he preferred to keep his books digitally, but he had spent a couple of hours perusing the shelves, as close to contentment as he got these days, bringing himself up to date on the latest horror titles (he liked to think of himself as a purist, favouring the works of H. P. Lovecraft and Edgar Allan Poe, but he was not beyond reading the occasional Stephen King or Clive Barker) and checking out what was newly published in the world of criminology.

He made for Henry Street. It was a bright, warm day, and he thought he might buy some fruit – his appetite was poor but he tried to balance his diet so that, even if he did not eat particularly healthily at every meal, his consumption over a week managed to hit all points on the food pyramid.

He was standing at a stall, examining some Granny Smith apples, when he heard his name called. 'David Dunnigan.'

He turned, and found himself face to face with Clive Carlton, his brother-in-law, Beth's father. They had not seen one another in ten years. Carlton was a middle-sized man, with a round face and curly dark hair. He usually wore conservative suits, as would be expected of a school principal.

'Hello, Clive,' Dunnigan said, but before he got another word out, his brother-in-law punched him hard in the stomach.

Dunnigan doubled over, as much in surprise as in pain, but as soon as he did, Clive brought his knee up, striking him square in the right eye and knocking him backwards so he landed hard on the flat of his back, his stomach heaving and his head reeling all at the same time.

He tried to get up, but a foot was placed on his chest.

'Keep away from my wife, you fucking weird asshole,' Clive said. 'Have you any idea what you've done to us?'

'I'm callin' the guards,' the woman who ran the fruit and veg stall chipped in. 'You can't go beatin' up me customers!'

'I'm going in a second,' Clive shot back.

'I'm sorry, Clive,' Dunnigan wheezed. 'I don't know what to do to put this right—'

Clive kicked him in the side of the face with vicious force. 'It's you who should have been taken,' his brother-in-law hissed, and then he was gone.

Dunnigan forgot about the fruit, and limped home.

10

GINA CALLED TO SEE HIM LATER THAT EVENING. 'Clive told me what he did,' she said. 'I'm so sorry, Davey. Did he hurt you badly? God, you look awful.'

His right eye had come up in a glorious shiner, and the left side of his face, where Clive had kicked him, was red and swollen.

'Do you have any ice? Any disinfectant?'

'No. I'll be fine.'

'I'm really angry with him – I can't believe he would treat you like that! I mean, this is Clive! I've never known him to even raise his voice! This is so out of character!'

'He had every right,' Dunnigan said.

'Davey, we've been over this.'

'I've accepted my guilt. Why can't you?'

'Because it's not true.'

'Mother and Father blame me. Clive blames me. It's pretty simple.'

'You're talking nonsense!'

'Beth was in my care. I don't see how we can point the finger at anyone else. It seems like an open-and-shut case to me.'

'Whichever evil monster took her, that's who's to blame!' Gina said. 'Now, would you stop beating yourself up and understand that you did not do this, and that Clive is just angry at the world, and you got in his way? Please?'

'I'm trying, Gina. I truly am.'

'I need you, Davey. I always have, and I always will. I'm back in Dublin, and we're starting again, but you're not really back being *you* yet. It's driving me crazy!'

'Your husband has asked me to keep away from you.'

'He had no right. And we're divorced, Davey. He's not my husband any more.'

'He's trying to protect you.'

'I don't need protecting from you!'

'That's what you thought about Beth.'

'Stop this, Davey, right now! That little girl worshipped the ground you walked on, just like I did when I was small. Don't you use her memory to twist our relationship. You're better than that.'

Tears obscuring her vision, Gina ran from the flat.

Gina Dunnigan-Carlton

When she was a child, she thought her brother was a superhero. He was only a few minutes her senior, but he had doted on her from when they were tiny. Her earliest memories were of him reading her Enid Blyton books – The Enchanted Wood *had been their favourite; she had loved the idea of a magic tree, the topmost branches of which reached other worlds. When Davey read to her, anything seemed possible. He read the stories with such passion and excitement, it was like she was really there with Moonface and Silky and the Old Saucepan Man, and Davey was right alongside her, having the most amazing adventures.*

When her first tooth fell out, it was Davey who told her about the Tooth Fairy, and helped her to wrap the tiny white gem in tissue paper and leave it under her pillow, and it was to him she ran the following morning, with her shiny pound coin held aloft.

He insisted on travelling to her all-girls boarding school when she made her confirmation (their parents' relief was almost palpable when they saw their two children off to school and could get their lives back), and he helped her pick out her new name: Faye. She knew it was the name of one of the actresses in those old films he loved so much, but he told her it was also another word for a fairy, and she loved that. She thought he was so clever to think of a name that fitted her like a glove.

She was heartbroken when he went to college in Cork and she had to go to UCD, but he promised her he would come home every weekend, and he kept his word, and never failed to arrive with some small present for her, and even though she was a teenager, and would have been mortified if any of her friends found out, she kept a calendar in her room and crossed off the days until she would see him again.

When she realised she was in love with Clive, she rang Davey to tell him.

'So it's serious with this bloke, then?'

'I think he's going to ask me to marry him.'

'That's pretty serious.'

'I know. What do you think?'

'He treats you well?'

'You know he does. You've been out with us loads of times. He treats me like a princess.'

'No more than you deserve.'

'If he asks me, I'm going to say yes.'

'If that's what you want, I couldn't be happier for you.'

When Beth was born, she saw, in his complete dedication to the child, the same love he had always shown her. She knew – had known maybe from as young as five or six – that Davey was a little bit different from most people, but that just added to her belief that he was super-powered. His dedication to those close to him was a part of that difference: when David Dunnigan loved you, it was complete and unerring.

And it was a love that had never had to deal with loss before. When Beth disappeared, something vital in her brother broke.

And, try as she might, she could not repair him.

11

THE DUNNIGAN FAMILY HAD LIVED IN AN OLD renovated farmhouse just off the Longmile Road since before David and Gina were born. The house sat in about five acres of land, and Stuart Dunnigan, David's psychoanalyst father, had planted fir trees, some of which he allowed a Traveller family who lived nearby to sell at Christmas (an arrangement that garnered him an annual financial loss), and some of which he allowed to grow as nature intended.

This meant that the three-storey house, which had been built in the eighteenth century, seemed to sit on the edge of a large forest. Dunnigan had loved that, growing up, and the books he read to Gina were always chosen to feature woods and wild places to make them more real for her.

He parked the BMW on the gravel in front of the house he had always thought of as home. As he walked to the front door, he was struck by the ever-present sounds of the rooks and jackdaws that habitually nested in the trees all about. They had provided the soundtrack to his youth, those crows. His mother had told him that corvids were highly intelligent birds, with developed social structures and complex behavioural patterns.

'They will always know you,' she told him. 'Rooks can live well into their fifties, and it is believed they can pass quite detailed information down to their progeny. You will be remembered by the colony that lives here – *they* will always welcome you home.'

With the sounds of the rookery ringing in his ears, Dunnigan lifted the old brass knocker, and rapped smartly, three times, then once more – his old signature knock.

His father's 1955 Jaguar was parked out front, as was his mother's battered old MG. He knew they were at home. From his knock, they would now know he was, too.

Eventually footsteps could be heard approaching, and the door swung open. Crystal Dunnigan, his mother, stood before him for the first time since Beth had been lost to them – and they to him.

'Hello, Mother,' he said.

'Davey,' she said. 'Why in all creation are you here?'

They sat in the old kitchen, where she had watched him bake and where the family had always eaten their meals.

'Stuart is out walking the land,' she said, the term they always used when Dunnigan's father went out to tend the trees.

'How has he been?'

'I have no idea,' she said, pouring herself a glass of wine from a dusty bottle. 'He doesn't speak much any more. He sits in his study – I hear the sounds of those awful bloody films you and he have always loved. Sometimes I hear music, Bach usually. I bring him food, he goes for his walks. But we don't talk, and we don't spend time together. To be honest, we don't have what could be called a marriage now.'

'But you and Dad – you were always so close.'

'And then you lost our granddaughter and destroyed your career. Your father had such high hopes for you. I think he grieves the loss of that almost as much as he does Beth.'

Dunnigan felt something in him give. He had long ago learned not to expect much from his parents, but this still hurt, almost more than he could bear. 'I see.'

'Have you progressed one level since starting at the university or the police?'

'No.'

'I see. Aren't you ashamed of that?'

'I hadn't really thought about it very much.'

'Clearly.' She sipped her wine, her eyes never leaving him. 'Your father doesn't know how to deal with what happened. You were always so like him – to you the world was black and white, great goods and terrible evils, and you fought the good fight against all that was wrong, and you made the world a better place. He did it through his practice, fixing those who had been wounded by the bad things in the world, and you did it by hunting down criminals and putting bad people in prison. But when a true evil was visited upon our family, neither of you knew how to cope. You ran away and so did he, in his way – he disappeared into his own world, and he hasn't come out.'

'I'm sorry, Mum.'

'So am I. I have lost a grandchild, I have lost a son, and I have lost a husband. I don't think I have very much left.'

'You haven't lost me. I'm here. I've come home.'

'What do you want me to say?'

'I don't know.'

'Did you think I'd be happy to see you? That I don't blame you for the pain we've been through, each and every person in this family? The pain, and the disappointment. I mean, I can say that, and perhaps, on an intellectual level, I even believe it, but the truth is I *do* blame you. I'm not angry with you any more, Davey. That burned out years ago. All that is left, really, is a sense of loss and a feeling of emptiness. I'm not sure if they'll ever leave me.'

'Mum – don't, please.'

'You should not have come here, Davey. It was a mistake.'

He stood up. 'I'm going to talk to Dad before I go.'

'As you wish.' His mother stood, brushed down her skirt

and, wine glass in hand, walked past him into the hallway. 'Davey?'

'Yes?'

'It might be better if you don't come here for a while. A *long* while.'

'I won't. Goodbye, Mother.'

She did not respond, just disappeared into the shadows of the house.

He found his father sitting on a stump of a tree almost in the centre of their demesne. He was smoking a clay pipe, as he sometimes did, dressed in a greatcoat, jeans and scuffed workboots. His grey hair was thinning on top, and his usually neatly trimmed beard had grown out since Dunnigan had seen him last.

The old man watched his son approach through half-closed eyes.

Dunnigan stopped ten yards away, raising a hand in salutation.

His father watched him for a few moments longer, then, standing, turned his back on his elder child and walked away from him into the trees, the cries of the birds echoing all about.

Dunnigan watched until he had disappeared from view.

Ernest Frobisher

The Yellow Man came to him one evening, just before sleep claimed him.

'There is someone asking questions.'

'About what?'

'The After Dark Campaign.'

Frobisher would have raised an eyebrow if he had one. 'Who?'

'A criminologist. He works for the Sex Crimes Unit of the gardaí.'

'How close is he to finding us?'

'I don't know. He had dealings with us in the past without ever knowing. It is not him I fear. There is the priest.'

'He is in this too?'

'I think he suspects something.'

Frobisher closed his eyes, but he was not asleep. He lay like that, silent, for a long time. The Yellow Man just waited.

'Do you think we should act?' Frobisher asked finally.

'I think we should watch them closely. If we need to move, we can do so, but I would prefer to act cautiously. We do not want to draw unnecessary attention to ourselves. So far, everything is going exactly to plan. It would be easy to ruin it.'

'Very well. But don't be over-cautious. If they get too close, end it. Hard and fast.'

The Yellow Man bowed, and was gone in the shadows.

It took Frobisher another hour to drift into a fitful doze. He felt as if something were hanging just at the edge of his consciousness.

It made him nervous.

PART SIX

In the Warrens

1

HE FOUND HE WAS THINKING ABOUT DIANE A LOT. It was interfering with his work, with his films, with everything. He dreamed about her too, and that made him very uncomfortable because some of the dreams made him feel hot and sweaty and agitated. When that happened he had to get up and go for a walk or do some push-ups to burn off the feeling of being out of control.

He didn't know what it was about her that disturbed him so much. He had never been drawn to physical beauty – he believed himself to be a man completely driven by intellectualism – but he had to admit he found her very beautiful, and he liked to look at her. He liked how she moved, he liked how she smelled and he liked the fact that, except for the other night, she did not plaster herself with makeup.

She did have a tattoo – he had seen it when she had worn the small dress: it was a drawing of a bird, some kind of wader, and it was done in a tribal, ethnic style, in black and red ink. It was just below the shoulder on her left arm and he found himself thinking about it particularly. In some of his dreams, she was lying with her arms above her head, and he was touching the tattoo, tracing its shape with his fingers.

That dream really upset him, much more than the others.

He went online, and discovered that the bird was a heron, a tall, wading species very common in Ireland. 'Does Diane like wildlife?' he asked Father Bill.

'Yes, I believe she does,' the priest said. 'She and her husband used to go on birdwatching holidays – they'd go down to Wexford to look at puffins and the like.'

'Does she have a favourite bird, do you know?'

'Now, you'd have to ask her that,' Father Bill said.

No, Dunnigan thought. I won't have to ask her at all.

'Is this some kind of code I don't know anything about?' Miley said, looking perplexed.

'No. Would you just ask her for me, please?'

'You want me to ask Diane what her favourite bird is?'

'Yes. Or animal, or whatever. Her favourite wild thing, for want of a better term.'

Miley ate a chip. They were having a late lunch in Eddie Rocket's City Diner, in Donnybrook – the Palace Theatre in Ballsbridge was now showing *To the Devil … a Daughter*, an old Hammer classic with Christopher Lee and Richard Widmark. This time Dunnigan had asked Miley to join him, and his request had been met with delight. They had caught the matinee, and Miley suggested lunch afterwards.

'And you can't ask her?'

'I want to take your advice, and make my best play. So far in our relationship, I have focused on doing things I like, and that doesn't seem to be working very well. I think I might encounter more success if I do something she likes. It's a theory I'm working on, anyway.'

'And you don't want her to know about this theory?'

'I'm hoping to utilise the element of surprise.'

Miley took a bite of his hot dog. Dunnigan had a Caesar salad, no dressing, in front of him, but he had barely touched it.

'I can ask her,' Miley said. 'D'you mind telling me what you're going to do with this information once you have it?'

'That bit still needs a little work,' Dunnigan admitted.

'Fair enough. How are things going in the search for Harry's family?'

'Slowly.'

'Want some help with that too?'

'Yes, please. I'm going to head out again this evening.'

'I'll tag along, then.'

They ate in silence for a while.

'How's the apartment?' Dunnigan asked, out of the blue. 'It's been a couple of months, now.'

'Oh – good, really good!' Miley said, nervously smiling.

'I'm glad to hear it,' Dunnigan said, although the criminal interviewer in him noted his friend had answered a little too quickly.

2

THE EVENING YIELDED NO MORE INFORMATION. The duo spent three hours visiting all the main gathering spots in the Warrens, but no one seemed to want to talk to them. They made their way back to the Project feeling dejected. To add to all this, as they arrived at Widow's Quay, Father Bill was ejecting a very irate man, who was not taking 'no' for an answer.

'You're drunk and you're wound up, Philly,' Father Bill said, shoving the man back as he tried to force his way in again. 'You know my rules, and they haven't changed. You don't get to sleep here when you're in that state, and you surely don't get to stop everyone else from taking their rest in a peaceful, safe place.'

'You can't leave me out here, Father! It's not safe, and you know it!'

'Go on over to Alan Connor's refuge in Smithfield. He might have some beds.'

'You know damn well he won't at this hour! You have to let me stay! I was here early!'

'And I didn't know you had a bottle of paint thinner in your bag – I thought we knew one another well enough at this stage that I could trust you. Now go somewhere and sleep it off and come and see me tomorrow.'

'I'm going back in there and you're not gonna stop me!'

Father Bill sighed and drew himself up to his full height. 'We both know I can and I will,' he said sadly. 'But I don't want to. We've managed to do this so far without my having to hurt you. Don't make it any worse than it has to be, Phil.'

The man's face crumpled and, sobbing, he turned tail and ran up the quays.

'Damn it all, it's a part of what we do here, but it's the part I wish to God I didn't have to do,' Father Bill said, and went back inside.

Half an hour later Dunnigan and Miley went into the office, where Diane was writing up a report on the incident with Philly.

'Can I get you some coffee?' Dunnigan asked her.

'What? Oh, no. I want to get this finished and then go home. It's been a bugger of a day.'

'*Ask her now!*' Dunnigan mouthed at Miley, none too subtly, but luckily Diane was too busy to notice.

Miley wandered over to a shelf of books and pretended to look at them, while Dunnigan withdrew.

It seemed an age before Miley emerged, giving Dunnigan the thumbs-up.

'So?'

'Her favourite bird is a Purple Heron,' Miley said. 'They're very rare in Ireland, so she's only ever seen one once. But her favourite wild animal is a hare.'

'A hare? Like a rabbit?'

'Hares are much bigger.'

'Yes. I suppose so.'

'She says she loves their grace and their … what did she say again? … their beauty and their wildness. Something like that.'

'Thank you, Miley. I appreciate your help.'

'Are you going to buy her a hare as a present?'

'No.'

'So what's your plan, then?'

'I'll tell you when I have one.'

'That does not fill me with confidence, Davey.'

'Me either.'

Dunnigan was locking up when he noticed someone standing in the shadows across the street by the railing on the waterside. He thought nothing of it initially, figuring it to be someone having a cigarette or stopping to make a phone call. Half an hour later, though, he happened to look out of one of the windows as he pulled down a blind, and saw the figure was still there.

He peered through the glass, and saw it was a tall, slim man, dressed in what seemed to be a beige trench coat, the collar pulled up to his ears. He was gazing unflinchingly at the Project. There was something familiar about the figure, but he couldn't place what it was.

Shuddering, Dunnigan went back to completing the evening chores. The man was nowhere to be seen when he was going home.

3

BERNARD, THE OLD HOMELESS MAN, ARRIVED AT Widow's Quay with Philly the next day.

'Father Bill isn't here,' Diane told them. 'There's been a bereavement and he's gone to spend time with the family.'

'I wanted to come over and apologise,' Philly said. 'Bernie knows Father Bill real well, and he said he'd come and speak up on me behalf, like,'

Bernard, for his part, was muttering ominously, his eyes darting here and there as if trying to follow the flight path of an insect.

'Hello, Bernie,' Diane said. 'How are you today?'

'I'm well. In good form today,' the old man said, suddenly laughing and doing a little jump. 'You let Philip here back in. He's proper sorry for bein' mean and grumpy.'

'He was mean and grumpy and off his head on paint thinner,' Diane said ruefully, but she stepped aside. 'Why don't you come on in and have some lunch? I don't suppose we're going to bar you over one little upset.'

Dunnigan had been listening to all of this from the hallway, and grabbed Diane as she went past. 'I thought Bernard Roche had Alzheimer's disease!'

'He does. He's still in the early stages, though, so he has days when he's quite lucid, and others when he doesn't know who he is or which end is up. It looks like he's with us today. He might not be by teatime, so let's try and make him comfortable while we can.'

'Yes. Of course.'

'I have a client at three. Will you get the two lads some lunch and sit with them for a bit?'

'I'd be happy to.'

She smiled, and her face softened. 'There's the Davey I like so much. Why can't he be around a bit more?'

'I … I'm sorry, Diane.'

'Sssh. Go and have lunch with our guests. I'm going to spread some mental well-being. I'll catch you later.'

The two men were sitting in the TV room when Dunnigan found them, watching an episode of *Homes Under the Hammer*, a show where two grinning, perma-tanned presenters went to auctions all over the UK and followed the purchasers of various properties as they either renovated their new buys or left them to rot.

'Now I'd say you'd rent that one for seven hundred pounds a calendar month,' Philly was saying to Bernard.

'Only if you fix that bathroom. It's terrible old-fashioned,' Bernard said, although he seemed not to be watching the show at all.

'The ladies in the kitchen tell me they have a pot of stew almost ready,' Dunnigan said.

'Lovely,' Philly said, his eyes still glued to the television.

'It's good to see you again, Bernard.' Dunnigan sat down next to the older man.

'Yes. It's nice to see you again, too.'

'Have you thought any more about those dark people you told me about?'

'No. I don't know about that,' Bernard said, his hands starting to flutter in front of him nervously.

'I just want to help the Grants – you remember them, don't you?'

'*Leave him alone!*' Philly stood up so quickly, he knocked his chair over. Before Dunnigan could move, he was nose to nose with him. '*He told you he doesn't know about it, so you just back off, okay?*'

'I was only asking him a question!'

'You don't know what you're doin', so you don't! Come on, Bernie. We were wrong to come here today.'

The old man took Philly's hand, and allowed himself to be led out of the door. Dunnigan sat where he was, deeply confused.

Which was a feeling he was starting to get used to.

4

LATER THAT EVENING DUNNIGAN AND MILEY found Philly. He was sitting on the pavement outside the Pro-Cathedral, a flagon of cider half drunk beside him.

'Can I please speak to you for a moment?' Dunnigan asked.

'No. Leave me the fuck alone, will you?'

'He just wants a quick word,' Miley piped up.

Philly squinted down at him, and seemed to soften. 'Hey, fella,' he said, his whole demeanour changing.

'Hey,' Miley said, casting a glance at Dunnigan, and deciding to play along if it helped.

'He your brother or somethin'?' Philly shot at Dunnigan.

'Something. He's my friend.'

The homeless man unscrewed the lid of his bottle, and took several deep gulps. 'My brother, Dominic, he was like that, y'know?'

'Where is he?' Miley asked.

'I don't know. Haven't seen him in five years. He was a good lad, though. We always had laugh, him 'n' me.'

Dunnigan motioned with his head, and he and Miley sat, one on either side of Philly. 'I didn't mean to upset you or Bernard today,' Dunnigan said. 'I've got some of that stew in a Thermos here, if you'd like some.'

'Thanks – me stomach prob'ly wouldn' be up to it. I've had a lot to drink, and I reckon I'd just throw it all up, if you know what I mean.'

'I don't see how you could mean more than one thing,' Dunnigan said, puzzled.

'I can put it in a container for you, and you can have it later,' Miley said, cutting across his friend. 'I'm sure it'll keep. The containers are tin foil, so they can be heated on a fire or whatever.'

'Thanks, lad,' Philly said, patting Miley on the shoulder. 'I knew you were a good 'un. I could tell.'

'Do you mind my asking you why you got so angry earlier?' Dunnigan said. 'I don't want to get you worked up again, but Miley and I are trying to find the parents of a young boy who have gone missing, and he is, as you can probably guess, very anxious to be reunited with them.'

'Oh, I'm sorry about how I was,' Philly said. 'I di'n't mean nothin' by it. It's jus', well, ol' Bernie has been good to me, over the years, and he's none too chipper now, and I gets vexed if I see people try'n'a take advantage of him. Sometimes he don' know what he's sayin'.'

'He told me about dark people. He said they take you to a house on the moon.'

Philly took another long drink and belched loudly. 'He said that, did he?'

'Yes, he did.'

'Poor ol' fucker. He gets confused an' muddled. He wouldna said that, if he was in his righ' mind.'

'What did he mean? Can you tell me?'

Philly looked at Miley. 'What are you doin' here, fella?' he asked him. 'Why aren't you safe at home, watchin' the telly?'

'I wanted to come out and see you,' Miley said. 'From what Davey said, I thought maybe you needed a friend.'

Philly's face creased up and tears ran down his cheeks. 'That's right good of you, fella. I don' d'serve that sort o' kindness.'

'The dark people?' Dunnigan pushed.

'I don' know 'bout no house on th' moon,' Philly said. 'But I reckon the dark ones he's talkin' 'bout are these fellas from a group called Dorcha. They been around the city for this past year, and people don' like 'em none.'

'Why not?'

'They come across as bein' sorta like you and your friend here and Father Bill – they say they wants to help. And they say they got more than just some soup or blankets – they talks about jobs and houses and a new life.'

'They're offering some kind of supported accommodation?' Dunnigan asked. 'How come I've never heard of this group before? Do you know them, Miley?'

Miley shook his head.

'I don' think they're legit,' Philly said. 'No one does. We're all afraid of 'em.'

'Why?'

''Cause no one who goes with them ever comes back.'

'But isn't that a good thing? It means their process is working – people are staying off the streets. That's the real test of an initiative like that.'

'No – you don't get me. My buddy, Simon. He went with them six months ago. Him 'n' me, we been roughin' it together for a long time. We were …'

Philly paused, and Miley (although possibly not Dunnigan) knew the nature of the bond Philly and Simon had enjoyed. Miley saw the loss in the man's eyes, and his heart went out to him.

'… we were real close, like. He went with them, and he said he'd get himself on his feet, see if the job was all they said it was gonna be, and then he'd come 'n' get me.'

'What kind of work were they offering?' Dunnigan asked him.

'All kinds. They talked about jobs in hospital'ty, in the trades – sparky and chippy and blocks, the whole lot. They said there'd be work on the boats, too.'

'What did Simon want to do?' Miley asked.

'He useta be a plasterer, in the old days, before he started on the smack. He was real good, too. He was gonna get back doin' that, and we was gonna get a place t'gedder.'

'So what happened?'

'He went with them one night last December, just 'fore Christmas. They met him at the squat we was in, near Ballymun. Two fellas, big lads in dark suits, an' a man in a long yella coat.'

'I beg your pardon?'

'There was three of 'em, two fellas in black and one in a yella coat – one o' them ones you tie in the middle with a belt, like they useta wear in th' ol' films.'

Dunnigan nodded. 'And?'

'And I never seen him again. We was to meet three weeks after that, at the top of Parnell Street, near the Luas stop. I waited, but he di'n't come. I waited the next night and the next.'

'Maybe he ... maybe he revaluated your friendship,' Dunnigan said. 'He could have met someone else.'

'I'm sure he didn't, though,' Miley said, glaring at his friend.

'It happens,' Dunnigan persisted.

'I thought of that,' Philly said, opening his bottle again. 'Even if he did, he wouldn't've jus' gone off. He'd've had the balls to come an' tell me. Anyways, he ain't the only one. I know four other people who went off with the Dorcha guys and ain't been heard of again. I don' know where they're goin' but it don' seem righ' t' me.'

Dunnigan pondered this information. It didn't seem right to him, either.

5

'WHAT DO YOU WANT, DAVEY? I'M ABOUT TO HEAD out.'

'It's called a mobile phone so you can carry it with you as you go about your business. The fact you're going out shouldn't preclude you from talking to me.'

'God, you are infuriating. Well? Talk then.'

'I'd like to take you out next Sunday afternoon.'

'Been there, done that, wore the dress and got no reaction or thanks for it. I think I'll pass, Davey.'

Pause.

'You're saying no?'

'I'm saying no. I really appreciate the fact that you're asking me, and I know how difficult it must be for you, but I'm not putting myself through it again. Thank you, but no.'

A longer pause.

'If you *had* said yes, I would have asked you to wear outdoor clothes, and walking boots, and to bring your binoculars.'

'You'd have asked me to do what?'

'Um … do you want me to repeat the entire last sentence?'

'No … What have you got planned, Davey?'

'I'd prefer to maintain a degree of secrecy.'

'Did my conversation with Miley last week have any part to play in this? I thought it was a bit random, but – well, you know Miley.'

'He may have been acting on my behalf, yes.'

'Davey, I am going to give you the benefit of the doubt this one last time. Okay, I accept your invitation.'

'I would like to pick you up. That's what people do on dates, isn't it?'

'Sometimes, yes.'

'I want to do things properly. You deserve that, Diane.'

'I'll text you my address.'

'Thank you.'

'I'll see you on Sunday, then.'

6

'FATHER BILL?'

'Yes, Davey?'

'He's out there again.'

The priest had just finished taking out the bins, and was washing his hands, singing 'Till the Morning Comes'.

'Who is?'

'I think it's the Yellow Man.'

Father Bill took a towel from the rack. 'What are you talking about, Davey?'

'Do you remember what Bernard said? To beware the Yellow Man?'

'I remember your telling me he said that.'

'A man in a cream trench coat has been outside by the river for the past two nights. He's there now.'

The priest folded the towel and put it back. 'Show me.'

They looked through the window at the dark waterfront. Sure enough, his hands in his pockets, standing mostly in shadow, there was a figure in a long coat.

'Do you know him?' Dunnigan asked.

'No.'

'What should we do?'

'I suppose I'd better introduce myself.'

'That's your plan?'

'I have always found the direct approach suits me best.'

Father Bill was pulling on his leather jacket, and already heading for the door.

'I'll keep watch,' Dunnigan said.

'Thanks.'

The stranger did not move as Father Bill opened the door and stepped out.

'Can I help you with something?' the priest asked, as he crossed the street.

Suddenly the shadowy figure turned and began to walk briskly away, in the direction of the 3Arena.

'Hey, hold on,' Father Bill called and, breaking into a run, caught up with the fleeing man and grasped his shoulder.

In a trice the man had dropped to the ground and, with a deft movement, knocked the legs from under the priest, sending him sprawling head over heels. By the time he was upright again, he was alone on the street.

'How'd the direct approach work this time, Father?' Dunnigan asked, as he came back in and locked the door.

'Not funny, Davey,' Father Bill said.

7

WEXFORD WILDFOWL RESERVE IS AN AREA OF SALT marsh and pasture reclaimed from the sea and then walled off from Wexford Harbour in the 1840s as a famine relief project. Dunnigan parked the BMW in a gateway about five hundred yards from the entrance to the reserve and took off his seatbelt.

'So this is the secret destination,' Diane said.

'Yes. I had initially planned on going to Bull Island, but on closer investigation, this seemed more appropriate.'

'Really?'

'Come on. We have an appointment to keep.'

'Curiouser and curiouser,' Diane said, and followed him.

They walked up the narrow tarmac road that led to the visitors' centre – it was a warm, early-summer day, swallows soaring above them like miniature jet planes. Trees rose on their left, behind which were the fields and salt-flats of the slobs. On their right was the sea wall, which the poor people of the area had constructed during the dark days of the Famine, working fourteen hours a day for a bowl of broth and a handful of barley.

'I think this is the place,' Dunnigan said, reaching a gate and holding it open.

'I don't think we're supposed to go in there,' Diane said. 'Most of this land isn't open to the public. There's a hide just a little further on – we can see the birds from there.'

'Please trust me,' Dunnigan said firmly. 'You won't be sorry.'

Diane decided to go along with whatever scheme he had concocted.

A passage had been worn through the scrub of the field they entered, and Dunnigan led the way along it for several hundred yards until they came to a broad, grassy area that stretched for several acres in all directions. 'There's our man,' he said, and Diane saw a tall, angular figure coming along the perimeter of the field towards them.

'Who's this?' she wanted to know.

'I'd like you to meet a colleague of mine from the university,' Dunnigan said, extending his hand to shake as the man reached them. 'Peter Byrne, from the biology department. Dr Byrne has been researching mountain hares on this reserve for the last five years. He'd like to show you something.'

'I'm very pleased to meet you, Ms Robinson,' Byrne said – he was about fifty, lean, with the rugged colouring of a man who spent most of his time outdoors. 'David tells me you're a big fan of our Irish hares.'

'Yes, I am,' Diane said, embarrassed.

'Well, so am I,' the biologist said confidentially. 'If you come this way, I'd like to introduce you to someone I think you'll like.'

He led them in a straight line across the field, chatting easily about the work he'd been doing with the animals there. 'Hares are nearing extinction in Ireland,' he said. 'It's mostly down to intrusion on their habitat, but the increase in the numbers of people keeping domestic dogs has had an impact too. We believe the disintegration of the population is almost totally down to greyhounds being allowed off their leash while being walked close to their habitats – we don't think it was organised coursing, just dog owners being thoughtless, and dogs doing what dogs do. Here, though, the hare is allowed to be.'

They reached a point where the grass was higher, and saw, almost immediately, ten very large hares dotted about the pasture

– all were russet-coloured, with very long ears, loping about or just sunbathing. Dunnigan realised that, while they bore a similarity to rabbits, they were quite different.

'Oh, my God, they're gorgeous,' Diane said, almost involuntarily.

'They are, aren't they?'

Byrne bent down, and plucked a blade of meadow grass, put it between his two thumbs, and blew, making a high-pitched whistling, keening sound. Dunnigan watched the animals all stand bolt upright. Most either took off across the meadow, helter-skelter. A couple dived for cover, disappearing into the undergrowth, but one ran at top speed towards them, coming to a juddering halt right in front of the biologist, who knelt down and held out his hand, in which he now had what looked to be salad leaves and some seeds. 'This is Jack,' he said. 'Jack and I are old, dear friends.'

Diane looked at Dunnigan, barely able to believe what she was seeing, then knelt down so she was at eye-level with the animal. 'How did you …' she began, and Byrne held up his hand.

'Keep your voice low – hares are very nervy creatures, prone to startling at the slightest sound.'

'I'm sorry.' Diane spoke now in a virtual whisper.

'I found him when he was a leveret, caught in a snare. I was sure he would die, as hares react very badly to severe shock – their heart rate increases to such a speed they simply keel over from cardiac arrest. I didn't think he'd make it, but I untangled him, bundled him up in a scarf and brought him home. I hand-fed him with milk and micro-herbs I blitzed up in a food processor, and after a few days, he was still alive. A week later he was starting to hop about my kitchen, and after a month he was rushing up and down the hallway. I waited until he was fully weaned, which was about three months, then let him go with the drove here.'

'And he still knows you?'

'He imprinted on me.'

The hare, which was about as big as a medium-sized dog, was sitting upright, occasionally leaning over and nuzzling Byrne's hand for more food.

'Can I touch him?' Diane asked.

'If you're very gentle,' Byrne said. 'Just move slowly. He's quite relaxed and he trusts me, so he will extend that to you too, since we're together.'

'Does he think you're his mother?' Dunnigan wanted to know.

'I don't believe so. Hares, especially males, don't stay with their family groups, so he wouldn't keep coming to me for that reason. He comes for the food, mostly.'

Diane was gently stroking the hare's long back. The animal was making occasional clicking noises, and she was suddenly struck by how alien it seemed. Yet a bond had developed between the man and the utterly wild thing.

'He obviously likes you,' Diane said.

'I don't know that he does,' Byrne said. 'We can't put human emotions on animals. I don't know that they like and love and hate and obsess the way we do. I think he feels safe with me and knows I will usually have some rocket and sunflower seeds for him, so he's happy to spend time with me, and allow me to be around him. With hares, that's as good as it gets, and I'm okay with it.'

Diane continued to run her hands over Jack's fur. She looked at Dunnigan who was standing a little apart from them. 'Thank you, Davey,' she said. 'Thank you for this.'

He nodded and smiled – a real smile that went right to his eyes.

8

LATER DIANE AND DUNNIGAN SAT SIDE BY SIDE IN a hide overlooking the ocean.

'That was, maybe, one of the nicest things anyone has ever done for me,' she said, her chin resting on her hands, gazing out at the heaving blue-grey waves.

'I'm pleased,' Dunnigan said.

'How the hell did you arrange all that? I mean, if you'd asked me what I'd love to do, like one of my top five bucket-list things, that would have been one of them – probably top three. Like … how?'

'Your tattoo.'

'My what?'

'You have a tattoo of a heron on your arm. I saw it when we went to see *The Bride of Frankenstein*.'

'And, by a process of deductive reasoning, you came to hares?'

'That, and getting Miley to quiz you in his discreet manner about what animals and birds you like best.'

'You haven't had a Purple Heron flown in too, have you? Managed to train it to do the dance from 'Thriller'?'

'No. I did some research and found that the leading authority on hares worked out of Maynooth. I emailed him and asked for his advice, and he told me about Jack, and that was it, really.'

'Well, it was quite the date. You've more than made up for

disastrous outing number two, and almost-disastrous outing number one.'

'I appreciate the positive feedback.'

'D'you see those birds out there?'

'The crows?'

'Yeah. Those are ravens.'

'Oh.'

'Do you see how those two are wheeling and diving and shooting back up into the air?'

Dunnigan watched the birds – huge, muscular and black, they rode the thermals on broad wings, engaged in frantic aerial acrobatics. 'Are they fighting?'

'No. That's their courtship ritual. Ravens mate for life, but their engagement can go on for two or even three years. During that period they can split up and spend time apart – it's almost as if they need to feel their way, get to know one another before they're convinced they're a good match and commit. They have to make mistakes and iron out the kinks.'

'I see.'

She sat up and gazed at him. 'I was about ready to give up on you.'

'I know.'

'But you weren't ready to give up on me.'

'I really like you, Diane. I know I'm difficult and not the same as other people. But I like you.'

'I like you too, Davey. Would I have let you drive me to Wexford without any real explanation if I didn't?'

'I'm trying really hard not to say anything wrong,' Dunnigan said, and she saw that he was rigid with tension. 'I don't want to mess today up, and there are so many things I want to say to you, but I'm frightened that any one of them might make you annoyed, and I so want this afternoon to keep going well.'

'Oh, you poor thing,' she said, and threw her arms around him.

At first, it was like hugging a board but, gradually, she felt him begin to let go, and then to relax, and then he was holding her, too, and to her surprise, she realised he was crying.

And she held him close, and they stayed like that for a long time.

9

THEY LAY ON THE SAND STARING UP AT THE STARS, the sound of the sea punctuating the silence. Diane was holding his hand, and he couldn't remember when he had last felt so content, so grounded.

Above them the universe wheeled, below them the earth turned, but for David Dunnigan all that mattered was this point in time, this moment, which was perfect and unique and had come upon him unbidden.

Somewhere in the darkness a fox barked.

'So what does this mean for us?' Diane asked him.

'I don't know,' Dunnigan said. 'I would like to try to be … with you.'

'And what is your definition of *with*?'

'I don't have the appropriate language,' Dunnigan said. 'I mean, I'm forty-one, you're … What age are you?'

'I'm thirty-seven.'

'So we're not going to be girlfriend and boyfriend, are we?'

'No. I think we're a little past that.'

'And *partners* sounds very officious and legal.'

'It does.'

'Lovers has a lascivious ring to it.'

'Lasciviousness has its place.'

He swallowed. 'Does it?'

'It does. Haven't you ever thought about being lascivious with me?'

'I ... um ... I ... ah ... I probably have wondered how something like that might proceed ...'

'That is a good question. I imagine you'd have to kiss me, to begin with.'

'Is that the proper first step?'

'I don't think there is an agreed series of steps, Davey, but it would be the accepted norm.'

'I see.'

'So, are you going to kiss me, David Dunnigan?'

'If you want me to.'

'I'm just short of getting a small aircraft to write the words "KISS ME NOW" in fluorescent letters in the sky.'

'Is that a yes?'

'It is.'

And then she leaned down and kissed him.

It was not his first kiss – Dunnigan had been with girls in college – but it was the first kiss that meant anything, and it had been more than two decades since he had last felt another's lips on his own.

When he replayed the experience (which he did often during the days that followed) he felt he had done quite well.

Afterwards, as they held one another on that night-time beach, he realised he was happy. It was a strange and joyful feeling.

10

'HAPPY BIRTHDAY.'

Gina and Dunnigan sat opposite one another in Musashi Noodles, a Japanese restaurant situated across the road from the Beacon Hospital, in Sandyford, above a Subway shop. Dunnigan had been interviewing a nurse who had been attacked by a serial mugger he believed might also be involved in a paedophile ring the Sex Crimes Unit were closing in on, so he'd asked Gina to come out and meet him. They had taken a table by the window, which had a panoramic view of the street outside and the hospital frontage.

An untidily wrapped parcel sat on the table between them.

'What's this?' Gina asked.

'It's your birthday present.'

'You haven't bought me a present in nineteen years. And it's your birthday too – I haven't got you anything.'

'I know. I wanted to buy you one this year.'

'Why?'

'I thought you'd be pleased. Was it wrong of me to do this?'

Gina ran her hands through her short hair. 'No – I mean, I'm pleased, Davey, really pleased! It's just so *unexpected*.'

'Aren't you going to open it?'

Dunnigan had always made a fuss of the special events that punctuated their childhoods – Christmas, Easter, the first day of the summer holidays – but he had made a special effort with their birthday.

They both received a small allowance from their father, who enjoyed expensive antique books and vintage British cars, but was frugal in most other ways. Rather than spend his pocket money on comics or sweets or *Star Wars* action figures, her brother saved it, and when the anniversary of their birth rolled around in July, he would always buy her something special.

From their mother the children would get a voucher for some clothes shop or other, whichever was considered the most fashionable at the time, and their father would present them with a first-edition copy of a children's classic, which had to be put on the correct shelf in the library with all the others as soon as it was unwrapped. Her brother, though, had paid attention to her reactions to advertisements for toys on TV, or had noted conversations they'd had about games she might like to own, and it was his gift she always looked forward to the most – Dunnigan always pretended the present was for them both, but it wasn't: it was his gift to her.

He was terrible at wrapping presents – the package always looked as if the paper had been thrown at it and half a roll of Sellotape used to hold it all together, but the clumsy attempt to make it look nice was all part of the experience. She would rip open the present, and there would be whatever she had wanted most. Her amazing brother would have found a way to get it for her.

Her mother always disapproved greatly. Dolls were sexist, she informed her children. They reinforced inappropriate gender stereotypes. My Little Pony was an anthropomorphic representation of a horse and therefore unrealistic. Gina and Davey didn't care. They would listen and nod and smile, and giggle about it afterwards. Most birthdays involved a diatribe from Mother about how Maria Montessori had demonstrated that fairy tales and imaginative play caused children of Gina's age to adopt unhealthy intellectual habits and unattainable expectations of the world. Dunnigan would always politely ask her questions about this or that aspect of the lecture, to make it look as if he was interested, and that generally appeased her – she was often more than a little drunk at that stage of the afternoon.

Then it was off to the kitchen, where Dunnigan would have a chocolate cake waiting, which he had baked and decorated for her, all bedecked with candles. When he was ten, her brother had carved figures of the whole family, using wood he found in the forest at the back of their house. These would be on the cake too, with Gina front and centre.

The twins would sing 'Happy Birthday' (their mother and father stood, tight-lipped, watching it all), then Gina would cut slices for everyone. Mum and Dad would hurriedly consume theirs, then disappear to their respective office and study, and she and her brother would spend the rest of the afternoon playing together.

She loved those birthdays. When he left to go to college, one of her few comforts was that the anniversary of their birth was in the summer holidays.

When it came round after Beth had vanished, and Dunnigan had disappeared into himself, she had stayed in bed.

And now this.

The package was about six inches across and five tall. Gina tore the paper away, to reveal something enclosed in a couple of layers of bubble wrap. She gently removed it, revealing a framed photograph. She remembered the day it had been taken – their father had just bought an ancient Box Brownie camera and wanted to play with his new toy. His two children were recruited to sit on the couch in the family's rarely used living room, and he took a few shots of them before he got bored with his subjects and went out to immortalise his beloved trees on celluloid.

The photo Dunnigan had had reprinted and framed was of Gina and him, aged eleven. He had his arm around her shoulders, an awkward smile on his adolescent face. She was grinning, delighted with this unusual attention from their father. Both children were dressed in their respective school uniforms.

'Where did you get this?' Gina asked, her voice catching, tears springing to her eyes.

'The summer before I started teaching at Maynooth I went up into the loft and found a box of old photos going right back to when we were babies – there were even some of Mum and Dad when they were young, before we were born. I took them and had them scanned, brought them back before either of them noticed they were gone.'

'They probably never would have,' Gina said, sniffing and wiping her eyes.

'No. Possibly not.'

'She called me the other day, you know. Mother.'

'Did she?'

'I tried to talk to her about you. She didn't want to know.'

'Really?'

'She's hurt. You should go and see her and Dad. I mean, you and he were close … sort of. As close as he ever got to anyone. I bet he'd really love to see you. He's just too much of an arsehole to admit it.'

Dunnigan sighed and sipped some water. 'I visted them. Shortly after I ran into Clive. It was a mistake.'

'Oh. I didn't know that.' Gina seemed bereft for a moment, then a smile brightened her face. 'Well, who cares about them? It's our birthday, and all we've ever needed on our birthday is one another. As usual, you've given me what I want most. Thank you.'

'You're welcome.'

The waiter, looking a bit apologetic, brought their food.

'I have something I want to tell you,' Dunnigan said, as Gina tucked into her ramen and he picked at a bento box.

'I'm all ears.'

'I've met someone.'

She paused, chopsticks halfway to her mouth. 'What do you mean you've met someone?'

'Is that the incorrect terminology? I'm really struggling with the language.'

'Are you telling me you have a girlfriend?'

'Well, I don't like that label but, inherently, yes.'

Gina opened her mouth, then closed it again. 'Who? Where? When?'

'In the order you asked: her name is Diane; we met at the Homeless Project; and we formalised our relationship status last weekend – we'd been out a couple of times with very mixed results before that.'

'I thought you were joking when you said you were volunteering at a shelter.'

'I don't usually tell jokes, Gina.'

'Not any more, no.'

'Well, I am and that is where I met Diane, and she asked me to go out with her, and now we're together.'

Gina narrowed her eyes. '*She* asked *you* out?'

'Yes.'

'Is she one of the homeless people?'

'She's a therapist and she works and volunteers also.'

'She's a goddam shrink? Like Dad and Mum?'

'Dad is a Freudian psychoanalyst and Mum is a sociocognitive educational psychologist. Diane is trained in the Rogerian method, which makes her a humanist, as I understand it.'

'But she's a shrink.'

'Again, I don't really like the word but, yes, I suppose she is.'

Gina snorted and sat back. 'Why did she ask you to go out with her?'

'I wondered the same thing. It seems she likes me.'

'Davey, you know I love you, and I'd do anything for you, but let's face it, you don't really come across as a great catch.'

'She likes me. What can I say?'

'I'm just a little puzzled, that's all. I mean, tell me a bit about her.'

'She's … well, she interested in wildlife. And she enjoys working at the shelter. She lives in Wicklow, and Miley is very fond of her.'

'How does Miley know her?'

'He comes to the Project too.'

'I just don't want you getting taken advantage of. You've had a very tough time these past years. You haven't been well.'

'I've not been sick.'

'No one could say you were in the fullness of your health, either. I think maybe I should meet this Diane.'

'I'm sure we could arrange that.'

Dunnigan had a piece of sushi, and happened to glance out of the window. There, across the street by the door to the Beacon, was a trenchcoat-draped figure. By the time the criminologist got down to street level, he was gone.

11

FATHER BILL SAID MASS EVERY SUNDAY MORNING in St Jude's, a small Georgian church near the Four Courts. Dunnigan found him there that evening, sitting in the front pew, his head bowed in prayer. The church was simply decorated inside – an unadorned crucifix hung above the altar, and the stations of the cross were represented in line drawings carved then stained on pieces of lacquered wood. The smell of incense and candle-wax hung in the air, and Dunnigan realised he could not recall when he had last been in a church.

The priest looked up slowly at the sound of his footsteps.

'Hello, Davey,' he said, smiling in a tired sort of way.

'Am I disturbing your prayers?' Dunnigan asked.

'No. Please, sit down.'

He did.

'This is nice,' Dunnigan said.

'I like it. I've tended four different churches since I was ordained. The biggest and grandest was over in Dolphin's Barn, could hold a thousand of the faithful, and we could probably squeeze in two hundred more if we ignored the fire regulations. The smallest was a wee hut in a village in the desert in Nicaragua, and that one could only hold ten people in comfort, so we usually went outside. But you know, Davey, it was no better and no worse than any of the others – a church is always special, in its own way.'

'It must be good to have your own place,' Dunnigan observed.

'This isn't mine. My ministry is with the homeless now. I'm considered too troublesome to have my own parish. I help out here, and I say mass once on a Sunday because the canonic rules say I must. But, yes, I'm happy to do so and to be attached to this house of God.'

'I don't think I believe in God, Father.'

'Oh, most people either don't or are very undecided about Him, these days, Davey. I don't think it matters much. God believes in you.'

'He hasn't been very nice to me, then.'

'I didn't say He had. The Lord can be a very tough friend to have, at times.'

Dunnigan said nothing for a bit, and the two men sat in the quiet.

'Who or what is Dorcha?' Dunnigan said, after a time. 'And who is the Yellow Man?'

'I wondered when you would come to me with those questions,' Father Bill said.

'That would be now.'

'I wish you hadn't.'

'Please answer. I think I've started something, and I'd like to know what it is.'

Father Bill took out his box of cigarettes and, standing up, lit one from one of the candles burning by the altar. 'There are those who will tell you Dorcha is just an old story, a legend made up to frighten children.'

'Is it?'

'Maybe it was, once. But I don't believe it is any more.'

'Tell me.'

'It's an old, old tale, Davey. Dublin in the eighteenth century was a city drowning beneath the weight of the urban poor.

Families were starving in the streets, bodies were stacking up, and typhoid, cholera and other diseases were rampant – there was talk of another plague if something wasn't done.'

'Something was done,' Dunnigan put in. 'The city's Board of Guardians established the Foundling Hospital and the workhouses, didn't they?'

'That they did,' Father Bill agreed. 'But you have to remember, politics wasn't that much different then than it is now. You had your left-leaning liberally minded, who wanted to support the poor and alleviate their suffering, but you also had the more conservative voice, those who saw the lumpen, uneducated, diseased masses as a problem that needed wiping out.'

'Wiping out?'

'Oh, yes. You're an academic – next time you're in the National Library look at the newspapers of the day. When Jonathan Swift published *A Modest Proposal*, his satirical pamphlet, where he suggested as a dark joke that the children of the poor could be eaten by the rich as a way of "giving something back", he was initially taken quite seriously. People wanted them eradicated. And that was how the After Dark Society came about.'

'The After Dark Society?'

'The American South had its Ku Klux Klan, Russia had its pogroms, Germany had the Nazis. We had the After Darkers.'

'Why haven't I heard of them before?'

'You've lived in Ireland all your life, Davey – you must know how good we are at brushing uncomfortable truths under the carpet.'

'Go on.'

'Their mission was to get rid of the destitute poor – those who were cluttering up the streets. And their methods were straightforward. They dressed in black, with handkerchiefs tied about their faces, like highwaymen. They armed themselves with swords and cudgels and clubs and pistols, and they went out into the streets at night. I've heard you using that old term, the Warrens, well, they had Warrens in the seventeen hundreds, too. They went to where homeless families congregated and they butchered the people who lived there.'

'They didn't think they could kill every homeless person,' Dunnigan said.

'No. But they did think that, once the word spread, those left alive would flee the city. And it worked, many did, and the establishment of the Foundling Hospital, the workhouses and county homes took up the slack. The problem was never wiped out, but it was surely lessened. And one hundred years later, the Famine got rid of most of what was left.'

'So you think Dorcha is the modern equivalent of this group?'

'They resurfaced in the mid-eighteen hundreds, in Limerick. The city was a mess: prostitution, begging, hundreds of people sleeping rough. There are reports of the After Darkers taking street walkers – there was a syphilis epidemic, and they were seen as the root cause of it. The rural people, who were flooding into the city as the industrial revolution and Poor Laws took their land, still spoke a lot of Irish, and they began calling them Dorcha, after the Irish word for "dark". The name stuck.'

'That still leaves us with a gap of more than a hundred years.'

'I have heard they were active here in the nineteen thirties also, and again in the fifties.'

'There are no bodies, Father. If they were killing people, there would be corpses.'

'They may be burying them somewhere. Incinerating them. I don't have the answers for you, Davey. You asked me about Dorcha. This is what I know. And it frightens the bejesus out of me that they have resurfaced.'

'And this Yellow Man?'

'He's new – but my guess would be he's a message from them. You've started asking questions, you're looking for them. He's found you, and he can get to you if he wants to.'

'I'm going to hand this to my bosses in the Unit,' Dunnigan said.

'This has nothing to do with child abductions or paedophile rings, Davey. And all you have is the word of a heroin addict and an old man with Alzheimer's – the Yellow Man hasn't done anything. What are the police going to do with it?'

'I don't know. But they need to do something.'

'I believe we've reached a point where *we* need to do something.'

12

DUNNIGAN DID WHAT FATHER BILL HAD suggested, and the following day he was in the National Library, poring over ancient newspapers. They told him nothing the priest had not already: in the eighteenth century the educated ruling classes harboured a lot of anger towards the vast and rising numbers of destitute poor in Dublin, and the poverty-stricken masses were no less angry at their circumstances. The pages he examined were full of stories of violent clashes and riots, but there were no reports of murders he could attribute to the After Dark Society – so many people were dying of cold, disease and starvation, he supposed that such deaths were hardly going to warrant many inches of newsprint.

After two hours, in which he wrote only three lines of notes on the neatly folded sheet of paper he had brought for the purpose, he gave up and looked through the library's digital index for books of social commentary about the time. After much searching he came across a tome by James Kelly and Martyn J. Powell, entitled *Clubs and Societies in Eighteenth-Century Ireland*. And he found his first mention of the After Darkers.

They were listed under a section that dealt with political groups, and the few paragraphs dedicated to them described them as 'an organisation of various business owners and citizens of Dublin who wished to address the problem of destitution, criminality and overcrowding, through force if called upon to do so'. The society met, according to the book, in the offices of a lawyer, Walter Frobisher, Esq., who kept premises at Eden Quay.

Further searching brought up numerous mentions of Frobishers, the most recent being Ernest, who was listed as a board member of Merchant Banking, an American-owned company with offices in the city, but he could find no other reference to him in the register of businesses.

He went back to Garda HQ, and fired up his computer. There were three businesses registered under the name Dorcha – one was a security firm that specialised in burglar alarms, and misspelt the word, calling themselves Doracha. Another was a gay Irish-language nightclub that operated out of rooms above a costume shop on South Great George's Street.

The third claimed, on its registry papers, to be involved in 'speculation'. There was a short list of trustees and directors, but he recognised none of them. A quick internet search showed that two were accountants, one a tax lawyer, one a former (and short-lived) minister for finance and one a 'business consultant', whatever that was.

The company had been running, with various degrees of success, since 1954, but over the past ten years it had been declaring profits of several hundreds of millions each year. Dunnigan ran through their business interests – most were vague: shares in various hotels dotted all over the world; futures in oil, coffee, tobacco, and a lead mine in the Wicklow Mountains. He double-checked this – there were no mines in County Wicklow that were currently in operation. The one mentioned in Dorcha's papers was an offshoot of an old network of pits at Glendassan, which had closed in 1957 – yet Dorcha was claiming it had earned two hundred thousand euros in 2014 from its interests in it.

Dunnigan paused, staring at the screen. Mining was not his area of expertise – he supposed it was possible to earn money from a closed lead mine: guided tours of the old shafts, perhaps. But there were no such tours advertised, so this seemed unlikely.

He got his coat, and headed for the car park.

PART SEVEN

Into the Dark

1

GLENDASSAN WAS ABOUT FIVE KILOMETRES FROM the monastic site of Glendalough. The old mine was situated in a wide valley, and Dunnigan had to park the BMW at a tourist viewing point and walk the remaining distance across a rocky heath. The mine Dorcha owned shares in was not part of the original excavation, which had first been opened in the 1740s, after first gold and then lead were found there, but was a series of tunnels hewn into the rocks adjacent to it. According to Dunnigan's research, these had been closed when the mine finally stopped yielding any ore in 1957, but the writing had been on the wall when two miners were killed in a tunnel collapse the year before.

It was six o'clock in the evening, the sun starting to dip in the sky, the quality of light changing to a subtle pink, as Dunnigan climbed a drumlin, and stood overlooking an area that had originally been levelled to create access for trucks and other vehicles, but was now empty of any such transport. He climbed down and approached the tunnel mouth. The remains of corrugated-metal sheds could be seen off to the west, and a low stone building, without a roof, stood against the sky on the edge of a steep incline, a pit that had fallen in at some point since the mine's closure.

A curlew made its whooping cry in the early evening, and

two ravens watched him from an escarpment. Dunnigan squatted down – the ground all about was pitted and furrowed by the comings and goings of many wheels and the tracks were recent. He followed them, walking stiffly over the uneven ground. A makeshift road had been cleared in the turf. Dunnigan broke into an awkward jog, and followed it.

An hour later, the road, which ran to the north-east in a more or less straight line, stopped at the entrance of a large, gated yard, surrounded on all sides by walls with razor fences on top. The yard was attached to what Dunnigan took to be a farm.

Using his phone, he checked his position on Google Maps – he was six kilometres from where his car was parked, and the nearest public road was a fifteen-minute walk across farmland.

He might as well have a thorough look around now he was there.

He went to the large gate, lay down on the earth and peered under it. The wheels of what looked to be either large trucks or agricultural machinery were visible, but from that angle, he couldn't be sure.

It took him several attempts to find a foothold in the bricks of the wall, but finally he did, and with no little effort he managed to haul himself up. He had no intention of trying to circumnavigate the razor fence, so he sort of hung near the top, straining to see what was inside.

The yard beyond was filled with trucks and containers.

'Hey – what the fuck are you playin' at?'

The cry caused Dunnigan to lose his grip and he tumbled to the ground in an undignified heap. Looking up, he saw a pair of blue-trousered legs approaching him, and then the world exploded with pain and white noise, and he knew nothing else for a time.

2

AWARENESS RETURNED SLOWLY TO DAVID Dunnigan.

The first thing he knew was that he was lying on a hard, flat surface that smelled of disinfectant. Then he heard voices, one of which had a Dublin accent, the other some kind of Eastern European inflection. He hurt all over, as if he had just fallen down a flight of stairs and hit every single one of them with a different part of his anatomy on the way.

He rolled on to his back, and took in his surroundings.

He was in what looked to be a prefabricated building lit by a single fluorescent bulb. A metal desk was at the end opposite, and two large men in uniforms of some kind were standing at it, speaking rapidly.

'You heard the boss – we don't have much fuckin' choice, do we?'

'I no like, Robert. I did not agree to such as this when I took job. I work long hours for small money, and I do all I am ask. I no do this!'

'You'll get the sack, Yuri. You know that as well as I do. And you need this job.'

'I no need that much!'

Dunnigan had been deposited on a filthy duvet on the floor of the room. He tried to sit up.

'Our friend is back with us!' the one called Robert said.

'What happened?' Dunnigan asked.

'I Tasered you.'

'Why?'

'I asked you to come down from the wall. You didn't.'

'I came down right away!'

'You were too slow.'

The man was about six feet tall with receding blond hair, a roll of flab thickening his waist, which caused his shirt buttons to look as if they were ready to pop off at any time. His partner was slimmer and in better shape, and both wore short-sleeved blue shirts, blue slacks, and had utility belts laden with torches, walkie-talkies, Tasers and mace.

They were obviously security guards.

'I was on the ground,' Dunnigan said. 'I need your help. I'm a consultant with the Sex Crimes Unit of An Garda Síochána. I'm here investigating a missing-person report – two missing people, actually.' He reached into his pocket to get his ID, but it wasn't there.

'You looking for this?' Robert asked, holding up Dunnigan's ID card. 'I took the liberty of searching you. Where'd you get this made? It's very realistic.'

'It is real. Would you please ring the number on the back? They'll confirm who I am.'

'Someone has already done that. From what I heard, no one there knows anythin' about you or why you're snoopin' around our property.'

'Ask to speak to Detective Inspector Frank Tormey.'

The man suddenly strode the length of the room and grabbed Dunnigan by the hair, dragging him into the centre of the floor. 'We've gone beyond that, pal! What the fuck are you doin' here? Who sent you to snoop around?'

Dunnigan tried to wriggle loose, but the big man had a firm

grip on his hair, and he felt it begin to rip at the roots. 'I'm a consultant with the Sex Crimes Unit of An Garda—'

Before he finished the mantra, Robert slammed him face first on to the linoleum. Something went 'pop' in Dunnigan's nose, and fireworks exploded behind his eyes. The pain was spectacular – he hadn't known such pain could exist, that the universe held such agony.

'Are you gonna just stand there, you Ukrainian fucker?'

'I tell you, I no like this. We no know this man. He could be just by accident at yard.'

'I am not doin' all the work on me own. Hit him a dig!'

'I no do this.'

'Hit him a dig, you cunt!'

'I will not!'

'If you don't hit the bollix, I'm tellin' Murphy you've been skippin' shifts and makin' me cover for you.'

With a sigh of vexation, the Ukrainian strode over and kicked Dunnigan on the hip, causing him to slam over on to his side.

'That's the spirit. Do him again!'

Robert tried to haul Dunnigan back up, but this time the criminologist was ready, and, grabbing the arm as it came close, he caught the little finger of the man's hand and wrenched it to the left, feeling it come out of its joint with a satisfying crack.

Robert wailed. 'You fuckin' cock-suckin' bastardin' fucker! My hand – I'm gonna kill you!' He drew his leg back and lifted Dunnigan from the ground with a kick. 'I cannot believe you broke my fuckin' finger, you shithead!'

He was about to kick him again, when the door of the office opened, and Detective Inspector Frank Tormey walked in.

Dunnigan had seen Tormey angry before – he had often been on the receiving end of Tormey's annoyance. He had, in all fairness, regularly been the cause of it. But he had never seen the look that was in his boss's eyes that evening – there was a madness, a ferocity radiating from him that was frightening to see. He took one look at the prone figure of Dunnigan on the floor, and another at Robert, nursing his injured hand, and finally at the man Robert had called Yuri, who was standing at the desk, looking as if he wished he were somewhere else.

'Who the fuck are you?' Robert asked.

'Two,' Tormey said. 'Two big chaps against him. Do you feel brave?'

'I asked you who the fuck you are.'

'Two big lads, and it looks like it still wasn't enough.'

'I'm not askin' you again!'

Robert clumsily tried to take the Taser from his belt with his left hand, and Tormey, quite casually, knocked it from his grip with a single slap, then kicked him on the side of the knee in a rapid, perfectly executed motion, causing the leg to buckle. Making a mewling noise, the big man sat down on the floor next to Dunnigan.

'I am Detective Inspector Frank Tormey,' Tormey said, holding out his badge. 'This gentleman you have beaten to a pulp is one of my men.'

'We di'n't know!' Robert sobbed, holding his leg, now at an odd angle, with his left hand, his right still useless.

'Someone rang our office and asked about Mr Dunnigan, and you were told we would send someone out. Do you think we're going to tell half-witted rent-a-cops like you our business, or what investigations we're currently engaged in? Do you?'

'No! I'm sorry!'

Tormey turned to Yuri. 'What's your part in all this?'

'I know nothing.'

'Are you from Barcelona?' Tormey shot back.

'I say I no like. No my job.'

'Take a hike!' Tormey said. Yuri bolted for the door and was gone.

Tormey got his arms around Dunnigan and hoisted him up,

half walking, half carrying him to the office chair. 'Are you all right, Davey?'

'I'm pressin' fuckin' charges!' Robert wailed. 'Police fuckin' brutality! I'm maimed!'

'Shut up!' Tormey shouted back at him. 'I mean it! Shut the hell up! I will deal with you in a moment.'

He lifted Dunnigan's face to the light. 'Your nose is fractured,' he said, 'but not badly. Where else are you hurt?'

'Hard to breathe,' Dunnigan wheezed.

Tormey probed his mid-section. 'I think you might have a cracked rib too. Are you okay for a couple more minutes? I need to finish talking to our friend.'

'Yes. I'll be all right.'

'Good lad.' Tormey turned back to the big security guard. 'What's your name, son?'

'I demand my phone call!'

'You're not under arrest,' Tormey said gently. 'I am an officer of the gardaí, and I am asking your name. Are you refusing to tell me? Because if you are, you might be needing that phone call very soon.'

'Robert Hayden. My name is Robert Hayden.'

'Good. Now, tell me, Robert, why did you open up a can of whup-ass on my friend?'

'I am in a lot of pain here! I need a doctor!'

'I'm sure you do, and I'll call one as soon as you answer my questions. Why did you beat up Davey?'

'We were told to find out why he was snoopin' around the yard.'

'The yard out back of here?'

'Yes. Where they keep the trucks.'

'And what is so secret in that yard that you would beat a fella half to death to protect it?'

'I don't know! Just trucks! Trucks go in and trucks go out!'

'Who gave you the order?'

'My boss. Come on, man, I'm really sore.'

'Who's your boss?'

'Murphy. Brian Murphy.'

'And he's the guy who owns the trucks?'

'No. He's the boss of the security firm I work for.'

Tormey looked at the insignia on the man's shirt. 'Baltic Security. I've not heard of ye. Big company?'

'Big enough.'

'And where might I find this Brian Murphy to express my unhappiness with his treatment of my associate?'

'Our main offices are in Dublin. Near the Red Cow.'

'Okay.'

Tormey went back to Dunnigan and gently helped him to stand. 'Robert, I may not be finished with you, so don't go off on any holidays, all right?'

'Are you callin' an ambulance?'

'I'll ring someone once I'm in the car. You fucked up today, Robert. You think you're a tough fella because you're big and you've got a belt packed full of toys, but you're not. I'm a tough guy. Davey took a beatin', but he's a tough guy. If I hadn't arrived, he might have left you a lot worse than a dislocated finger to contend with. Think about that, while you're on the crutches.'

And they left him on the floor, nursing his wounds.

3

TORMEY SAT WITH HIM IN A & E FOR FOUR HOURS. Being in the company of a police detective didn't make them see him any quicker, but once he'd been given some morphine to numb the pain, at least he didn't care.

'What were you thinking, Davey?' Tormey asked him, when the drugs kicked in.

'I was trying to find that kid's parents. The mine came up in my research.'

'Tell me,' Tormey said, so he did.

'What you've got isn't a whole lot. It's barely even circumstantial.'

'I know. But my gut tells me there's something really bad going on.'

'Will this homeless gent – what did you call him? Philly? – will he file a missing-person report on his friend?'

'I'll ask him.'

'Good. I've asked some of the lads to roust Baltic Security, but I don't think we'll get much from them – they're just the hired help. I'll look into Dorcha, see if there's anything dodgy there at all. CAB have forensic accountants that can work magic with the books these people keep. I don't understand how they do it, but if there's a body buried in the numbers, they'll dig it up.'

'Thanks, boss.'

'And I'll do what you should have done, and get a warrant to search the yard. You probably wouldn't have got one, because there was no real cause, but the hiding you just got has given us some, so we might as well use it.'

'Every cloud has a silver lining.'

'So it seems. We're both going to catch hell for this.'

'Yes.'

'I don't know why I keep you around, Davey, I truly don't.'

'I don't either, boss.'

'I mean, we've had our ups and downs, but there will come a time when I can't bail you out any more, you know that, don't you?'

'Yes.'

'I mean, I know I owe you.'

'You don't owe me anything.'

'I do. Ten years back, when I was drinking … you covered for me then and you didn't have to. I haven't forgotten that.'

'The Unit had to run, boss. I was only doing my job.'

'You could have told management I was pissed at my desk.'

'I knew you'd come out of it.'

'How did you know that?'

'You're … well, you're tougher than that.'

'I appreciate your confidence. And, like I said, I owe you. But I don't owe you everything. And they're very close to letting you go, Davey. I can help you so much, but beyond a certain point …'

'You must like me, boss.'

'I must be off my fuckin' head.'

4

'OH, MY GOD, WHAT THE HELL HAPPENED TO YOU?' Diane asked.

She was sitting on the couch in his flat – he was too sore to attempt to go to the Project, and Tormey had told him to take at least a week off work at the Unit. He wasn't due at the university until the following week, but was in no hurry to explain to William Clarke why he wouldn't be coming in to teach – not that Clarke would care much about his absence.

'I had a disagreement with a security guard at an abandoned mine in the Wicklow Mountains.'

'Excuse me?'

He explained as briefly as he could to her about the chain of information that had ended with him in A & E.

'What do you think it means?' she asked, when he had finished.

'I don't know.'

'You must have some ideas.'

'My process when it comes to investigations is to keep following the evidence until you can't go any further. Once you reach that place, you've usually got the answer you've been looking for. I try not to make any judgements or pre-empt that result until I have as much information as possible and, just now, I have almost none.'

'Not even a teensy little baby of a thought?'

'No.'

Dunnigan was standing at his spot by the window, half watching the people go past on the street. He didn't know why he had invited Diane to come over – he'd thought he wanted to see her, but now she was here, in his space, he wasn't so sure.

She patted the couch beside her for him to sit there. He paused, considering it, then did so gingerly. She took his hand. 'Are you very sore?'

'I took some painkillers. I'm all right.'

'Maybe looking for Harry's folks isn't such a good idea.'

'I promised Miley I'd find them, but it's bigger than just them. A lot of people are missing.'

'They'll have to take a stronger role in it now, won't they?'

'I hope so. I promised Miley I'd get to the bottom of it.'

She sighed and took his arm in hers. 'I know you did.'

The doorbell buzzed downstairs.

'You expecting someone?'

'No one ever calls here except my sister.'

'Could be her, then.'

Dunnigan went to the window again and peered out. 'It's my boss.'

'Which one?'

He opened the door and pressed the buzzer to open the one to the street.

Frank Tormey came in looking apologetic.

'This is my … um … my lady friend, Diane Robinson.'

'Oh. Hello. I'm pleased to meet you.'

'Likewise,' Diane said, shaking his hand.

'Do you mind if Davey and I have a chat for a moment?'

'Not at all. I'll put the kettle on,' Diane said, and went into the kitchen closing the door after her.

'How're the war wounds today?' Tormey asked, looking about the room.

'I'm okay. Why are you here, boss?'

'I made an application for a warrant to search the yard in Glendassan. And I made a request for the accountants to look into Dorcha.'

'Thank you.'

'I was refused on both counts.'

Dunnigan blinked and sat down. 'Is that usual?'

'It's not *un*usual. All departments are overloaded and resources are thin on the ground, but I don't like it.'

'What do you want me to do?'

'Officially, I'm telling you to leave it alone.'

'Yes, boss.'

'But I was given a name by a detective from the CAB, who has an interest in this group, Dorcha, but has also been told to leave it alone. I thought that if someone did some digging on a private basis, and didn't tell me about it, there wouldn't be a whole lot I could do, would there?'

Dunnigan nodded. 'What's the lead?'

'There's a bar on the road to Ashbourne. It's called the Moon Behind the Hill.'

'The Moon …'

'I thought that might make your ears prick up.'

'And why would an imaginary person be hypothetically interested in this bar?'

'Let's just say there are monies flowing in and out of that pub in amounts that match monies flowing in and out of Dorcha's finances. My associate in the CAB thinks they're connected.'

'So CAB has been looking into Dorcha too?'

'From what I've learned this morning, various detectives have had suspicions about them for years. Every time they start to investigate, someone higher up blocks them. Which is exactly what has happened now.'

'That's awful,' Dunnigan said. 'And not good enough. Who do we complain to about it?'

'Aw, Jesus, Davey – I'm throwing you a bone here! Why don't

you and Father Bill check out this bar and see what you can find? But tell the psycho priest not to go torching the place or going all fucking Chuck Norris on the locals, all right?'

Dunnigan shook his head. 'We can't allow them to stop us doing our job,' he said. 'We are the police – we catch criminals, we don't collude with them.'

'From what I've been told, this is coming right from the top. Could go right to the minister's office.'

'Which minister?'

'I don't bloody know. Leave it alone. Can you do that?'

'Maybe. I'll try.'

'It doesn't matter, anyway. We have no official capacity in this from here on, so if you want to go digging, you're on your own. Are we clear?' Tormey saw himself out.

'He seems nice,' Diane said, coming out of the kitchen.

'What? Oh, yes, he is,' Dunnigan said, pulling over his laptop.

'What are you looking for?'

'The itinerary of the minister for housing, planning, community and local government.'

'Why?'

'Because I need to speak to him, and I don't think they'll let me make an official appointment.'

5

DUNNIGAN DID SOMETHING HE HAD NEVER DONE before: he fell asleep on the couch that evening. Diane had made them some chicken soup, and its warmth, combined with the effects of the pills he'd been given at the hospital, caused him to drift off.

He was awakened by voices, and sat up to see Gina and Diane standing in the doorway, looking at one another with undisguised distaste.

'Hello, Gina,' Dunnigan said.

'Your friend Diane wasn't very happy about waking you up to see me,' Gina said tersely.

'Davey has been hurt and needs to sleep. I said you could wait!'

'I'm awake now.'

'If I want to see my brother, I'll see him.'

'I never said you couldn't!'

'Um … I'm awake now …'

'I don't know how you feel you have the right to screen who sees him and who doesn't!'

'I wasn't screening anyone! I only said I'd rather let him sleep – God knows, he doesn't get very much shuteye, so I wanted to make the best of it!'

'What do you know about his sleep habits?'

'Enough to know that they're all over the shop!'

'Gina! I am awake!'

She shot him a look. 'What happened to you?'

'Workplace injury.'

'Are you all right?'

'I'm fine. Would you please sit down?'

'I think I'll come back when the atmosphere is a bit warmer.' And she stomped out.

'I'm not sure that went well,' Diane said.

'No.'

Father Bill Creedon

Before dawn every morning he ran eight kilometres along the river, his feet pounding the pavements as he felt the blood pumping and the oxygen infusing him, like water might a flower. It was a ritual he had been observing since his teens, and it was one of the few times during any day when he was truly alone.

He liked the last shimmer of stars on the surface of the water, the feel of the early-morning breeze on his face, the occasional greeting from people he might pass.

He would finish his run at the Phoenix Park and spend a few minutes sitting on the bench nearest the gate, feeling the warmth of the sun as it gradually climbed over the horizon and took charge of the day.

Father Bill loved Dublin City. Other than his brief stint in South America, he had never lived anywhere else, and he had no desire to. The people of the town were his people, the Liffey was in his blood, and the bells of the cathedral were his heartbeat.

He knew he was considered a rogue element by his superiors in the Church, but that caused him little concern. By his second year in the seminary he had understood he was never going to be able to toe the party line on many of the issues that exercised his fellow theologians. Their God was one of rules and regulations, of sanctions and punishment, a figure who was as likely to abandon a lost sheep as He was to welcome it back to the fold.

Father Bill could not accept this. The Jesus he loved was as much human as divine: He welcomed the poor, the disenfranchised. He sat down with beggars, shared food with prostitutes, and the only people He rejected were the businessmen who tried to turn His home into a marketplace. In the gospels, Father Bill found a blueprint for living, and he had held true to its message his entire life. He was not going to compromise that moral code for anyone: not the bishops, or the cardinals, not even the Holy Father himself.

There was a time, early in his priesthood, when he had considered leaving the Church. There had been a woman in Nicaragua, a young mother, whose husband had been killed in the guerrilla fighting. She had come to him for sanctuary, protection, and their friendship had rapidly blossomed into something more.

Elisa – her name was Elisa. She was slim and lithe, her dark hair hanging almost to her waist. Thinking of her even now he experienced a thrill in his stomach. She had roused feelings in him he had never known he could have. To him, she was like a drug, and he would have done anything for her.

One humid night as they lay together, he told her he wanted to give up his calling for her and her child. They could be happy, he whispered, in his broken Spanish. They could go up into the mountains, away from the fighting and the politics and the squalor, and live a simple life – he could keep sheep or goats, she could tend a garden.

Elisa would not hear of it – he belonged to God, she told him. She would not be the one who sundered the vows he had made with the Almighty. She loved him – and because she loved him, she would not ask him to make that sacrifice for her.

So he had remained, and she and the boy had gone. He never saw them again.

He had no photos of her and no letters, for she could neither read nor write. But he had the memory of how she felt, of how she smelled, of what it was like to be touched by her. These things he remembered every day.

The Church he served was an imperfect, human thing, but then he was imperfect and human, too.

Father Bill thought they might muddle along together for a few more years.

6

BARTLEBY FITZHENRY TD TOOK THE PODIUM TO give his address to the Construction Workers and General Labourers Guild luncheon at two o'clock sharp the following day. He was a florid-faced man, his white hair cut neatly, his navy-blue pinstriped suit tailored to mask the bulge of his stomach, a silver pin holding his red tie in place just so.

That afternoon he intended to congratulate the assembled group, all dressed in their best bib-and-tucker, some with their wives, some with other people's wives, all of whom had just dined as well as might be expected at the Shelbourne Hotel. He planned to thank them for the sterling work they had done in bringing the building industry back from the Armageddon it had experienced in 2007, when the economic bubble, which had been inflated by ludicrous property prices and reckless borrowing, burst, bringing everyone down with it.

He was going to express his belief that things were on a rocket-like trajectory skyward, and there was little that could happen to prevent a return to the wondrous days when Irish construction was the envy not just of Europe but of the world.

He was going to say these things, but before he could even introduce himself, a strange man dressed in a long grey coat, jeans and a Judge Dredd T-shirt, looking as if he had just done a few rounds with Conor McGregor, shouted at him from the back of the room, 'Minister Fitzhenry, could you please explain to me why you and your office have been blocking the official investigation of a right-wing group linked to unexplained disappearances of countless homeless people from the streets of this city?'

All eyes in the room turned to the scruffy stranger who had gatecrashed their gathering.

Fitzhenry peered down at the man. Was he from one of the other parties? From the way he was dressed he looked like he might belong to People Before Profit, but then, with the state of his face, he was probably a Shinner. 'And who are you, sir?' the minister asked, smiling jovially.

'My name is David Dunnigan. I am a civilian consultant with the Sex Crimes Unit of An Garda Síochána.'

'Well, I'm always happy to help the gardaí out in any way possible,' FitzHenry said. 'But, as you can see, I do have to talk to these people.'

A girl in her early twenties, wearing a business suit and large earrings, was suddenly at Dunnigan's side. 'If you'd like to come with me, sir, we can arrange a more convenient meeting with the minister.'

'But I'm here now,' Dunnigan said. 'I'm happy to wait until he finishes his speech. It can't take that long, can it?'

On the podium, Bartleby Fitzhenry had already started addressing the crowd.

'Please, could you just step outside for a second?'

Dunnigan allowed himself to be led from the room, expecting to be sat down and given tea in the Horseshoe Bar while diaries were consulted. Nothing like that happened. The moment he was outside the dining-room doors, a tall man with an earpiece had him by the arm, and he was whisked into what seemed to be a linen closet.

'What seems to be the problem, sir?' the tall man said.

'I would have thought that was pretty clear,' Dunnigan said. 'Was my question poorly worded?'

'Can I see some identification?'

'Can I see some from you?'

Both men took their respective cards and badges from their pockets.

'David, do your superiors know you're here today?'

'I'm not sure,' Dunnigan said. 'But I don't think they'll be surprised to hear I showed up.'

'I bet they won't. I'm going to have to ask you to leave.'

'I thought I was to be given an appointment with Minister Bartleby.'

'No, David. That was a lie.'

'Oh.' Dunnigan was genuinely disappointed.

Frank Tormey

'Come in, DI Tormey. Please sit down.'

'Thank you, Commissioner.'

'Shut up, Tormey.'

'Yes, sir.'

'Do you know who I received a call from yesterday?'

'I can guess, sir.'

'I got a call from the minister for housing, planning, community and local government. Not from his parliamentary assistant, not from his handler, not from his secretary or the girl who presses his suits. I got a call from the man himself. And he was a very angry man, Tormey. He was fucking beside himself with rage, in fact, because of the behaviour of one of my employees. Do you know which one he was speaking about, DI Tormey?'

'I think I do, sir.'

'Shut up. David Dunnigan walked into an engagement this elected representative of the people of Ireland was attending, and accused him, openly, of trying to suppress a police investigation. Something about missing homeless people. Do you know anything about this?'

'I did put in requests for a warrant to enter and search a premises in Wicklow, sir, and for some hours from the forensic accountants. Both were declined.'

'How many other requests have you had declined this week alone?'

'Three, sir.'

'And do you, or any other of your men, believe there is a cover-up going in in relation to those cases?'

'No, sir.'

'Shut up, Tormey. I want David Dunnigan off the streets. If you must employ him, I want him office-based from now on. What's this about some security guard beating the snot out of him?'

'That has been resolved, sir. Dunnigan does not wish to press charges.'

'I'm not looking to prosecute the bloke – I wanted to shake his hand!'

'I understand you're frustrated, sir—'

'Shut up, Tormey! This Dorcha thing is as old as I am, older. It's a copper's fairytale, nothing more. I do not want any more fuss caused, and I'm not kidding when I say that if Dunnigan's name comes across my desk one more time, I will see him disciplined. Do you understand me, DI Tormey?'

'I do, sir. Loud and clear.'

'And I might knock you down a few pegs while I'm at it. You specialist squads can get to believing that you're laws unto yourselves. You're not – you're still on my force, and I won't stand for you continuously ignoring my direct instructions. Put your house in order, Tormey, or I'll send in someone who will. Now get out of my sight before I get really ticked off.'

'Yes, sir.'

'Shut up, Tormey.'

7

MILEY TIMONEY PUSHED THE BUTTON ON THE intercom in his apartment. ''Lo, yes, who is it?'

'Get your coat, we're going out.'

'And who is this, please?'

'You know who it is. Come on.'

'It might be someone doing an impression. Or a robot.'

'Miley, will you get your coat and come on?'

'Where are we going?'

'To a pub.'

'Are you the designated driver?'

'You aren't able to drive, Miley.'

'Which is why I want to be sure you're staying on the Lucozade tonight.'

The Moon Behind the Hill was a long, single-storeyed building with a flat roof, just off the main Dublin to Ashbourne road. Dunnigan immediately spotted three large transport containers in its spacious car park, and wondered if they might be some of those he had (sort of) seen in Glendassan. He noted that they were without cabs – the trailers had been left and the trucks taken somewhere else. It was as if the pub's car park was being used as a storage area.

'You take me to such nice places,' Miley said. 'What are we looking for?'

'I don't know,' Dunnigan admitted. 'Tormey told me one of his friends in the Criminal Assets Bureau has found links between here and the Dorcha group.'

'Links?'

'From what I can gather, they seem to believe this place is being used to launder money. But some of those trailers look familiar. I only saw the ones in the mine yard for a second, but if I'm right, there might be more going on here than processing funds.'

'The plot thickens,' Miley said.

'It does.'

Inside, the pub was crowded with people drinking, eating and listening to Smokie on an old jukebox. Dunnigan and Miley pushed their way to the bar.

'Well, hello there.' The barman was an elderly man with his yellow-white hair brushed none too artfully over his bald pate. He was giving Miley the half-indulgent, half-pitying look Dunnigan was getting used to seeing when out with his friend. 'What can I get ye?'

'I'll have a glass of sparkling water,' Dunnigan said.

'Pint of Guinness,' Miley said.

'Will I put a drop of blackcurrant in that for you?' the barman asked, winking conspiratorially at Miley.

'Why would you do that?' Miley asked.

The barman paused, then went and got their drinks.

'Living Next Door to Alice' ended, and a short, bearded man fed some more coins into the jukebox. 'Needles And Pins' began.

'I like this song,' Miley said, tapping his fingers on the bartop.

'Why?' Dunnigan asked, genuinely puzzled.

'It's catchy. And it has a happy tune.'

'If I'm interpreting the lyrics correctly, it's about an unhappy love affair.'

'Well, it's got a good rhythm.'

The drinks arrived, the barman looking less friendly this time. 'Guinness, no blackcurrant,' he said, putting the pint on a beermat in in front of Miley.

'Do you mind if I ask you something?' Dunnigan said.

'Not at all.'

'A friend of mine used to do some work for a group called Dorcha. It was an outreach programme for the homeless, trying to get them involved in employment, you know.'

'Well, fair play to them,' the barman said.

'Yes. He told me he and some of his workmates used to come in here for a drink sometimes. I owe him some money, and I need to pay him back – do you know if any of the Dorcha people are here this evening?'

'I'm sorry, sir, I can't help you.'

'Are you sure?'

'Certain. You two boys enjoy your drinks, now.' He went to serve another customer.

'That was smooth,' Miley said. 'I love your interview technique, how you reeled him in like an angler landing a prize fish.'

'Do you have any better ideas?'

'I'm going to take a whizz,' Miley said, and slid off his barstool.

'Not much of an idea, but thanks for letting me know,' Dunnigan said, and sipped his fizzy water.

People flooded in in dribs and drabs, mostly men in work clothes. 'Needles and Pins' ended. The bearded man added more money, and 'Living Next Door to Alice' began all over again. Dunnigan shuddered.

He wondered if he should have asked Diane if she might like to join them. He hadn't seen her in a couple of days, and he missed her. Of course he didn't want her involved in anything dangerous but, then, she had been in the army, and she looked to be very strong – her arms and legs had clearly defined muscles. He had noticed.

Miley was taking a long time.

A group in the corner were joining in enthusiastically on the choruses of the old country rock song, adding in the line 'Who the fuck is Alice?' at the appropriate time. They seemed to be having a good time. Maybe he should take Diane to a pub. Perhaps she liked music. He did not. Every time he thought about singing, he was reminded of that choir they had been listening to when Beth disappeared. How he wished he had never stopped to hear that song. What if he and Beth had just kept going? Would things have been different?

'Davey?'

He jumped, startled at having his thoughts interrupted.

Miley was standing beside him, a look he couldn't read on his face. 'Come and have a look at this,' he said.

The car park was now half full, and about one third of that space was taken up with trucks and containers.

'What is it?' Dunnigan asked.

'Just watch,' Miley said.

They leaned against the bonnet of the BMW and waited.

A truck had just pulled in, and was reversing into a spot in the furthest corner, beside the three other containers that were there already. The process took a good five more minutes as the large vehicle angled and manoeuvred into place. Finally, the driver hopped out of the cab and went inside.

'Let's go,' Miley hissed.

'Where?'

'You got beat up trying to get a look at the trucks in the yard by the mine,' Miley said. 'No one can stop you having a gander at these.'

Dunnigan nodded, and they jogged over to the cab that had just arrived. The three trailers were tall, and were constructed from some kind of thick metal that had been painted purple. There were some numbers stencilled in black ink on the side: 13346226, DRCA.

'Could be Dorcha,' Miley said.

'It could be,' Dunnigan agreed, snapping a photo of the stencil on his phone's camera. 'And if it isn't, it's quite the coincidence.'

'What do you think is inside?'

'I don't know. Is there any way we can have a look?'

Miley climbed up onto the rear of the container closest, looking at the locking mechanism. He kicked at it a couple of times.

'Sssh!' Dunnigan said.

'What?'

'Just listen.'

They did. Nothing at first, then, as if from far away, a distant tapping, coming from inside the container.

'What the hell . . .' Miley said.

'You pair have got to be kiddin' me!'

They spun around to see the truck driver, his arms folded, glaring at them.

8

'GET THAT FELLA DOWN OFF ME TRUCK, WILL YOU?'

Miley was still standing on the footrest, his leg drawn back to kick the door again.

'Truck!' Miley said, in a goofy, slurred voice. 'Me like de truck!'

'For fuck sake, he's one o' them retarded lads, isn't he?'

'Me drive inna truck?' Miley said, stepping awkwardly down and falling on his behind in the process.

'Um ... please excuse my brother, he's just out of the residential home for the evening, and he loves trucks and trains and things,' Dunnigan said, following Miley's lead.

'Boop! Boop!' Miley said, pulling an imaginary cord in the air. 'Boop! Boop!'

'The air horn,' Dunnigan explained. 'It's his favourite.'

'If I give him a blast of it, will ye feck off? I'm in there tryin' to have a bit of grub when the landlord tells me you two are interferin' with me load.'

'We really didn't mean any harm,' Dunnigan said, feeling himself relax – through Miley's ingenuity, they had got away with it.

'One blast and then I'm goin' back inside, right?'

'Boop! Boop!' Miley said, and burst into loud guffaws.

'I cannot believe you played that card and it worked,'

Dunnigan said, his eyes on the road as they drove back to the city.

'It's what people think, so why not?' Miley said, through his giggles. 'I've learned that it can be useful sometimes.'

'Well, it certainly was this evening.'

'Yes, it was.'

They drove on, Miley singing the chorus of 'Needles and Pins' gently to himself.

'What do you reckon was in the truck?' Miley asked when he had gotten bored singing by himself.

'I don't know. But I don't like it.'

'What are you going to do?'

'I'm going to tell Father Bill.'

'That sounds like a good idea to me. "Needles and pinsah!" *Boop! Boop!*'

'Will you stop doing that?'

9

FATHER BILL LISTENED AS DUNNIGAN AND MILEY took turns telling the story of their trip to the Moon Behind the Hill. 'You heard tapping from inside the container.'

'Yes.'

'Was it regular, or irregular? Did it sound like Morse Code, or someone beating the side in panic?'

'It sounded like tapping,' Dunnigan said. 'I don't have enough experience to be able to characterise it as anything more than that.'

'Did it sound as if it was being made by a person, or an animal, or a piece of machinery?'

'I thought it sounded like somebody knocking on the metal wall,' Miley offered.

'What makes you think that?'

''S just what I think.'

'What do you want me to do with this?' Father Bill asked them.

They were sitting in his office at the end of the night, the rest of the Project silent except for some distant snoring.

'Help us to look into it,' Dunnigan said.

'To what purpose?'

'Hopefully to find Harry's parents.'

'I got a phone call today from a social worker,' Father Bill said. 'She's coming out on Friday to talk to us about Harry's future.'

'What does that even mean?' Miley said.

'He needs to be in care, Miley,' Father Bill said gently. 'He can't keep sleeping in that warehouse, and you can't continue spending your life looking after him. The only reason they haven't sent someone out before this is because we were involved with the boy, but the situation can't continue. You both deserve better.'

'You can't take him into care,' Miley said, his voice getting thick with tears. 'He's a nice kid – you shouldn't put nice people in places where they get treated bad.'

'I'm really sorry about what happened to you, Miley,' Father Bill said, his eyes on the mug of Scotch whisky-laced tea he was drinking. 'But there are lots of good children's homes, too, with people working in them who really care about the kids. Harry is being neglected, sleeping all by himself in a ruined building. Even if he would come here, we couldn't promise him a bed every night. You know that's not how it works.'

'Can't he come and live with me?'

'No, Miley. I'm sorry, but he can't.'

'Why?'

'You'd need to get trained as a foster-parent, and then there's the fact that you're just out of care yourself and … and, well …'

'And my stupid fucking genetic condition!' Miley shouted.

Dunnigan and Father Bill took a breath. Miley had plenty of reasons to be angry, but they had never seen him be anything other than upbeat and happy. That he would eventually blow was probably inevitable, but it was still shocking, now it had happened.

'You know I don't have any truck with that kind of prejudice, Miley, but Tusla and the Department of Children do. We can always fight for visitation rights for you – I know Harry would want to see you.'

'Fuck visitation rights! Has anyone asked him what he wants? Have you even told him you're planning on locking him up?'

'He's not getting locked up, Miley.'

'That's easy for you to say! Davey, did you know about this?'

'Well, I knew it was on the cards—'

'Back-stabbers! You are both two-faced, lying hypocrites.'

'Miley, please take a breath,' Dunnigan said, but his friend was already on his feet, his face flushed with anger and tears running down his cheeks.

'You were supposed to be my friends,' he said. 'Why didn't you just leave me in that fucking nursing home, eh? At least when I was in there, I knew where I stood. The people in there didn't pretend to like me and then treat me like shit – one thing you can say for them, they were consistent!'

And then he was gone out of the door and into the night.

Dunnigan and Father Bill sat in the wake of his anguish.

'Neither of us spoke to him about Harry going into care,' Father Bill said.

'No.'

'Have you talked to Harry about it?'

'No.'

'Neither have I.' Father Bill had some tea. 'Miley's right,' he said. 'We are a pair of hypocrites.'

10

'YES. WHO IS IT, PLEASE?'

'Davey, it's Father Bill.'

'It's five thirty in the morning. Why are you calling me?'

'I'm at the Moon Behind the Hill bar.'

'Is it open this early?'

'I managed to persuade them to make an exception. They were most accommodating.'

'What have you done, Father?'

'I've stopped being a hypocrite. Can you come out?'

'I'll be there as soon as I can.'

'Good. I should warn you, we'll be needing the presence of some of your law-enforcement friends, but perhaps not right away. I'd like to have a chat with some people here first, and I thought you might like to be involved in the discussion.'

'I don't follow.'

'You will. See you soon.'

'Okay.'

Dunnigan hangs up.

11

FATHER BILL WAS WAITING FOR HIM OUT FRONT of the pub when he turned the BMW into the wide, and now mostly empty, car park. The containers were all gone. Only Father Bill's decrepit Ford Capri and a couple of Toyotas took up any of the spaces. The priest looked as fresh as ever, though he mustn't have slept at all.

'Good to see you. Come and meet my new friends.'

As they approached the side door to the bar, Dunnigan noticed it was hanging on its hinges.

'I had to use a little brute force,' Father Bill said apologetically.

Inside, the place was in complete disarray: tables and chairs overturned, glasses broken. The barman who had served Dunnigan and Miley the night before was sitting at one of the tables holding a blood-stained cloth to his head. Lying on the floor just under the bar, unconscious amid the remains of a couple of tables that had been smashed to bits, was a large man dressed in a brightly coloured shell suit. Propped up against the wall near the jukebox was the small, bearded Smokie fan, one of his legs folded under him at an angle it wasn't meant to achieve. He looked up when Dunnigan and the priest came in, and a wave of fear crossed his face.

'This is Ross,' Father Bill said, motioning at the Smokie fan. 'Ross works for Alec,' a nod to the barman, 'who runs this place.

Alec, though, works for someone much higher up the food chain, don't you, Alec me lad?'

'Fuck youse,' Alec said, spitting blood at the two men.

'That's not very hospitable,' Father Bill said. 'Do you want me to get aggressive again? I'm not in a very good mood this morning, and it wouldn't take much to tip me over the edge.'

'Do what you fuckin' like. When my people hear about this, and they will, your life won't be worth livin', anyway.'

Father Bill was at the man's table in a second, and with no apparent effort tipped it and him over on to the floor. 'Who do you work for, Alec? Who's funding all this? Give me a name and I'll go, leaving you to people less likely to break any more of your bones.'

'Fuck. You.'

Father Bill sighed. He reached down, grabbed the man by the nose, then twisted and lifted at the same time. 'It's not as tough as most people think, the shnozz,' he said. 'I don't think it would take a great deal of effort to rip it off.'

The barman was bellowing at the top of his lungs. Father Bill gave him another shake, and then dropped him – he hit the floor with a thud. 'Who are you working with? The next time I ask, I won't be so gentle.'

'I don't know all the names! There's a man called Andrews – he calls me when a consignment is coming in.'

'He telephones?'

'Yes.'

'Write down the number.'

'He's a fucking freak, so he is! He'll kill me!'

'And I won't?'

The man took a pen and a phone from the large pocket of his apron, and copied a number down onto a beer mat.

'What consignment is he talking about?' Dunnigan asked. 'Are they dealing drugs?'

Father Bill nodded at a door behind the bar, which led,

Dunnigan assumed, to the cellar, where the kegs were stored. 'You'd better take a look.'

A flight of narrow steps descended to a low-ceilinged concrete room. Kegs lined most of the walls, and there were cardboard boxes of crisps and peanuts in abundance. At first, he couldn't see much through the gloom, but as his eyes adjusted, Dunnigan made out some figures huddled on a mattress in the furthest corner. 'Um … hello,' he said.

One of the figures said something rapidly in a language he did not understand, but which sounded like Romanian. Using the torch on his phone, he illuminated the murk, and saw five women, two of whom looked to be in their teens, gazing in terror at him. They were all wearing grubby, flimsy clothes, and were thin and very dirty.

'It's okay,' he said, holding out his ID card to them. 'I'm the police. You're safe now.'

If the women understood, they didn't show it. One started to sob as he dialled the number for Harcourt Street.

By the time the police arrived, Father Bill was gone.

12

'YOU'RE SUPPOSED TO BE ON INJURY LEAVE,' Tormey said, as they watched the five women being helped into an ambulance.

'I got a lead about this place,' Dunnigan said, with no hint of irony. 'I felt it couldn't wait.'

'According to Alec Potts, the owner of this establishment, six guys came in and smashed the bar up, then beat him and his two associates fairly badly.'

'Must have been a rival gang,' Dunnigan said.

'That's what I thought. It's a stroke of luck you got here after they'd gone, or you could have got another hiding.'

'Yes. Very lucky. Do we know what was to happen to those girls?'

'No. Brazaite, from the Drug Squad, speaks Romanian, and he'll act as an interpreter when we get back to base. My guess would be the sex industry, but they're as likely to have ended up working as chambermaids in hotels or picking mushrooms in Monaghan. The slave trade is alive and well, Davey. You just have to look a little harder to find it.'

'Alec wasn't running this on his own.'

'No. But he's already refusing to speak until he sees his solicitor, so I doubt we'll get much more out of him. Did he say anything before we got here?'

'Um … no. Not a thing.'

'Are you sure of that, Davey?'

'Yes. I'm sure.'

Tormey pursed his lips. 'That's how you want to play it?'

'I'm not playing, boss.'

'Now we've got those girls, someone is going to have to pay attention.'

'To what degree, though? We've managed to save five women, and I'm very pleased to have done that, but this is just one piece of the jigsaw puzzle. I don't trust they'll want us to find any more. Someone doesn't want us to see the full picture.'

Tormey nodded. 'I'm a career cop, Davey. I can turn a blind eye to so much, but this is starting to make me feel very uncomfortable.'

'Me too.'

'When you unleash Bill Creedon on a situation like this, you never know what he's liable to do. He's a blunt instrument, Davey, and I genuinely think he's more than a little unbalanced.'

'You told me to bring him in.'

'I was wrong to do that. I'm scared of where this is all going to end.'

'I am too,' Dunnigan said. 'But it *is* going to end, one way or another.'

Ernest Frobisher

He screamed at the nurses, raged at the doctors and called for the Yellow Man to be brought to him. 'Make this stop! Make them go away!'

'As I said when we last spoke about it, one of them works for the police.'

'You have dealt with the police before! Do what you do!'

A detective named Goodison had tried to stem the flow of their money, once, and had come close to succeeding. He had created a great deal of trouble for them, and the Yellow Man had been sent to make him see the error of his ways.

He had gone to the detective's house as he and his wife slept, and had awakened the woman by cutting off one of her fingers with a hedge trimmer. The detective had desisted immediately.

'This one is different – he has no wife and hardly sees his family. I think he wants to die. I've seen it before, and it's hard to scare a man with no fear of death.'

'Find something he fears.'

'I'll do what I can.'

PART EIGHT

Tell it to the Mountain

1

THE MAN NAMED ANDREWS MET DUNNIGAN across the road from the Project, at a bench that overlooked the Liffey. He was slim and sallow-skinned, wearing a beige suit that looked to have been very expensive. His light brown hair was freshly cut, and he exuded an air of civilised menace – there was something reptilian about the set of his eyes, and he seemed rarely to blink.

He was the Yellow Man.

'You wished to meet me, Mr Dunnigan.' His voice was dry and completely accentless.

'Yes.'

'You recognise me, I think?'

'Yes.'

'You truly know me?'

'You've been hanging around outside the Project, and I've heard the homeless talk about you.'

'I see.'

'And you know who I am?'

'I know you work for the police, and are involved with the homeless shelter behind us.'

'Correct. Now who are you – really?'

'I am simply an employee. I represent Mr Frobisher, and am here because he requested that I meet with you, as we seem to find ourselves at cross-purposes. Put more simply, I work for the Dorcha Campaign.'

'Campaign?'

'We see it as a political movement.'

'Trafficking vulnerable women is an act of political engagement?'

Andrews cleared his throat and looked surreptitiously about him. 'May I speak candidly, Mr Dunnigan?'

'Yes.'

'The men and women you try to help in the Project – and who have been the cause of our disagreement – are part of a social group that has been a drain on Ireland's resources for many hundreds of years. They are largely uneducated, they have no transferable skills, and they are, more often than not, unable to care for themselves and their families. They make no contribution to the running of this country, yet they expect handouts through social welfare and support payments. Many of these individuals do not even hold an Irish passport!'

'So you offer them slavery and death?'

'We offer Ireland an alternative to supporting them with taxpayers' hard-earned money and never-ending requests for charity.'

'How thoughtful.'

'Capitalism is not a system that can support those who are unable to support themselves. If you wish to be a member of a society, you must be prepared to contribute to that society. The people you would have us cosset and mollycoddle have no true desire to move above their circumstances. We force them to. Tough love, you might call it.'

'I call it abduction and murder.'

'Who has been murdered? Dorcha is about the movement of assets. Transport, if you will.'

'You're not making sense.'

'You're familiar with the term "an Irish answer to an Irish problem"?'

'Yes.'

'We're using the same methodology: Dorcha wants the scum gone.'

'So you are forcing people to leave? This is Fascism – you're banishing them from the country because they don't suit your vision of how Ireland should be.'

'We do what many would wish but are afraid to ask for. I'm not ashamed of that.'

'Good for you. I'm looking for a number of people who were taken by your men, but let's start with two: Pauline and Tom Gately.'

'I don't recognise the names.'

'I want to know where they went, and I want them returned.'

'What you ask may not be possible.'

'Why not?'

'In certain instances, contracts are signed, terms agreed. These people could be anywhere in the world.'

Dunnigan considered this. 'I want you to make this happen, Mr Andrews. I have only started to poke the hornets' nest that is your "campaign". I'm not going to stop until I've found the Gatelys and half a dozen others who have been reported missing to the police. You seem to have some powerful friends, but I am in the happy position of not caring if I lose my job or even get sued – I don't have any money and my reputation is so tarnished that another smear won't make any difference.'

'Be that as it may, Mr Dunnigan, my employer is very unhappy with the attention you have been attracting. He has asked me to convey to you that, should your activities continue, we will be forced to take action. Such action may not be directed at you, Mr Dunnigan. But we know you have a sister. And there is the young man with Down's Syndrome, whom you seem to be quite fond of. Would it not be a great tragedy if something were to befall either of them?'

Dunnigan felt fingers of ice claw at his insides. And a sudden surge of anger.

'Do we understand each other, Mr Dunnigan?'

'I work for the police, Mr Andrews. If anything happens to my sister or my friends, I will make sure the full force of the gardaí comes down directly on your head.'

'The gardaí need proof, Mr Dunnigan. I and my people are very experienced in covering our tracks.'

'We'll see about that.'

'I trust we won't have to. You will, I think, not be insulted if I hope we do not meet again. I wish you a pleasant day.' He stood and, in moments, was swallowed by the crowd on the quay.

Father Bill sat on the bench beside Dunnigan. 'What did we learn?'

'That they're scared of us.'

'I've asked Philly to follow our friend at a safe distance. Let's see where he goes.'

'Probably nowhere good,' Dunnigan observed.

2

A SOCIAL WORKER NAMED KARLA GAMMON called to the Project later that day to talk to Father Bill, Dunnigan and Diane about Harry. Diane had sent Miley a text asking him to come to the meeting, but he had not responded. In fact, none of them had seen him since he had stormed out, almost a week earlier.

Karla, who dressed like a hippie, her long dark hair in dreadlocks, sat and listened to the story of how they had first encountered young Harry Gately, interspersing their narrative with questions about how the boy seemed developmentally. 'And he comes here most evenings?'

'No. I would say we see him once, twice a week,' Father Bill said. 'Miley goes to him, generally.'

'And Miley is one of your volunteers?'

'Yes.'

'He has established the strongest relationship with him?'

'Oh, by far.'

'But he's not here.'

'Miley has mixed feelings about Harry going into care,' Dunnigan said. 'He was in care himself, and didn't have a very nice time.'

'I'm sorry to hear that,' Karla Gammon said. 'Shall we see if we can meet Harry, then? I'd like to have a chat with him about what our options are. Did you tell him I was coming, as I asked?'

'We did – well, we asked Miley to,' Diane said sheepishly.

'I'm sure he knows, then,' the social worker said, and they made the short walk to the warehouse.

'Miley, Harry, we're coming up,' Father Bill hollered up the stairs as they began the climb. 'Watch your step there, Karla – the footing can be a bit treacherous.'

They got to Harry's room to find it empty.

'It looks like Harry's decided he doesn't want to meet me today,' Karla said.

'It does,' Diane agreed.

'Well, I think it's important he feels he's in control of the process. We can afford to give him a little time – within reason.'

'That's very understanding of you,' Father Bill said.

And they trooped back the way they had come.

3

DUNNIGAN WALKED KARLA GAMMON TO HER CAR. 'Miley has become very attached to Harry,' he told the social worker.

'That can happen, particularly when you're working one-on-one with a child. It tends to go either of two ways: you can end up detesting the sight of the child and want to get as far away from them as you can, or you find yourself wanting to adopt them.'

'Miley really cares about him. The idea of placing him in care is breaking his heart. Is there any way we can explore the idea of Miley fostering Harry?'

'Over the long term, it is a possibility. But your friend would have to be vetted, go through training, and even then there would be no guarantees. You say he was in care himself?'

'That shouldn't preclude him from being a carer.'

'I'm not suggesting it would. But his background must be taken into consideration. We would want to know about his experiences of being parented – how he was raised. Why was he in care to begin with?'

'Miley has Down's Syndrome.'

Karla Gammon tried very hard not to react, but Dunnigan's trained eye saw something flicker across her face, just for a moment. 'Again, that would not preclude him from taking care of Harry, but I have to tell you, it lessens the likelihood of a successful application considerably.'

'Miley is not intellectually disabled.'

'Intellectual disability is not a box-ticking exercise. He may be literate and numerate, but what about his emotional intelligence? How well able is he to tend his home, or deal with the challenging behaviour Harry is bound to exhibit?'

'He's been doing just fine for the couple of months before you deigned to arrive.'

'Has he? How do you know? It seems to me you have allowed a mildly disabled man to wander off and do God knows what with an abandoned, neglected boy.'

'Miley is the best thing that's happened to that kid in a very long time.'

'Perhaps – or is Harry the best thing to happen to Miley? A playmate, so the rest of you didn't have to keep him entertained.'

'You don't know what you're talking about.'

'Sadly, I do. All too well.' She opened her car door. 'I'll be back in a week. Have Harry here when I arrive, or I'll be coming back with an emergency care order, and there will be no slow transition into a residential home – I'll just take him.'

Then she was gone, and Dunnigan wished he had kept his mouth shut.

4

RECORDS SHOWED THAT ERNEST FROBISHER, THE direct descendant of the Walter who had founded the After Dark Society, had no children, and had addresses in five different countries, not including Ireland. Dunnigan ran searches through every existing database, but could find no relatives, either by blood or marriage, who might be using the name.

The problem he had with Ernest Frobisher being the head of the snake was that, according to his birth certificare, the man had been born in 1917 – making him ninety-nine years old. It was not impossible that a man of that age was running a criminal enterprise on this scale, but Dunnigan thought it unlikely.

He was sitting at his desk in Garda HQ, staring into space, when Derek Cole, a detective he had worked with on several cases in the past, found him. 'They need you in Interview Room Six.'

'Why?'

'They want you to take a crack at your man Potts.'

'Okay.'

'He's a proper cunt, if you get my meaning.'

'Is there more than one way to interpret it?'

Potts was sitting with his feet up on the table, which, along with a couple of chairs, was the only furniture in the room.

Dunnigan switched on the camera, and stated the date and time. 'Mr Potts, how did the five young women I found in your cellar come to be on your property?'

'The Tooth Fairy put them there.'

'The containers that I saw parked outside your bar are being used to traffic people, whom you hold in your cellar until they're ready to be moved. Isn't that right, Mr Potts?'

'I have no comment on that.'

'Your bar has been used to launder monies for the Dorcha Campaign – what exactly is your relationship with Ernest Frobisher?'

And so it went. Within three minutes, Dunnigan knew he was not going to get one shred of information from Alec Potts.

'Oh, well, you tried,' Cole said. 'He's not gonna crack. He'll do whatever time gets handed down and he'll not say one word. He's scared shitless, if you ask me.'

'There were two other men brought in with him,' Dunnigan said. 'One was called Ross Something-or-other.'

'Little beardy guy,' Cole said. 'He's in Room Two. Want to see him? He seems pretty low down the peckin' order, if you ask me. I think he's a bit simple.'

'It can't hurt, can it?'

Ross, whose surname was Tuohy, had his right leg in plaster and was in a wheelchair, the legacy of Father Bill's ministrations.

'All I done was drive trucks,' he said, when Dunnigan enquired about his role in the affair.

'Who's your boss?' Dunnigan asked him.

'I works for Mr Kennedy at the depot, but he works for Mr Frobisher. Mr Frobisher owns the company.'

'Does he?'

'Oh, yeah. He does.'

'Tell me about Mr Frobisher. Is he young or old or middle-aged?'

'He's old. I don't know what age, but he's old, all right.'

'You've seen him?

'One time. He came to the yard in Drogheda to talk to Mr Kennedy.'

'Would you say he's in his sixties?'

'I'd say older.'

'Seventies?'

'Maybe. Maybe even older than that.'

'Interesting. And the depot is in Wicklow?'

'Yeah, in Glendassan. We used to work from Drogheda, but they moved two year ago.'

'Why?'

'I dunno. There was some row over one of the drivers pickin' up hitchers, I think. We ain't suppose to do that. Insurance don't cover it.'

'That wouldn't be a reason to move your operations.'

'That's what I heard. There was a right fuss, and that was when I met Mr Frobisher, y'see, so I remembers it.'

'Tell me about that.'

'My mate, Danny, he was the one who got into trouble. Me 'n' him, we was on the same roster, so we usually worked together. We'd come into the yard at four and we'd fuel up, check the tyre pressure, hitch up the cabs – you know, all the stuff everyone does.'

'You never loaded up the containers?'

'No. We would pick them up empty, and then we'd bring 'em to different places – some in Dublin, one in Wexford, one in Cork – and we'd park up and there was always a team of people there who would load for us. It's what I like most about workin' for Dorcha, see. I'm only small, and mosta the time I finds the loadin' real hard. An' I'm shite with a forklift.'

'So you would arrive, park in a designated location, go away, and when you came back the container would be loaded and you'd move out?'

'Yup.'

'Isn't that irregular?'

'What d'ya mean?'

'It's not the usual way of operating, is it?'

'Sometimes. Depends, really.'

'You were saying about your friend Danny?'

'Oh, yeah. I come in one day, and we'd usually go an' get breakfast after the trucks are ready, but this day, I have mine all done, an' he ain't there yet. So I goes to the office to ask Mr Kennedy if he knows where he is, an' I knocks and goes in, 'cause that's what we always did, only when I go in Mr Kennedy ain't alone – there's this old man in the fanciest suit I ever seen sittin' in Mr Kennedy's chair, and Mr Kennedy is standin' where we usually stood, an' he don't look too happy. And there's this other guy, in a cream-coloured suit, an' he's standin' back, by the wall, and I don't like the look of him at all. He had a kind of a mean look to him.'

'Yes. I think I know who you're talking about.'

'Well, I says I'm sorry, that I didn't mean to interrupt no meetin', but Mr Frobisher, he was real friendly, like. "Who is this fine gentleman?" he asked Mr Kennedy, and Mr Kennedy, he says, "This is Ross Tuohy, one of my best drivers" – that's what he said! An' he gets up, all slow, like, 'cause he's so old, but he come around the desk an' he shook my hand. He had a kind of a cane with a glass top on it that he used to help him walk. I remember that.'

'Did he say anything else?'

'He just told Mr Kennedy to remember their conversation, then him and the other man left. I thought he seemed real nice, but Mr Kennedy, he was in a state. He had to have a sit-down and I went and got him some tea.'

'Why was he upset?'

'He said that Danny had been caught with people on board his truck what shouldn't have been there.'

'Which you took to mean hitchers,' Dunnigan said.

'You think I was wrong?'

'It doesn't matter. What else did Mr Kennedy say?'

'He said that Danny wouldn't be coming to work for us any more, and that we would all have to be very careful to do things by the book, because if anyone else got nicked, we'd all be in the shit. He said Mr Frobisher had come to make sure we all understood that.'

'I see.'

'I told him Mr Frobisher seemed like a nice old fella, and he laughed – a real sick-soundin' laugh it was, like he didn't really think it was funny, you know? He said Mr Frobisher was an evil old bastard – pardon me, but that's what he said – and that he was just glad to see the back of him.'

'Did he say why he had such an opinion of the old gentleman?'

'He told me a story, but it wasn't a very nice one.'

'I love stories.'

'You won't like this one.'

'Try me.'

'Okay. If you really want. He told me that, when he started out workin' for Dorcha, he was in charge of runnin' a yard they had in Belfast. He said that his daddy had worked for Dorcha as well, and he pulled in a favour to get Mr Kennedy a job when he left school. Well, he worked hard, and on the day of his twenty-first birthday, he got promoted and was made manager. He told me he was real good at havin' all the papers in order and keepin' his mouth shut, an' that was what was needed.'

'In many jobs, I would imagine,' Dunnigan said.

'There was a little dog that used to hang around the yard – no one knew who owned it, but some of the lads used to feed it scraps and it just stayed. Mr Kennedy said they put some old blankets down in one of the sheds, and it would sleep there at night. Do you like dogs, Mr Dunnigan?'

'I don't really have an opinion on them.'

'I like 'em. I don't remember what he said they named it, but all the fellas workin' in the yard loved havin' this little dog around. They'd play Fetch with it when they were waitin' for a load, and they taught it tricks an' stuff. It was like a pet to them.'

'Lovely,' Dunnigan said.

'Yeah. Well, one afternoon this big fucker of a car pulls up, and Mr Frobisher gets out. He didn't have the Yellow Man with him then, but he had another guy just like him. They had come to pick up some files Mr Kennedy was to have ready, and when they got them, Mr Frobisher asked for a look around the yard, to see how things were runnin'. Well, Mr Kennedy di'n't mind that, none, 'cause he had everything just spot on. So they finish the tour, and they're all happy, and Mr Frobisher starts to tell Mr Kennedy about his new car. It's a Rolls-Royce, he says, brought over from England special. Only five others in Ireland, he says. Mr Kennedy told him it was the beautifullest car he'd ever seen. They came around this pile of pallets, and there was the car, all shiny and new, parked outside the office, and there, with his leg cocked, pissin' all over one of the front tyres, was the little dog.'

'Oh dear,' Dunnigan said.

'Mr Kennedy said Mr Frobisher done blew a gasket. He started shoutin' and screamin' and yellin' for all the world like the dog had pissed on him. He hit Mr Kennedy right in the face, grabbed him by the shirt and shook him, and he yelled at the man who was with him to get that dog. Well, while all this was goin' on the mutt had taken off and was hidin' under the blankets in his shed, but Mr Kennedy he showed the bad man where it was, and he went in and got the dog.'

'What happened?'

'Mr Frobisher told Mr Kennedy to get some petrol for him. They mostly used diesel in the yard, but they had a petrol pump as well, for some of the company cars. The poor dog was tied to one of the gate posts by a bit of rope, and Mr Frobisher, he poured the petrol all over him, and then he set him on fire. Mr Kennedy said the poor thing squealed like a small baby for ages before it fell down and died. He told me Mr Frobisher laughed and laughed. That don't seem right to me.'

'No, it doesn't.'

'What's gonna happen to me, Mr Dunnigan?'

'That's not for me to decide.'

'Did I do somethin' wrong?'

'Someone did, Ross,' Dunnigan said. 'And I think I'm starting to get a sense of who it was.'

5

FROBISHER'S IRISH ADDRESS WAS LISTED AS Moonshine Meadows, and was a large, walled compound in the Dublin Mountains. According to the Ordnance Survey, it covered close to twenty acres, and the satellite image showed a large L-shaped house right at its centre.

The next morning Dunnigan parked outside it at seven thirty, in full view of the gate.

He was working on the assumption that the threats Andrews had made were designed to scare him off, and that the fact he worked for the Sex Crimes Unit, and was therefore capable of making life very difficult for them, would preclude them from making good their promises. He had asked Tormey to have a patrol car keep a regular eye on Gina's house, and he had left a message with Miley, who was not returning his calls, to be careful. He was worried about his friend.

It was his promise to him and, by extension, Harry, that prevented him from just giving up this whole business, as his word was something that meant a great deal to him. There was also the fact that none of them had seen Miley since his outburst. He knew his friend felt let down by him, and that there was some justification for that.

Dunnigan did not think of Miley as disabled – he never really had, after he'd got over his first impressions. But he was guilty of buying into the front Miley presented: the happy, ebullient, easy-going façade that they all knew was simply a device to hide the pain, the grief and the cripplingly low self-esteem Miley lived with.

No one had discussed their plans for Harry with Miley because everyone thought that, whatever they did, Miley would just bounce back with a grin and a smart comment, and everything would be fine.

Dunnigan felt like a heel for the way he had treated his friend, and he knew Father Bill and Diane did, too. He was determined to find Harry's parents as a way, he hoped, to make up for his lack of sensitivity.

That caused him to stop – *his lack of sensitivity*! When had he started caring about being sensitive? And when had he given a damn about the feelings of anyone other than Gina? He wondered if this was a step forward for him or a step back.

The road on which he was parked was lined with trees on both sides, the wall of the compound made of dark wood that had been stained even darker. Every now and then he heard a screeching, rattling call. He knew it was a jay, a member of the crow family. He had started learning about birds over the past few weeks – when this business with Dorcha was done, he planned to take Diane birdwatching at the Comeraghs, in Waterford. He had read online that a mating pair of osprey, a large bird of prey, had been sighted there. He thought Diane might like to see them.

An hour passed. He had brought a flask of tea and a ham sandwich. His appetite had been returning somewhat of late, and he thought he had better bring something, in case he got a bit peckish. He poured himself some tea. He wasn't hungry yet, but he liked tea.

Another hour passed by. The big metal gates opened and a gold-coloured Peugot 405 came out and drove past him. He did not recognise the driver, but took down the registration number.

His phone rang.

'Davey, it's Father Bill.'

'Hello.'

'Guess where I am.'

'I hate guessing games, Father.'

'I am at Hall's Wharf.'

'Why would I care about that?'

'You've never heard of it?'

'Should I have?'

'No. That's the point. It hasn't been used for shipping of any kind since 1918.'

'Why are you at an abandoned wharf, then?'

'Do you remember that I asked Philly to tail Andrews?'

'I do.'

'He followed him back here. It's nice and secluded, in an inlet that was once part of the frontage in Ringsend, but when they reclaimed a chunk of the land around the Dodder they rerouted the channel, so you have to go out of your way to come here now.'

'Why did Andrews go there?'

'Because the wharf isn't abandoned any more. There's a great big bloody ship here now, and trucks have been coming and going all morning.'

'Dorcha trucks?'

'Well, I can't tell, but I'm just about to follow one back to base – and I think we can both guess where it will go.'

'Glendassan,' Dunnigan said.

'I might be wrong, but I don't think so.'

'Keep me posted.'

'I will to be sure. Any word on Miley?'

'No. I'm concerned about him.'

'Me too, but we have to give him some space. He's had a lot of change in a very short time. He'll come back when he's ready, and when he does, we'll make a true apology and he'll forgive us.'

'Why are you so sure he will?'

'Because he got a beautiful soul, does Miley Timoney.'

Dunnigan smiled to himself. 'He does. You're right about that.'

'Okay – there's my mark. I'll call when I have some news.' And he hung up.

Davey stayed at his post for the rest of the day, but no other cars came or went. He headed for home at seven thirty, wondering if he had wasted his time.

6

DUNNIGAN AND DIANE WENT TO DINNER AT A place called Avenue. Diane had been dying to go there, because it was run by someone who had been on television. Dunnigan was hardly a gourmet, but he liked the fact that she was excited about the prospect of going, so he made the booking.

They were halfway through their starter when Diane asked, 'What are you and Father Bill up to?'

'We're still looking for Harry's parents.'

'That's it?'

'Yes.'

'And that involves what, exactly?'

'You know – asking around about them. Going to places they might have gone. Following leads.'

'And those guys who beat you up before – there's no risk of anything like that happening again, is there?'

'Why do you ask?'

She put down her knife and fork. 'I ask you about it, and you dodge the question, or give me the kind of vague bullshit like you just spouted. I ask Father Bill and he does something similar, only he's better at lying than you are so he's more convincing. Will you please tell me what's going on?'

'Why?'

'Number one, because you are my man-friend, or whatever

we're calling it, and I care and worry about you. Number two, I am one tough bitch, a decorated former Ranger. Which means I can kick most people's arses, so I might actually be a help.'

'I hadn't thought about it like that.'

'Most people don't.'

'All right, then. I'll tell you.'

And he did.

She listened carefully, occasionally asking questions to clarify certain points. When he had finished, she sat back, watching him thoughtfully. 'This is quite a mess.'

'I know.'

'I think you're dealing with some very dangerous people.'

'I believe so.'

'I want to help. I'm *able* to help.'

'Are you sure?'

'I'm positive. You need a plan of attack, and I think I'm just the person to help you formulate one.'

A waiter came and began to clear away their plates. When he had gone, she started to talk about tactics, and contingencies, and consolidating their position, and Dunnigan wished he had asked for her help weeks ago.

7

HE LOOKED AT THE PHOTOGRAPH OF BETH AND HIM taken on the day she vanished. There she was, frozen in time as a smiling four-year-old. She would be twenty-three, he thought, if she were still with us today.

He barely needed to look at the picture any more – he knew the details of it by heart: her hair was tied back in a ponytail, and she had clips with plastic snowmen holding some unruly strands in place. She was wearing a pink scarf and a puffy blue anorak to keep her warm, and she had blue and pink woollen mittens on her hands. On her feet she wore pink and white trainers with lights around the trim of the soles that had flashed when she walked, the effect triggered by the impact of the shoe on the pavement.

Beth had loved those shoes!

Dunnigan realised he no longer knew the version of himself he saw in the photo. There was a time when he had wished to be that person again, had mourned the man he might have been had things gone differently, had the trajectory he was on all those years ago been permitted to continue uninterrupted. Now he knew he could never be that person again, and did not want to be. He traced the smile on his niece's face with his finger.

'She was the person I loved the most,' he said to the poster of the Doctor. 'I would have given my life for hers without hesitation or regret.'

Some beads of rain hit the windowpane. A summer storm was gathering. Dunnigan put the photo on his mantelpiece above the fireplace he never used. 'Time to go to work,' he said to the emptiness.

He paused and looked at the photo of Beth. 'I'll be seeing you later,' he said, kissed the tips of his fingers and placed the kiss on the glass pane over her forehead.

Then he left the flat to start his war.

PART NINE

Taking Care of Business

1

'SO WHAT DID YOU DO IN THE RANGERS?' Dunnigan asked Diane.

They were parked a hundred yards up the road from Moonshine Meadows in the early evening. A slow, gentle rain was falling, and it made the mountain road dream-like, as if all that mattered was the world inside the car. Dunnigan was sipping some tea from his Thermos; Diane had a large cappuccino in a cardboard cup she had bought at a petrol station on the drive over.

'I was a field nurse and the battalion counsellor. I applied to be in the ranks, but I didn't make the grade – the selection process is unbelievably hard. I was good enough to be asked to stay on as support staff, though, which is still pretty damn good.'

'Where did you serve?'

'With the Rangers? Chad, mostly. We did some work in Ireland, too. In the North.'

'What kind of work?'

'I could tell you, but I'd have to kill you.'

'Did you like being in the army?'

'I loved it.'

'Do you miss it?'

She looked at him and smiled. 'Sometimes. Not today, though.'

At nine they heard the sound of the metal gates grinding open. A red coupé came out and turned onto the road.

'Here we go,' Diane said, and got out, holding up her hand to stop the sports car as it approached. 'Sorry, sir, I won't keep you a moment,' she said, as the window rolled down.

'What's the problem?' The driver was a skinny man with a thin moustache.

'You've just been to the Frobisher place?' Diane asked.

'Yeah.'

'We're passing out these, today,' Diane said handing the man a sheet of paper with the words in large bold print: *In case you didn't know, Ernest Frobisher is a pimp and a people trafficker and he will be going out of business very soon.*

'*What the fuck?*' the man spluttered, balling up the page and throwing it at her – she caught it neatly in her left hand.

'Have a nice day, now! And feel free to tell Mr Frobisher we were asking after him, okay?'

'Get outta me way,' the man said, and, gunning the engine, sped away.

The following day, they gave out ten more of the sheets. That evening, Diane scaled the wall of the estate and managed to get into one of the tall trees that grew right beside it. Using its branches, she was able to clamber onto another tree and made her way into the estate. After ten minutes' scrambling, she was overlooking a well-tended lawn that spread out in front of the house. She took a bag from her back, zipped it open, and shimmied out as far as she dared on a broad limb. She took parcel wrapped in oiled cloth from the bag, and carefully dropped it into a bush that grew beside the door to the house. Satisfied her bundle was completely obscured from sight, she helicoptered the bag around her head, spilling the five hundred A5-sized pieces of paper inside it onto the breeze, which dispersed them across the garden. Many stuck to the windows of the sprawling, L-shaped house.

These pages were all emblazoned with the lines: *This house was built with dirty money. We're going to blow it down.*

Then she made her way gingerly back along the branch.

She had been in the car for five minutes when the gates ground open, and Andrews walked slowly out into the road. He simply stood, his hands in the pockets of his beige suit, looking at them. Diane waved and grinned. 'That's what I wanted. We've smoked the Beta dog out. And it's enough for today. Let's go.'

Dunnigan turned the car slowly and drove away at a dignified speed. He could see Andrews in his rear-view mirror until they turned a bend in the road.

At five next morning, Diane used a spray can to paint *Pimps and Pushers live here – but not for long!* on the big black gates of the house.

'You have very nice handwriting,' Dunnigan said, as he watched her.

'Why, thank you, Davey.'

'The curve on your *r* is particularly pleasing.'

'I didn't know you had a letter fetish.'

'Neither did I!'

The gates opened at eight and a large man in a blue and red tracksuit got out of a green Nissan and looked at the graffiti. It seemed to take him a long time to work out what the message was, as the gates were now open and it was divided in two.

'Jesus Christ, they send out one that can't read!' Diane said, as they watched from the BMW.

'He'll work it out,' Dunnigan said.

The man walked first one way, then another, leaning his head to one side as if that might help. Then, as if the idea had just occurred to him, he got in and moved the car forward a bit. The gates' motion sensor activated and they closed.

'Hallelujah!' Diane said, clapping.

The man did an almost comic double-take when he finally read the full message, took out his phone and called someone. Then he got into the Nissan and sped away.

At ten, a white van with *Mick the Painter* written on the side, next to a cartoon image of a man in overalls holding a roller, pulled up. He must have called the house from inside the van because the gates opened, and out he got, looking uncannily like the image on his vehicle.

'Okay, this is the really risky one,' Diane said. 'You sure you're up for it?'

'No,' Dunnigan said. 'But I'm going to do it anyway.'

'Let's go.'

Mick had parked at an angle to the gate, and was taking out tins, brushes and trays to begin his work when Dunnigan's BMW shot past him and up the drive. Diane rolled down the passenger side window, a wine bottle in her hand, a piece of old dishcloth shoved into the top. As they reached the end of the drive and hit the open space in front of the house, she lit the rag and tossed the bottle indiscriminately at the building.

'Now get us the hell out of here!' she shouted at Dunnigan, who twisted the wheel and executed a perfect U-turn.

He saw the flames erupt in the rear-view mirror, and then they were screeching back down the avenue.

'Little trick I learned from some nice chaps we had to deal with in Chad,' Diane said. 'I've doctored the solution, so it'll burn out in a second and won't harm the place at all, but I want them to know we could.'

'I think they've got that message,' Dunnigan said, as they shot out of the gate and made their escape.

2

THEY MET FATHER BILL FOR DINNER AT THE Project. The dining hall was bustling, as it always was, and Dunnigan realised, for perhaps the first time, that he liked having all these people around him. He felt comfortable, as if he belonged. It was an odd feeling, but a good one.

'Well, you've been making a proper nuisance of yourselves.' Father Bill laughed, when he heard of their exploits over the past few days. 'Well done! I'd doff my hat to you if I had one!'

'Thank you very much!' Diane said, grinning happily.

'How is it progressing at your end?' Dunnigan asked.

'The yard at Glendassan seems to be only one base of operations for the trucks,' Father Bill said. 'You told me that Dorcha owned shares in the mine, so I expect they simply reopened the yards and some of the old service roads when things got too hot for them elsewhere. But I followed a truck to an industrial estate in Dundalk, and another to a small haulage company in Kildare.'

'They're keeping their interests spread out – harder to detect,' Dunnigan said.

'Undoubtedly. But all their exports seem to go through Hall's Wharf,' Father Bill said. 'Whatever they're shipping out, it seems to be too dangerous to go by air. They're not going to risk the heightened security.'

'Have you seen anything actually being loaded onto the ships?'

'No. The trucks go on board with their containers, then come off an hour or so later. But we can all guess what the cargo is.'

'People,' Diane and Dunnigan said in unison.

'I have a plan,' Father Bill said. 'But it's highly dangerous, completely illegal and involves some unsavoury characters.'

'Sounds perfect,' Diane said.

'I don't want either of you involved,' Father Bill said. 'You've shaken things up and I have no doubt Frobisher and his crew are running scared. That's what I want – they'll be jumpy and on edge, and they're going to think the house is our target. They won't expect me to hit the dock.'

'We're already involved,' Dunnigan said. 'You can't ask us to step aside now!'

'I can and I am,' Father Bill said. 'If you really want to help, take a last run at the house tomorrow night. Keep them occupied. Leave the rest to me and my friends.'

'I thought we were your friends,' Diane said, genuinely hurt.

'You are, Diane,' Father Bill said. 'But I have lots of different sorts of friends, and some I don't think you'd like.'

3

DUNNIGAN WENT OVER TO MILEY'S FLAT AFTER they had finished their meal with Father Bill. Both he and Diane had tried to get the priest to change his mind about their role in whatever he was planning, but he was immovable.

Dunnigan knew Father Bill had a way of compartmentalising his life, and that he, Diane and Miley fitted into one area and were not welcome in others. It was a part of the priest's makeup he understood but he was not wholly comfortable with it. It made him realise he didn't really know the man at all.

Repeated presses of the buzzer did not elicit a response from Miley, so Dunnigan did something he would never have contemplated six months before, and pressed all the buzzers at once – there were five apartments besides Miley's in the complex, and he figured someone must be at home. In a second he heard a buzzing, and the lock on the front door released. He was in.

Knocking on Miley's front door did not bring him any joy, either.

He went to the warehouse, but Harry's room was empty, not just of the boy but of any of his stuff. It looked as if Harry had moved on, and now Dunnigan was worried. Standing in the dusty, cold room, he took out his phone and rang Miley's number.

He thought it would not be answered, but after five rings he heard a click, and then, to his relief, his friend's familiar tones.

'What do you want, Davey?'

'How are you, Miley? I've been trying to get hold of you for ages.'

'I know. I've been screening my calls. I'm very busy. I don't have time for people who aren't honest with me.'

'I'm really sorry about what happened, Miley. So are Bill and Diane. We want to see you so we can make amends – show you just how sorry we really are.'

'I don't believe you, Davey.'

'Have I ever lied to you?'

'Yes. Lots of times.'

'I … I didn't lie. I just didn't tell you things, and not because I didn't want you to know – I just didn't think.'

'It's called lying by omission. It's still a lie. *I'm not stupid, Davey!* Stop treating me like I'm stupid! I thought you were better than other people. But you're not.'

'I'm in the warehouse, Miley. I think Harry's gone.'

'He has. We've both gone.'

Dunnigan slapped his forehead. He should have seen this coming. He'd been so wrapped up in the Dorcha case and his battle with the mysterious Frobisher that he'd taken his eyes off the ball with Miley and Harry. 'Where are you?'

'None of your business.'

'They're going to look for you, Miley. They'll find you, and you'll be in trouble I won't be able to get you out of.'

'They won't look. Who's gonna care 'bout a mongoloid man and some homeless kid? No one cares 'bout us, and that's fine. We care 'bout each other. I've got him and he's got me and that's all we need from now on.'

'Please, Miley. Let me come and get you.'

'Bye, Davey. I won't be seein' you again. I'm not comin' back, not ever. Say bye to Father Bill and Diane for me.'

And then he hung up. Dunnigan stood in the empty room in the derelict building and wondered how it had all gone so badly wrong so quickly, and how he had not seen it until it was far too late.

4

THE FOLLOWING EVENING DUNNIGAN AND DIANE drove to Moonlight Meadows separately. Dunnigan parked his beloved BMW up a laneway five kilometres from the compound, and met Diane on the road. She was piloting a 1992 Volvo 740 station wagon, and he got in beside her.

'You're sure you don't mind sacrificing your car?'

'I haven't driven this in years – I gave it to my uncle, because he said he wanted to use it around the farm but, sure, it ended up sitting in a shed. No one's going to miss it.'

'All right, then.'

'It's what we need tonight. These old Volvos are basically tanks – it'll take a missile to dent it, so we're going in as protected as we can be outside of a Hummer.'

'Comforting.'

The Volvo was longer than Dunnigan's BMW by about a metre, and when they reached the estate, Diane parked right across the gateway, making it impossible for anyone to get either in or out. 'Now we wait,' she said, and pushed her seat back, putting her hands behind her head.

They did. Nothing happened. No one came, no one went.

An hour passed.

'Miley's gone,' Dunnigan said.

'How do you mean "gone"?'

'He's taken Harry and run away.'

'He's not Tom Sawyer, Davey. He's an adult. Adults don't run away. He's moved.'

'He's taken the boy, though. Tusla and the social workers are going to be looking for him.'

'He's smart enough to know that himself,' Diane said. 'He'll work it out. Give him some time. He's entitled to his tantrum, in my humble opinion.'

'I just hope the tantrum doesn't end up hurting him even worse than we did,' Dunnigan observed. 'Hold on, someone's coming.'

The gates began to swing open, the lights of a vehicle showing behind them. As this happened, an olive-green Range Rover approached them from the road, stopping a yard shy of them.

'And it's on,' Diane said.

The gate finished swinging open, a blue Land Rover drove forward, and Andrews got out. This evening, he was wearing pale chinos and a light brown shirt. He approached the Volvo, and made a motion for the window to be rolled down. Dunnigan did so, by about an inch.

'This ends tonight, Mr Dunnigan,' he said.

'I would appreciate that,' Dunnigan said. 'Tell me where the Gatelys are, and we'll be on our way.'

Andrews seemed a bit befuddled. 'This is still about them?'

'It was always about the people you took,' Dunnigan said. 'I promised my friend I would find them, and I intend to do so. I have a list in my pocket of five others. Tell me where they are, and we'll go.'

'You are a very stupid man, Mr Dunnigan.'

'I've been told that before.'

'I am giving you one final chance to withdraw. I will not be held responsible for what happens after that.'

'Me either, Blondie!' Diane shouted.

'Very well,' Andrews said and stepped away, nodding at the drivers.

With a roar of engines, both jeeps rammed the Volvo simultaneously.

Dunnigan and Diane had their seatbelts on, and the car held remarkably well. They were buffeted around a bit, but the first strike proved mostly ineffective.

'Is this car insured?' Dunnigan asked.

'Third party,' Diane said ruefully.

The jeeps were reversing, the one on Dunnigan's side going a fair distance back up the driveway.

'Here we go again!' Diane said, holding on to the dashboard.

It was much worse this time: the driver's side door buckled in, shoving Diane half off her seat and almost on top of Dunnigan.

'Oh, shit!' she said, and Dunnigan looked to where she was gazing. Andrews had produced a sledgehammer from somewhere and, without pause, he swung it straight into the windscreen, causing it to shatter in a thousand spidery lines.

'I think we're in trouble,' Diane said, and the two Rovers struck a third time.

Dunnigan's door caved in, crushing him and Diane against one another, the car now like an accordion with all the air sucked out of it. The head of the sledgehammer appeared through the windscreen, and the entire glass pane was pulled out, showering the pair with shards.

'Can you reach my pocket?' Diane asked, her voice tiny due to the constricted space they were sandwiched into.

'No.'

'Damn.'

'Why?'

'I have Father Bill's number on speed-dial on my phone. Doesn't matter.'

They heard a thump, and suddenly Andrews was peering in at them – he had obviously climbed on to the Volvo's mangled bonnet. 'I can tell you that there is petrol leaking from the fuel tank,' he said. 'And one of my men is a committed smoker.'

Suddenly he had a knife in his hand. 'Unfortunately, Mr Frobisher would like to meet you.'

He cut through Diane's seatbelt, and, apparently without effort, hauled her from the wreckage.

5

ANDREWS TOOK DIANE'S PHONE (DUNNIGAN HAD left his in the BMW), then they were marched up the driveway and through a side door into the house.

It was deathly quiet and smelled like a hospital – Dunnigan noticed his feet whispering over deep pile carpets. Paintings in many different styles adorned the walls.

'In there,' Andrews said, and they went through double doors into what Dunnigan at first took to be an aircraft hangar, so wide was it, the ceiling seemingly three or four floors above them. It was dimly lit, except for an area in the centre, which was illuminated by huge overhead lamps, machines buzzing and hissing on all sides. At the centre of all this was a bed, and in the bed was what had once been a man.

'They are here, sir,' Andrews said.

'Bring them,' a harsh, guttural voice responded.

Dunnigan and Diane were pushed forwards.

Lying before them was the oldest person David Dunnigan had ever seen. The head seemed to be simply skin stretched over bone, all hair and lashes had long since vanished, and the lips had receded, leaving only a gash and cracked, yellowed teeth. A dressing had been applied to the right cheek, but something dark had already soaked into it. There was a smell of human waste and decay, and tubes pumped oxygen and antibiotics into withered veins, while a heart monitor beeped, sounding each pump that kept the creature alive.

Its eyes were terrifying – bloodshot pools of blue hatred and wicked intelligence gazed out of the mummified visage.

It spoke. 'I am Ernest Frobisher,' it said. 'And I want you to give me one good reason why I should not have you gutted like fish.'

'People know we're here,' Dunnigan said, trying to keep his voice from trembling. 'If I don't report in before ten tonight, they will come looking for me.'

'Fool,' Frobisher wheezed. 'I own several high-ranking members of your police force, and I confirmed days ago that you were not following any orders, or participating in any official investigation. You are here of your own volition, and no one, Mr Dunnigan, is looking for you or awaiting your call.'

'Who said he was talking about the police?' Diane said.

'Oh, you mean your friend the warrior priest? The one who has been watching my ships this past week? He wouldn't get through the door.'

'You don't know him.'

'Andrews put him on his arse before – he can do it again.'

'What's wrong with you?' Dunnigan asked, stalling for more time.

'Old age and cancer,' Frobisher said. 'In equal quantities.'

'Where are the Gatelys? What have you done with the Grants?'

'I don't know,' Frobisher said. 'And I don't care.'

'But you can find out – you must have records,' Dunnigan pressed on. He didn't know if he and Diane would get out of that room alive, but he was determined to come as close to the truth as he could before it all went up. He might not have the chance again.

'What the hell does it matter to you?' Frobisher hissed. 'You bleeding hearts make me sick. So what if a few drug-riddled homeless sacks of shit end up dying in some Czech coal mine or a Japanazi whore-house? Who gives a damn? At least they gave their lives to provide some sort of meaningful service instead of cluttering up the streets. I give them a chance to be something. You should be thanking me.'

'Are you telling me they're dead?'

'I told you I don't know! Don't you love your country? Don't you want to see it returned to its rightful place as one of the wealthiest nations in Europe? Wouldn't you wish to have our streets clean and healthy and free of vermin?'

'I thought this was all about politics,' Dunnigan said. 'It sounds more about money than idealism.'

'I am an idealist,' the old man rasped. 'Those leeches dragged this country to the edge of collapse. I've helped to bring it back.'

'By exploiting the weakest members of our society?' Diane said.

'We help them! We offer them work and a roof over their heads – those women you took from the pub were destined for a hotel in Thailand!'

'You were sending them to be prostitutes,' Diane said.

'For which they would have been paid. Better than rotting on the streets.'

'And how much were you paid for them?'

'I am following a long-established tradition. Two hundred years ago my family shipped the dregs of our cities and towns to Van Diemen's Land. They were paid a farthing a head, and no one batted an eyelid or said it was cruel or wrong! The nation of Australia sprang from it. Forced to do some work, given a purpose, all those beggars and thieves and wastrels founded a new country, tamed a savage landscape. Shouldn't we offer today's equivalent the same opportunities?'

'Shouldn't we ask them first?'

'You do not understand, and I do not have the time or the energy to explain it to you,' Frobisher said. 'Remember the coffin ships? My great-grandfather spoke of the lumpen poor lined up for miles to board those boats to new frontiers. They wanted out because they were afraid to stay. My family instigated that, and I am doing so again. I have brought back the coffin ships, and with them I will bring forth a new Ireland. And in so doing I have made myself rich.'

'So your family were responsible for the Famine?' Diane asked. 'I think you need to increase whatever meds you're on.'

'Put a knife in her eye,' Frobisher said, a horrifying leer taking over what was left of his face.

Andrews stepped forward and grabbed her, the blade he had used to cut them free of the car in his hand. Dunnigan, a strange coldness settling over him, flung himself at the man, but another of the thugs got in his way.

'Bring her over here so I can see,' Frobisher rasped. 'And do it slowly.'

Diane thrashed and cursed, but Andrews lifted her physically and carried her to the bed.

'Now do it,' Frobisher hissed.

Dunnigan heard someone screaming, and realised it was him. He wrenched himself free of the man who held him, but as he was about to charge at Andrews, the door to the room burst open.

'The Wharf has been hit!'

'Explain,' Andrews barked at the new arrival. He still had a tight hold of Diane.

'Rogers's crew. The ship is on fire and there's been shooting.'

'Go and fix it,' Frobisher said. 'Liam, take these two out the back and put them out of my misery.'

Andrews strode out, disappearing into the property, and the man who had come in with the news led Dunnigan and Diane back towards the garden. As they reached the door, Diane spun and hit him in the throat with the heel of her hand. Dunnigan heard him gurgle and then he was on the ground, clutching at his windpipe.

'Run and don't look back,' Diane said urgently.

Dunnigan did as he was told. He heard what he took to be gunshots behind them, but then he was on the driveway, and he saw with a wave of relief that the ruined Volvo was preventing the gates from closing. He then realised that the shots were coming from Diane, who had somehow got hold of a handgun. She fired twice in the direction of the gate, causing two men who were standing there to run for cover – and then they were through, sprinting in the direction of the lane where Dunnigan had parked the BMW.

6

'WHERE DID YOU GET THE GUN?' DUNNIGAN asked as they drove helter-skelter through the night.

'I dropped it into a shrub by the door when I threw the papers on the lawn a few days back. I thought it might come in useful.'

'You were right.'

'Where are we going?'

'Hall's Wharf. If there's any record of where they've been sending people, it'll be there. I want to try and salvage it before Father Bill burns the place to the ground.'

'He wouldn't, would he?'

'I don't know any more.'

They hit the outskirts of Dublin City fifteen minutes later. Dunnigan dialled Father Bill's number. It rang out. 'I hope we're not too late,' he said.

As they approached Ringsend, coming in through Ballsbridge, they could both see smoke on the horizon.

'Shit,' Diane said.

Father Bill Creedon

Tim Pat Rogers was taller than Father Bill by a head, and he walked with the air of a man who believed he owned the very ground he traversed. The priest had known him since they were boys growing up on the streets of the inner city, and even though life had led them in different directions, they retained a degree of respect for one another.

Joining the street gangs had never been an option for Father Bill – his dad would have tanned his hide if he'd thought for a second his son was involved in crime. But, as most of his peers were members of the various crews, it would have been impossible for him not to associate with them at all – his childhood would have been very lonely indeed – so he had become friends with Rogers and his associates through boxing or football or simply hanging around the local area.

As a priest in the inner city, Father Bill found keeping in touch with these men had been useful from time to time, so he had maintained the relationships.

Rogers ran one of the more successful – and tenacious – gangs in Dublin. A journalist in one of the less intellectual red-top tabloid newspapers had once dubbed him the Janitor because he had a habit of taking out the trash – anyone who got in his way – and the scenes of these operations were always so immaculately clean that nothing could ever be traced back to him.

Father Bill met him in Daddy Joe's, the club he ran on the North Wall.

'It's good to see you, Father,' Rogers said, embracing the priest.

'And you, Tim Pat.'

'I hear you were questioned over that dirty priest we neutralised.'

'An inconvenience. They chose not to pursue it.'

'Good. Can I get you a drink?'

'A cup of tea would be welcome.'

'Will I put a wee drop in to liven it up?'

'That would be nice.'

They reminisced about old times, then Father Bill cut to the chase. 'I need your help again, old friend.'

'Not another priest interfering with kiddies?'

'No. This one will, I think, benefit us both.'

'What do you need?'

'I need an army.'

'I think I can loan you one of those.'

7

THEY GOT TO THE WHARF BEFORE THE POLICE and the fire brigade. The ship that was anchored at the old dock was ablaze, clouds of black smoke billowing into the night sky. There were vehicles of all kinds parked about the waterfront – one of those was on fire too.

Dunnigan and Diane jumped from the BMW. A crowd of people had gathered in a cluster to their left, and they made for it. As they got closer, Dunnigan could see that many were holding semi-automatic weapons. 'Where's Father Bill?'

One of the men looked him up and down. 'What's it to you?' He spoke in a dense inner-city accent.

'He told me to meet him here.'

'He's over there, talking to the yellow lad.'

Dunnigan and Diane pushed their way through the crowd, who dispersed to allow them through.

They heard Father Bill before they saw him: he was singing 'Don't Let It Bring You Down' gently, almost like a lullaby. The priest was squatting on his haunches, singing quietly to Andrews, the Yellow Man, who was lying against a metal bollard, a gunshot wound in his chest. The knife was lying on the ground just out of his reach. He looked up at Dunnigan and Diane as they arrived – this he did by moving his eyes only, as if any other motion would hurt too much.

'We meet again,' he said, and coughed, causing blood to run from the corners of his mouth.

'What happened here?' Dunnigan asked.

'I've shut down Dorcha's operations,' Father Bill said. 'There were fifty people on that ship, about half of whom had been taken from the streets.'

'Where are they?' Diane asked.

'In one of the buildings over there. Perhaps, Davey, you might call your associates, and we can organise some help for them.'

'And him?' Dunnigan said, indicating Andrews.

'He and I were settling our differences, and he pulled a knife on me,' Father Bill said. 'The people I came here with didn't think that was very fair, so one of them shot him.'

'That will teach me to bring a knife to a gunfight,' Andrews croaked, his laughter turning into a racking cough, spraying blood down his front. Father Bill gave him a handkerchief.

The wound in his chest was bleeding profusely. Dunnigan could smell the coppery stench of it. 'Where do you keep your records?' he asked.

'Everything is in the office in the main building,' Andrews said, his voice thickening now – he was drowning in his own blood. 'And there will be documents on the ship.'

Dunnigan cast a look at Father Bill, who nodded. 'Don't worry – we have them.'

'I'm going to check,' Dunnigan said. He left Father Bill and Diane with the dying man.

One of the men with guns – he did not want to know who they were or where they had come from – helped him force the door of the building that seemed to be used for administration. There were a lot of mostly empty filing cabinets, a drawer full of receipts, and a single laptop computer. He took it.

Sirens were sounding on the breeze as he came back out.

'Time for us to go,' Father Bill said.

Andrews's head was slumped on his chest – he would never be a threat again.

'Take this,' Dunnigan said, handing Father Bill the computer. 'You'll deal with the boys in blue?'

'Yes.'

'You'll get promoted for this.' The priest grinned.

'I'll get locked up,' Dunnigan responded, only half joking.

8

IT WAS JUST LIKE WHEN THEY HAD QUESTIONED him after Beth's disappearance, except this time Tormey insisted on sitting in with him, and no one raised so much as a finger in his direction. He was as honest as he could be, telling them about Harry and Miley and the promise he had made, and how a series of breaks in his research had led him to Moonlight Meadows, and when he called there that evening, to ask Mr Frobisher some questions, he had been unlawfully detained and threatened by some of the old man's staff. During the course of their conversation, though, one of them had dropped the name of the Wharf, and he had managed to extricate himself and gone straight there. Unfortunately, the massacre had already happened, so he had called it in.

'We found fifty people in a shed on that dock,' Dockrell, the detective from Internal Affairs, said. 'Sitting there all in a nice row, with the door unlocked. They claim they don't know how they got there, or who took them off that ship before it went up. The place was clean as a whistle – no shells, no casings, no fingerprints or indentations – all we have are a lot of dead bodies, not a single one of whose owners is on the system.'

'It's very curious,' Dunnigan said.

'I'll say it is.'

'Davey has had a very busy night, Ian,' Tormey said. 'Don't

you think it's time we let him go home? I mean, if he'd been involved in this in any criminal capacity, why would he have still been there when we arrived?'

'Frank, I don't think even he knows what's going on in his head half the time,' Dockrell said, but he let Dunnigan go.

'What aren't you telling me?' Tormey said, as they walked to the car park.

'Nothing yet,' Dunnigan said. 'When I do have something, I'll tell you.'

'I don't know why, but I'm going to pretend I believe you,' Tormey said. 'Now, if you don't mind, I'm going to go and arrest Ernest Frobisher.'

'Bring some of the Armed Response boys with you,' Dunnigan said.

Then he went home and slept for fourteen hours.

9

WHEN HE WOKE HE MADE SOME TEA, POURED himself a bowl of Cheerios and plugged in the laptop – Diane had left it on his coffee-table beside his own computer, with a note written on a yellow Post-it that said, *Thought you'd want this asap – good luck!* stuck to it. It was sitting on top of the paperwork Father Bill had taken off the ship.

It took him less than five minutes to break the access code – he had key-finder software on his flashdrive – and once he was in, nothing was encrypted. It was simply a matter of trying to work out how the person who had used the laptop ordered their files.

He had always found that the direct approach was the best first step, so he simply entered the name, Tom Gately, into the Windows search window.

To his surprise, Harry's father was featured in three files, all of which, he discovered, were linked to a program for making fake passports – Tom, who, in the photo Dunnigan found, was the image of Harry writ large – had been given the name Derek Bentley. Pauline was now Amanda Murray.

Using these new names, it took Dunnigan an hour to discover that Tom had been sent to Calais, by boat, where he had been put on a truck and transported to the Czech Republic – he was simply listed as a forestry worker, with no further information on which part of the country he had been sent to. Pauline had sailed to Rotterdam and gone by rail from there to Amsterdam. She was listed as working in a club – again, no further details could be found.

He called Tormey. 'I have some news.' He told him what little he had learned, and where he had found it. He suggested that a similar search, using the names of the other missing people, might well turn up similar information.

'It's something,' Tormey said. 'We'll pass it to Interpol.'

'Do you think they can be traced?'

'It happens. But you know better than me the statistics on tracking them at this stage.'

'Very poor. Do you have Frobisher?'

'The house was empty when we got there.'

'Of course it was.'

'I do have *some* good news for you.'

'What?'

'The CAB issued proceedings this morning to seize all of Dorcha's assets. Your friend Mr Frobisher is going to be flat broke before the year is out.'

'That *is* good news.'

'I thought you'd like it.'

PART TEN

More Unwanted Visitors

1

DUNNIGAN CALLED IN AT THE UNIVERSITY TO PICK up a book he thought he had left in his desk: Michel Foucault's *Discipline and Punish*, which he thought Miley might enjoy. He planned to give it to him as a gift when he saw his friend again.

He was heading back out through the John Hume building when he heard his name being called.

'Davey, how are you?' It was William Clarke. The lecturer, twenty-five stone, dressed in a red jacket, blue shirt, green tie and mustard jeans, waddled towards him, peering through thick John Lennon-style wire-framed glasses.

'I'm on leave for another week, William. I just called in to get something.'

'As you are entitled to do! Just while I see you, there was something I thought we might be able to help one another with.'

'Really?'

'Yes! It's been on my mind that perhaps your teaching hours have been a bit *demanding*. You seem to have a lot of things going on – I mean, look at your poor face! Perhaps it would be a good idea to take some of the pressure off – to help you out, of course.'

Dunnigan sighed and put the book into the pocket of his jacket. 'You want to cut my teaching hours.'

'Just a little. To lessen your load.'

'And this was your idea?'

'We discussed it at the course board.'

Dunnigan stepped up very close to Clarke, and looked him dead in the eye. 'Dr Clarke,' he said, quietly but firmly. 'I have a contract with this university that guarantees me a certain number of contact hours with my students. I have tolerated your interference and your rudeness and your snide, underhand comments for long enough. Do you have a problem with me?'

'Of course not! It's just that—'

'*Do you have a problem with me?*'

'No.'

'Good.' Dunnigan stepped back, smiling pleasantly. 'I'll be back in a week, and I will resume my duties. I would be grateful if you would inform my classes that we will be resuming my old reading list – the one I was using before you changed it.' Then he walked out, feeling pleased with himself, leaving Clarke looking very flustered indeed.

2

DUNNIGAN FOUND MILEY AND HARRY LIVING IN a tiny bedsit in Naas. They had not proven difficult to locate – Miley was still drawing his payments, and it was simply a matter of finding out which ATM machines he was using, then asking around about a man with Down's Syndrome and a little boy. He had an address within thirty minutes of arriving in town.

'I am not coming with you!' Miley said.

Harry was watching *Blaze and the Monster Machines* on a small television. The room had a table, a couch, a single bed and the TV. It was like Dunnigan's own place, but smaller and seedier.

'Just hear me out, and then I'll go.'

'You have five minutes.'

'We all miss you.'

'Who's we?'

'Father Bill. Diane. Everyone at the Project.'

'What about you?'

'Me? Well, of course I do.'

'We have a good life. No one tries to tell us what to do. No one lies to us.'

'What do you do all day?'

'Stuff.'

'Is Harry going to school?'

'I'm letting him take a year out.'

'He's ten years old and you're giving him a gap year?'

'It'll be good for his development.'

They watched the young boy, who was engrossed in the television programme.

'I really do miss you, Miley.'

'You're full of it! You just feel responsible for me because you got me out of that home. I appreciate your effort, but you don't have to put up with me any more.'

'I don't put up with you, Miley.'

'All those times I asked you to go out for a drink, or meet me for lunch, and you always said no. It was okay if I was helping out at the Project, I was useful then, but if it was just you and me, hanging out, you didn't want to be next or near me.'

'I haven't always been fair to you, Miley. I know that.'

'I really looked up to you.'

'I know.'

Miley paused, his head lowered. 'Why'd you have to lie to me? You knew how I felt about Harry – how much I cared about what happened to him. Why did nobody talk to me about your plans? It's like I didn't matter.'

'I don't have an excuse, Miley. It was wrong.'

'When I met you, and when you helped me, and when I was around Diane and Father Bill, for the first time in my life I felt like I was a real person,' Miley said, and he was crying now. 'You all treated me like you cared. Like you wanted to know what I thought, and I really helped the people at the Project, and I thought I was making a difference with Harry. And then I found out it was all in my head, that you were all laughing at me behind my back!'

'We weren't,' Dunnigan said, and he suddenly realised he was crying too.

'That's what it feels like to me,' Miley said.

'You've got to remember,' Dunnigan said, 'I'm not a very good friend – I don't know how to be. I'm trying, though. And if you give me a second chance, I'll do my best not to let you down again.'

'I don't know,' Miley said. 'What about Harry? Are you still gonna put him in care?'

'Father Bill says he wants you to be part of the process – and the social worker has agreed. Harry won't go anywhere unless you're completely happy, and you can see him as often as you like.'

'I'll think about it.'

'That's all I ask.'

Suddenly Miley threw his arms around Dunnigan. The criminologist froze for a second, then hugged him back. 'There's one thing you have to remember, Miley Timoney,' he said.

'What?'

'I might have saved you, but you saved me, too.'

And even though he couldn't see it, he knew Miley was smiling.

3

SUNDAY MORNING

DUNNIGAN GOT UP AT TEN THIRTY, LEAVING Diane asleep, her arm thrown across her forehead and her legs splayed out, taking up most of the bed, and went out to get breakfast. He had bought a cafetière and learned how to make decent coffee, but Diane preferred cappuccino, so he got a large takeout one from a nearby café, as well as some Danish pastries and a couple of cream-cheese bagels – he had some good raspberry jam at the flat.

Back at the flat, he made tea, put the ingredients on the coffee-table, and gently shook Diane awake.

'Breakfast is served.'

'It's still the middle of the night.'

'It's a quarter past eleven.'

'You just made my point for me.'

Ten minutes later she emerged from the bedroom, wearing an oversized *Bat Out of Hell* T-shirt, and plonked down on the couch beside him.

'Would you consider getting a proper dining table?' she asked, as they ate.

'I'd consider it.'

'I thought it might be nice to have Miley and Harry over for a meal. Maybe Father Bill.'

'Mmm. I can't really cook, though.'

'That's why God invented take-out menus. Would your sister come?'

'She might. I could ask her.'

'Her husband still pissed at you?'

'Yes.'

'We can work on that.'

'Do we need to?'

Diane shrugged. 'Only if you want.'

'I don't.'

They applied themselves to their meal.

'D'you think they'll find Harry's parents?' Diane asked, after a time.

'Tormey isn't hopeful. It looks as if his dad was sent to a region of the Black Forest, which is known as a centre for people trafficking, mostly to different parts of the Arctic regions of Scandinavia, where they still have company towns, largely involved in either fish processing or mining. It's basically indentured slavery. His name will have been changed several times en route to wherever they send him. Interpol have his details and are looking, but it's an almost impossible task.'

'And his mum?'

'She has, without doubt, been channelled into the sex industry in Holland, and when she's used up there, the next step is often Eastern Europe.'

'Which doesn't bear thinking about.'

'No. Harry will be living with a foster-family, and Father Bill has swung it so he can work up to spending weekends, maybe even longer, with Miley. If his parents are found, that will be marvellous, but in the meantime, he's with people who care about him.'

The doorbell buzzed. Dunnigan went to the window, but could see no one. 'Probably a mistake.'

He was about to sit when it buzzed again. He pressed the unlocking mechanism and opened his own door, waiting for the caller to come upstairs, but no one did. 'Back in a moment,' he said, and went downstairs.

He pushed open the front door, and was about to close it again when he noticed the box on the pavement. He picked it up. *David Dunnigan* was printed in bold type on a piece of white paper that had been Sellotaped to the brown card of the box. He looked up and down the street, but everyone was hurrying on their way, oblivious to him.

Back inside, he sat down on the couch next to Diane. 'Someone left this,' he said.

'Were you expecting anything?'

'No.'

She took the box from him and shook it gently. From the weight, it was clear there wasn't much inside, and what was in there made a dull sound when she shook it. 'Seems safe.'

'And that is your professional opinion?'

'Yep.'

'What if it explodes?'

'It won't.'

'We made a lot of very unpleasant people very unhappy recently, or have you forgotten?'

'Open it!'

The package was a perfect square, fifteen centimetres on each side (he measured it later). It had no postmark, and his name and address had been typed, probably on a computer of some kind, then printed, the section with the words on cut out and glued to the exterior of the box. It was neat and precise, centred perfectly.

He got a pair of scissors and sliced open the packing tape. At first all he saw inside was some shredded newspaper that had been put there to stop the contents bouncing about while it was in transit. Removing the top layer of paper, he saw what had been sent to him, and froze.

It was a child's trainer, white with pink trim, a series of lights set into the sides, so that, as the owner walked, they would sparkle.

Dunnigan's mind went blank, his heartbeat loud in his ears. He did not have to look at the trainer to know it was a child's size six, and he did not need to examine it to see that it was old – it looked like it had been cleaned, but it showed wear at various points.

He realised he had stopped breathing, and stood up rapidly, hyperventilating fiercely. Diane was asking him if he was all right, but he could not answer – a single thought was screaming in his head, and he could not hear or comprehend anything but that one, unavoidable truth.

Someone had sent him one of Beth's shoes.

WHEN SHE WAS GONE

By S.A. Dunphy

COMING SPRING 2018

When criminologist David Dunnigan receives the shocking delivery of one of his niece Beth's shoes, it reignites the eighteen-year-old investigation into her disappearance. But is Dunnigan ready for what he might find?

New evidence links Beth's abduction to a series of suicides in an antiquated psychiatric hospital, and to an Inuit village in the frozen north of Greenland where the parents of Harry, a homeless boy Dunnigan and his friend Miley rescued from the streets, may have been trafficked.

Can Dunnigan survive the hunt, and will he find Beth after all this time?